HITMAN
DAMNATION

Books published by The Random House Publishing Group are available at quantity discounts on bulk purchases for premium, educational, fund-raising, and special sales use. For details, please call 1-800-733-3000.

HITMAN™
DAMNATION

RAYMOND BENSON

BALLANTINE BOOKS • NEW YORK

Hitman: Damnation is a work of fiction. Names, places, and incidents either are products of the author's imagination or are used fictitiously. Any resemblance to actual events, locales, or persons, living or dead, is purely coincidental.

A Del Rey Mass Market Original

Hitman is a registered trademark of Square Enix, Ltd.

Published in the United States by Del Rey, an imprint of the Random House Publishing Group, a division of Random House, Inc., New York.

Del Rey is a registered trademark and the Del Rey colophon is a trademark of Random House, Inc.

ISBN 978-0-345-47134-5
eBook ISBN 978-0-345-53585-6

9 8 7 6 5 4 3 2 1

Printed in the United States of America

www.delreybooks.com

ACKNOWLEDGMENTS

The author wishes to thank Peter Miller and the folks at PMA Literary & Film Management, Inc., and everyone at Del Rey (especially editor extraordinaire Mike Braff) and Io Interactive for all the splendid help and guidance.

PROLOGUE

The important thing was to keep Agent 47 alive.

That's what Diana Burnwood had told herself for years, even though it wasn't the Agency's prime directive for handlers. The unwritten law was that operators in the field had to be disavowed and abandoned if there was the slightest danger of the Agency being compromised. And yet Diana had always felt a connection to 47—as much as it was possible that anyone could bond with the man. She wanted him to succeed in his various missions, and she took great pains to watch his back. It was her job.

Well, it *was* her job.

Diana planned to disappear after the current hit was completed. She had no choice. Considering what she was intending to do, the Agency would stop at nothing to eliminate her. The escape route was in place and the travel plans were set in stone. She would vanish for a while and then make her move. Returning to the laboratory in Chicago would be terribly perilous, but it was absolutely essential for her to snatch the "package" and spirit it away from the Agency.

The trouble started when Benjamin Travis was appointed to be her superior. Diana was immediately at odds with the guy. Although not the ultimate boss of the International Contract Agency, Travis had proven himself to be a more than competent manager. He was tough, opinionated, intelligent, and ambitious. It was no wonder he had been promoted to his current position. Diana held no grudge against the man for that.

What she didn't like about Travis was that he was an unethical and dangerous asshole.

When Diana had confronted him about his new classified pet project, noting that it would cost many innocent lives, Travis scoffed and said, "Really? This, coming from a handler of an assassin? Give me a break, Burnwood. You alone have caused collateral damage in the hundreds. Don't go all high-and-mighty on me all of a sudden."

Normally she would have let it go and moved on. This time, however, the implications of Travis's venture were more than simply disturbing. In her opinion, the man was threatening the integrity of the Agency.

Diana was already working on the Himalayan assignment with 47 when she had decided to take action. Originally she wanted to wait until the mission was completed, but the situation had become too volatile. Something had to be done quickly, and she had decided to risk her life to take the package and run. But first she had to go off the grid for a while and carefully plan her next move.

Did they realize she had betrayed them? Most likely. She knew they would come for her at any moment. She should have left Paris hours ago, but she owed it to 47 to see him through the current operation.

Finish the job and then get out quickly.

She opened her laptop and switched it on. The encryption software was already in place; there was no way anyone could hack into her network. As she connected to the satellite over Nepal, Diana checked the small video monitors once again. The two miniature cameras she had installed in the hotel hallway outside her room were undetectable and state of the art. They each pointed in an opposite direction, so she could see anyone who happened to appear in the corridor. A third camera, mounted near the elevators and stairwell, would alert her to any newcomers on the floor. It wasn't perfect by any means, but at least the three monitors on the desk would give her fair warning should she come under attack.

The comlink securely connected to the satellite's signal. An image of a snowcapped mountain materialized on the laptop—Kangchenjunga, one of the most difficult climbs in the Himalayas. Diana checked her watch. Just after six in the morning. That meant it was close to one o'clock there. Nepal Standard Time was unusual in that it was offset by forty-five minutes from Coordinated Universal Time. If she was correct in her calculations, then 47 would be in place and waiting for her.

She zoomed in to the blinking beacon on the side of the peak. The homer 47 carried was undetectable to the naked eye but easily picked up by the satellite. *Quite ingenious, actually,* Diana thought. The Agency did indeed have cool toys.

Another marvel the satellite provided was the ability to analyze physical structures, whether they were manmade or natural. In this case, the program detected where the rock surface of the mountainside ended and the thick layers of snow began, so that she could easily identify areas susceptible to avalanches.

"Hello, 47," she said into her headset. "Do you read me?"

"Loud and clear," came the reply. There was no inflection of warmth or pleasure that he had recognized her refined British accent. Typical of the hitman. He was a man of few words and absolutely no emotion.

"Is the target in place?" she asked.

"Can't you see them?"

She moved the camera down the cliff and spotted the Chinese climbing party, some six or seven hundred feet below 47's perch.

"Affirmative. How was the climb?"

"Cold."

"All your carabiners and belay devices worked all right?"

"Yes."

"Have you done much mountain climbing, 47?"

"Where do I place the boomer?"

She smiled to herself. Agent 47 always cut to the chase. "The computer is calculating that as we speak. Wait . . . okay, here it is. You're very close. Move about forty yards to the east. You'll find yourself on a ledge of what looks like ice, but it's really very compact snow. That'll do nicely, and it's right over the target's head."

"I see what you mean. Give me a few minutes to work my way over there."

Diana watched the tiny figure use a rope, a pickax, and a series of carabiners to maneuver sideways across the face of the cliff. She admired how 47 seemed to be able to do anything. He was a superb athlete, trained to work in all the elements. Of course, he was genetically engineered to be a superman of sorts. Diana often wondered how strong his tolerance for pain and fatigue really was. The climb must have been terribly difficult, especially alone. Luckily, he wasn't so high in altitude that the helicopter she had arranged to pick him up couldn't reach him. If he had been another thousand feet farther up, 47 would have had to descend Kangchenjunga the hard way.

Then she saw them.

Diana furrowed her brow and squinted. She quickly maneuvered the mouse and zoomed in closer.

Two men. Almost directly above 47.

"47, I see two hostiles, maybe two hundred feet at one

o'clock." She focused the camera on the men as tightly as it would go. "They're Chinese, all right."

"I'm not surprised," 47 said. "I suspected the target sent a scouting party up the mountain to precede his own expedition. He wanted to make sure the path was safe. They don't like Nam Vo too much around here. Do they see me?"

"I can't tell. I don't think so . . . Wait—they're on the move. They must know you're there."

"How much time do I have before they're within shooting range?"

"Plenty. Just get the boomer in place and get the hell out of there. The helicopter will—"

A movement on one of the camera monitors caught her attention. Someone had come out of the elevator on her floor. No—two someones. They paused for a moment as the stairwell door opened and two more men came into view. They were dressed in suits and appeared to be ordinary businessmen, until one of them dropped a large bag on the floor and opened it.

"Diana?" 47 asked. "Are you there?"

"Hold on a second, 47," she snapped.

One of the men pulled out four Kevlar vests, which the quartet began to don.

No!

The Agency had found her.

No time to lose. She immediately severed the satellite link, pulled the plug on her laptop, and rose from the desk.

The men on the monitor armed themselves with assault rifles, M16s from the look of them.

Diana quickly grabbed her laptop and small traveling bag, which was packed and ready to go. She moved to the fire-escape window, opened it, and tossed the computer outside. The machine fell six floors and smashed to pieces on the ground below. She glanced back at the

monitors on the desk and saw that the men were creep-
ing quietly toward her room. Diana then tossed her bag
out the window and watched it drop to the pavement.
No damage; there was nothing inside but clothes, passports, and money.

As the men kicked in the hotel-room door, Diana was
already out on the fire-escape landing. The tall redhead,
dressed in an expensive Versace suit, scampered in her
bare feet down the metal stairs toward the street below.
She heard shouts above her.

Faster!

She took three steps at a time. When she got to the
first-floor landing, one of the men shouted, "There she
is!" Diana took hold of the railing, deftly catapulted her
body over it, and dropped twenty feet to the ground.
She landed hard on the soles of her feet, winced with
the pain, and kept moving.

That's when the gunfire began.

She grabbed her bag, rounded the corner of the hotel,
and ran into the traffic on the street. Drivers slammed
on the brakes and honked horns. Bullets whizzed past
her, dotting the pavement in her wake. By the time she
was on the other side of Rue Froissart, the men were in
hot pursuit down the fire escape.

Diana ducked into the Metro entrance at the corner,
practically flew down the steps, and reached the platform as the train pulled in to the station. The timing
couldn't have been more perfect. She climbed aboard
the train, pushed her way through the crowd of passengers, found a seat, and collapsed into it. The doors
closed and she was away. Opening her bag, she found
the Prada heels and put them on. Now she was just another ordinary classy Parisienne commuting through
the busy city. She was confident that the Agency would
not be able to trace her movements once she got to her

destination. The route was secure and airtight. Perhaps fate really was on her side.

She took a deep breath and then felt a pang of regret. She hadn't meant to abandon 47, but she'd had no choice.

Sorry, old friend, she thought. *I hope you'll understand one day. Send positive thoughts my way, if you're capable of doing such a thing.*

Goodbye—and good luck.

ONE

TWELVE MONTHS LATER

It was always a variation of the same dream.

This time I was, what, thirteen years old? Yes. Thirteen. I recognized the asylum's corridors and I passed a framed portrait of my father—one of them, anyway—Dr. Ort-Meyer. I saw my reflection in the glass, and it was how I remembered myself at that age.

But where was everyone? The asylum was empty. My footsteps echoed as if I were in a cavern.

I thought to myself that I should run. He was coming, but I hadn't perceived him yet. Usually I felt him coming. It was a sensation I was unable to describe, but I knew he was there. Just around the corner. Coming for me.

So I ran.

And then he was behind me, appearing out of nowhere. I could practically smell him. I could feel the coldness. It was always cold when he was nearby.

I dared to look over my shoulder as I ran. The dark figure was faceless, as usual. Almost as if he were only a shadow, but I knew better.

He was Death.

No question about it. Death had been coming for me in my dreams for a long time now.

I ran faster. I was fairly certain I could stay ahead of him, but the temperature around me grew colder. He was closer. How did he come to move so fast? He was getting better at the chase. He was learning.

But I was learning too. Wasn't I?

I turned a corner and faced an interminable hallway. It disappeared into nothingness, a long way away. Could I make it to the end before he caught me?

I pushed forward and felt my legs working to put distance between the shadow and me. Did I hear him calling me? How could he call me? I don't have a name. Or did I? I don't remember.

Things were always crazy in a dream.

Suddenly my legs struggled to move. As if I were waist deep in invisible quicksand. No matter how hard I tried, I could only step forward at the pace of a snail. The muscles in my thighs and calves hurt from the exertion.

The ice-cold breath was now on my neck. He was directly behind me, perhaps close enough to reach out and touch me.

No! I had to get away! I couldn't let Death touch me.

I sensed his hand, outstretched and ready to clasp my shoulder. The only thing I could do was fall forward, as if I'd just toppled like a stack of building blocks. But I didn't fall fast enough; it was more like I was floating! Then I felt the icy, stinging pressure of his fingers.

I screamed as I landed on the hallway's tiled floor . . .

. . . and I woke up.

The disorientation lasted for a few seconds, as always.

That unpleasant ball of bees in my chest felt as if it might explode. Some might call it anxiety. I don't know what it was for me. Whatever I chose to call it, I didn't like it.

I immediately sat up in bed. The hotel room was dark. No, it was light outside. I had the curtains closed. The digital clock on the nightstand read 5:43. I'd meant to wake from the afternoon nap at 6:00. This had been happening a lot. My internal alarm clock was all messed up. At least I awoke early and not too late.

I had a job to do.

I stood and walked to the window. I carefully pulled back the drapes and peered outside. The Caribbean sun was bright and hot. I saw men and women in bathing attire. The resort's pool was full of guests, splashing and cavorting. I knew the beach would be crowded as well.

What would it be like to put on swim trunks, walk outside, and join the other people for fun? Ocho Rios, Jamaica! Didn't every human being want to lie on a recliner and relax with a piña colada while the sun baked your skin and turned it into cancer cells? Attend the nightly dance and hook up with someone of the opposite sex? Enjoy a weekend fling in paradise?

What a stupid idea. I knew I wasn't capable of that.

I released the drapes and plunged the room into darkness again.

I noticed that my hand was trembling. This always happened when I woke up. After so many hours without a pill I got the shakes. Naked, I walked into the bathroom and turned on the light. I reached for the plastic bottle I kept in a pouch. I'd tossed it onto the counter after I'd checked in to the resort. I tapped out a pill into the palm of my hand and popped it into my mouth. Then I turned on the faucet, cupped my hands, and filled them with enough water to chug down the medication.

My reflection in the mirror stared back at me. I was certainly no longer thirteen years old. I wasn't sure *how old I was, although I was "created" in 1964. That was the downside of being a test-tube baby.*

I snapped the lid back on the pill bottle. There was no label. I'd obtained the oxycodone illegally, so there was no prescription information. Besides, no doctor in his right mind would have prescribed these powerful pain-killers for as long as I'd been taking them.

I supposed people would say I was addicted, but actually I could quit anytime I wanted. I just didn't want to. I was pretty sure that, because of how I'm wired, the oxycodone didn't affect me as it would a "normal" person. I started taking the pills after the injury. I really needed painkillers at the time. But even after I'd healed, I found I liked the effects. The pills didn't dope me up the way they would most people. Instead, they cleared my head and calmed me down.

Granted, if I didn't take one after so many hours, I got a headache that was unbearable, I became anxious and jittery, and I had vivid nightmares. I never used to experience anxiety. Never. Now I did if I didn't take the pill. Did that mean I was addicted? In my own way, perhaps.

I returned to the room. I had a boat to catch. I had a target to eliminate. I had a job to do. Time to get dressed.

I knew I wasn't operating at 100 percent. I wasn't at the top of my game. Ever since the accident. Ever since Diana . . . It wasn't good for me to think about it, but sometimes I couldn't help it.

The difficulty was avoiding the Agency. They'd been trying to reach me. Messages had come through the usual channels. I didn't answer them. I had no desire to work with ICA anymore. I was past my prime. I wasn't the assassin I once was. I knew that. It's why I worked freelance now. It's why I supported myself with easy assignments like the one tonight.

Hector Corado. Mediocre scum who specialized in human trafficking. And my employer, Roget, was just as sleazy. But it was a job. And it was money. Not as much as I made with the Agency, but it was enough. I really didn't care about the money. As long as I had the means to carry on each day and dress the way I liked, I was happy.

Happy. What a concept.

If I could laugh, I would have.

<u>TWO</u>

The festivities were palpable on the beach of the Sandals Grande Ocho Rios Resort. Swimsuit-clad men and women ran in and out of the warm blue-green water, others played volleyball on the sand, and the rest reclined with drinks in hand as the sun slowly descended to the horizon. It was the magical hour of the day in Jamaica, the twilight time when the sky was painted orange-red, before it turned coal black and was dotted with the twinkling of stars.

Agent 47 ignored it all as he made his way to the dock to board a small ferry that would carry select VIPs to Fernandez's yacht. Dressed in a black suit made of the highest-quality light wool, a white cotton shirt, black leather gloves, and the added accessory of a crimson-red tie, 47 knew that he looked exceptionally sharp. The assassin took great pleasure in what he wore. After all, there were so few things in the world he did enjoy. With his tall stature, sleek bald head, and an enigmatic bar-code tattoo on the back of his neck, 47 was indeed a striking figure. His appearance was appropriate for the occasion, since the party aboard Fernandez's yacht was by invitation only. The island's rich, famous, and infamous were to be the exclusive guests. 47's employer, a man he knew only as Roget, had secured an invite for 47 under the name "Michael Brant." His cover was simple—he was a European of undeterminable origin who had made a fortune in water. It was a subject 47 didn't have to know much about—water was water, and it was easily bottled and sold. He would have no trouble fooling Emilio Fernandez, the playboy billionaire who owned the yacht. Fernandez, who made his money through dubious means, normally resided in Nassau but spent most of his time on the boat, traveling from island to island and throwing extravagant parties.

47 didn't care about Fernandez or the party. His only interest was Hector Corado. The intel assured him that the criminal would be aboard as Fernandez's special guest.

It was a good thing 47's employer had warned him that guests would be frisked and would have to pass through a metal detector at the dock before boarding the barge. Thus, 47 had left any and all weapons behind. He was armed with only the clothes on his back and a thin line of carbon-fiberwire, which wouldn't be picked up by the metal detector or even a very intimate frisking. In many ways, the Fiberwire was 47's trademark weapon.

Approximately thirty people stood in the security line on the dock. Beefy guards armed with automatic pistols on their belts ushered the men and women onto the barge after clearance. Everyone was dressed to the nines. The men were handsome and exuded power and wealth; the women were beautiful and exhibited entitlement and wanton sexuality. The ferry had already made two round-trips to the yacht to deliver party guests. Nearly three hundred people were expected aboard the massive vessel. That was useful for 47. The more crowded the party was, the more likely his job would go unnoticed. More important, the barge would continue to make the return trip to shore every half hour for revelers who had reached their partying limit.

As the boat sailed slowly toward the yacht, 47 couldn't help but be impressed. He reckoned the *Daphne* was between three hundred seventy and four hundred feet long and its tonnage most likely around five thousand. He'd been told the *Daphne* traveled at nineteen knots per hour, which, given the size of the cruiser, was quite fast. Built and designed by Lürssen in Germany and outfitted by Blohm & Voss, the *Daphne* sported a large deck for parties, two swimming pools, and luxury cabins, which were usually off-limits to anyone but Fernandez's special overnight guests. There was also a helipad, and 47 could discern the outline of the Bell 206 sitting upon it.

Corado's helicopter.

The party was already going full swing by the time 47 stepped onto the *Daphne*'s deck, located forward, near the bow. A live band specializing in reggae and calypso tunes blasted Bob Marley hits and other familiar numbers as couples and non-couples alike covered the area designated as a dance floor. The liquor flowed freely from open bars located at stations around the deck. Guests also had no qualms about consuming drugs in front of anyone. Marijuana and cocaine were in plain sight. After all, this was a private party, with no chance of law enforcement showing up. None of this made any impact on 47. He had no interest in dancing or recreational drugs. He occasionally drank but never in excess. What captured his attention was the monumental layout of gourmet food—sautéed ackee, seafood, and steaks, steamed and sautéed vegetables of every color and type, a variety of salads, conch chowder, Jamaican jerk chicken, curry goat, fried plantain, and an abundance of tropical fruits. For dessert, guests could try other Caribbean delectables such as gizzada, grater cake, potato pudding, and banana fritters, along with the more traditional fare of chocolate cakes and fruit pies. 47 hadn't eaten dinner, so he allowed himself to blend with the crowd, fill a plate, and take advantage of the host's hospitality before he got down to the business at hand.

The hitman moved to a tall dining station, around which guests could stand and eat. From there he could survey the entire deck. Roget's intel was correct. Fernandez had employed several guards—all of whom were armed—and positioned them at key points on the ship. It was forbidden for guests to bring weapons aboard, but his own men? No problemo.

That was good. All was going according to plan.

47 scanned the crowd and didn't see Corado. But he spotted Emilio Fernandez, surrounded by young, gorgeous females, making his way through the throng and greeting familiar faces with handshakes and smiles. The man was about forty, resembled a friendlier version of Al Pacino in *Scarface*, and oozed smarminess. As the billionaire moved closer, 47 prepared himself for the cue to go "onstage."

"And hello to you, *señor*," Fernandez said to him.

"Good evening." 47 gave him a smile. He could play a part well if he had to. What was uncomfortable for 47 when he was *himself*, he was smoothly able to fake when on a mission. In many ways, it was something like a game to him. Could he pull off the deceit? That was the thrill.

"Emilio Fernandez. I don't believe we've met." The man held out a hand.

"Michael Brant." 47 shook his palm. The man's grip was somewhat clammy. Fernandez was obviously someone who got where he was through his money, not by any strength or *machismo*. Unlike Corado, wherever he might be.

"Oh, Mr. Brant. You're in . . ." Fernandez snapped his fingers in succession, trying to remember what he'd heard about his guest.

"Water. I have a water company in Luxembourg."

"Right! How canny of you to invest in water. How long ago did you do it?"

"My family has been in water since before I was born. I inherited the business."

"I see. Well, smart family! We all need water, don't we? Welcome aboard, Mr. Brant."

"*Gracias*. You have a lovely yacht, sir."

"The *Daphne* is my pride and joy." The man spotted someone he knew and waved. "I must move on. Please enjoy yourself, Mr. Brant. Many of the women aboard the yacht, I understand, are more than willing to make the acquaintance of a man such as yourself." He winked lasciviously and walked away with his harem. One of the girls, a dark-skinned, lithe model type, gazed at 47 over her shoulder as they disappeared.

An invitation?

47 paid no attention. Now sated, it was time for the hunt.

He circled the deck and finally homed in on Corado. The man sat with a lovely young Hispanic woman at a table near the bulkhead entrance to the cabins and lower levels of the ship. Two burly bodyguards accompanied him; both men stood behind Corado, with their arms folded in front of their broad chests. Corado was a small man, probably in his late forties. Most likely had a Napoleon complex. He had a walrus mustache and slicked-back black hair with touches of gray. A big fat Cuban cigar dominated his mouth. All three men wore tailored suits. 47 wondered if Fernandez had allowed them to be armed. Surely a wretch like Corado would never go anywhere without firepower for protection.

Right. Time to set the plan in motion.

47 needed a weapon.

He turned away from Corado's table and walked along the starboard side toward the stern, where the helipad was located. As expected, one of Fernandez's guards blocked his passage midway. 47 glanced behind him to make sure no one else was watching.

"Guests are not allowed aft, sir," the man said.

The noise from the party was nearly deafening, even that far away from the band and excitement. 47 put on his best act as a happy partygoer. "What did you say?"

The guard spoke louder. "Guests are not allowed aft."

"Oh, I wanted to have a look at that marvelous helipad. Is that Emilio's helicopter? I'm something of a chopper enthusiast. That's a Bell 206, isn't it? I thought those were used exclusively by the military and law-enforcement personnel."

"I'm sorry, sir, you'll need to go back to the deck."

47 slipped his hand into his jacket pocket and grasped the Fiberwire. "Aw, man, you can't let me see it?"

"No, sir, I'm sorry."

The assassin jerked his head toward the helipad. "Then how come *those* people get to go back there?"

The guard turned to see what the bald man was talking about. 47 swiftly threw the Fiberwire around the man's neck and tightened it with both hands. Since the device had small grips on each end, it didn't take much strength for 47 to choke the man to death.

It took all of fifteen seconds. The guard slumped into 47's arms. The hitman turned his head around again—all clear. Should he throw the man overboard? No, the body might be spotted as it floated away. A door leading to the hold was directly to his right, so 47 wrapped his arms around the corpse's barrel chest and dragged it inside.

The place was a storeroom full of life jackets. Hopefully, 47 thought, no one would need any and the guard wouldn't be discovered. He laid the body in the corner and covered it with several jackets, but only after he had taken the man's Glock 17. Not a bad weapon at all. 47 figured he could have done much worse. He checked the magazine, stuffed the gun into his waistband beneath the jacket, and, satisfied, left the room.

47 went back to the party and stood next to the bar closest to Corado's table. Most of the guests had to stand in line at the various bars to pick up drinks, but a designated waiter had been assigned to Corado. When he wasn't attending to the criminal, the servant stood at the bar with his eyes on the long, tanned legs of a tall blonde dancing nearby. But when Corado waved his hand, the waiter rushed to the table and took another order. The man then hurried back and barked the instructions to the busy bartender.

47 picked up a cocktail napkin and a pen from the bar and wrote a message in Spanish on it.

JUST LEARNED POLICE ARRIVING IN 10 MINUTES TO ARREST YOU! PLEASE LEAVE AS QUIETLY AS POSSIBLE, GET TO CUBAN AIRSPACE IN MINUTES, AND THEY WILL NEVER KNOW YOU WERE HERE. I AM SORRY, MY FRIEND. SEE YOU SOON. EMILIO.

When he was done, 47 put the pen down next to a circular drink platter and kept the napkin in his hand. The bartender placed a new napkin and one drink on the tray. "Here's the girl's," he said. The waiter ignored him, for he was once again gawking at the blonde's legs. The bartender quickly shook a martini, poured it, added an olive, and placed another napkin and the glass on the tray. "And here's the man's," he said. The busy bartender then turned away to serve other guests.

47 quickly picked up the martini glass, set his napkin

with the note on top of the clean one, and replaced the drink.

The waiter finally turned away from the blonde, grabbed the tray without noticing the hitman's napkin, and hustled back to Corado's table. 47 watched as the man first served the girl's drink and then placed Corado's martini—with 47's napkin—on the table. Corado barely acknowledged the waiter.

47 moved to a different position, still in sight of his prey. The criminal took a sip of the drink . . . and then saw the scribbling. He picked up the napkin, read the message, and gestured to one of the bodyguards. The armed man leaned over, scanned the note, and the two men conferred. Corado furrowed his brow. He said something to his girlfriend and stood. She made a face of protest, but he roughly grabbed her arm and pulled her up.

Agent 47 quickly headed back to the starboard side of the ship and made his way aft. The music was as loud as ever, which suited him fine. No one would hear what he was about to do.

He reached the helipad before Corado and his entourage did. 47 flattened himself against the bulkhead, the Glock in his hand. He didn't have to wait long.

Corado, the girl, and the two bodyguards appeared from the yacht's port side. They moved quickly and quietly, but Corado was obviously distressed, the girl angry. One of the bodyguards made for the pilot's side of the chopper. Corado had to pull on the girl as she struggled against him. She cursed at him in Spanish, and then Corado turned to slap her hard. That shut her up.

The bodyguard/pilot opened the door and started to climb in.

Now.

47 stepped into view, leveled the Glock in front of

him, and shot the bodyguard in the pilot's seat through the open door. Before the victim could register that he was shot, 47 swung his arm over, trained the sight on the second bodyguard, and squeezed the trigger. The man jerked and crumpled to the deck. It took precisely 2.3 seconds to eliminate Corado's protection.

47 was confident the gunshots and the girl's subsequent scream couldn't be heard on the other side of the ship.

Corado reached inside his jacket and fumbled for a pistol hidden there. Apparently he wasn't used to having to defend himself—he always had others nearby to do the job.

The hitman shot him with a double tap—one in the chest and one in the head.

Easy.

That left the girl, who was now hysterical. She started to run back to the port side, yelling bloody murder.

47 raised the gun again to eliminate her from the equation—but his hand unwillingly trembled. Nevertheless, he squeezed the trigger.

A miss! How could that happen?

By then the girl had disappeared behind the bulkhead, running along the port side toward the bow.

47 took off after her.

Even though she had long, muscular legs, 47 was taller, stronger, and was genetically engineered to be a superior athlete in every way. He caught her in six seconds, and they weren't halfway to the ship's midpoint.

The assassin picked her up by the waist, even with the Glock in his right hand. She continued to scream and struggle.

Only one thing to do.

Agent 47 lifted and threw the girl over the rail into the sea.

He paused for a moment to look aft and toward the

bow. Luckily, a guard, some forty feet away, was facing forward and didn't witness the act.

47 tossed the Glock overboard and then calmly walked back to the helipad. He picked up and piled the dead men, one by one, into the helicopter. The corpses slumped to the floor and wouldn't be discovered immediately. Satisfied, the hitman circled around to the starboard side and returned to the party. He smoothly merged into a line dance in progress. 47 put on his best happy face, performed the step in rhythm, and got lost among the partygoers.

The job was a success; nevertheless, 47 was angry with himself. The trembling hand had nearly cost him the mission. Was it the painkillers? Of course it was. The hitman knew it was so, and yet he obstinately refused to acknowledge the message this portended. Instead, he reached into his jacket pocket, found the plastic bottle, opened it, threw a tablet into his mouth, and swallowed it without water.

Over the next half hour, he calmed down and continued to act as one of the privileged guests at an exclusive Caribbean party. 47 saw no indication that his handiwork had been discovered. No one had a reason to go aft. If Fernandez missed his friend, he would figure the criminal and his girlfriend had gone below to a cabin.

Eventually, the assassin boarded the barge with twenty other exhausted and very drunk guests, and he sailed back to Ocho Rios and safety.

As big noisy parties went, 47 decided this one hadn't been too bad.

<u>THREE</u>

Another superyacht, coincidentally also built by Lürssen, slowly and aimlessly drifted in the waters west of Spain. At three hundred sixty feet long, the *Jean Danjou II* was not unlike the luxury vessels owned by the many wealthy socialites in Spain or France. After all, the Costa del Sol, especially the port of Marbella, was one of the most exclusive sailing destinations for the rich and famous. Thus, multimillion-dollar pleasure boats were a dime a dozen. Many of them navigated through the Strait of Gibraltar from the Mediterranean, into the open Atlantic, and back. The *Jean Danjou II* was no exception. Law-enforcement agencies knew she docked in Marbella but was registered to a corporation based in Switzerland. The owner was allegedly a major player in OPEC. This, of course, was false. The Swiss company was in reality the front for yet another business based in Portugal. This organization, too, was simply a cog in a third layer of deception, but it had connections to a conglomerate of banks in the Cayman Islands. In short, no one had any idea who really owned the yacht.

But if Interpol or other legal watchdogs of the world had an opportunity to visit the interior of the *Jean Danjou II*, they would discover a beehive of ex-military personnel, some of the world's savviest IT and encryption specialists, and the core middle-management team of a shadowy, secret international network.

Since she never anchored in one place for very long, the yacht was the ideal vessel to house the cerebral cortex of the International Contract Agency. And while high-level government officials, such as the president of the United States, the prime ministers of the United Kingdom and of Russia, and the king of Saudi Arabia, were certainly aware that the Agency existed, and although elite inner circles of intelligence organizations such as the CIA and SIS had reason and the ability to contact the Agency's leaders, these entities denied any knowledge of such an immoral but sometimes useful society. The ICA's services were sought after by the bad and the good alike. And yet, if America or Great Britain or Russia or any other nation on earth desired to actually locate the Agency's physical headquarters or meet its administrators, they might as well look on the moon. It was inconceivable that the ICA was right there in plain sight, moving from port to port on the open sea.

The *Jean Danjou II* was the perfect home for a necessary evil.

The twenty-eight-year-old Asian woman known only as Jade rechecked the figures on her notepad, glanced back at the monitor on the workstation labeled "Caribbean" to note any changes in the data, made some calculations, and then stood. The command center was buzzing with activity and distractions, but the woman had no problem staying focused. She looked at her steel-and-white-gold Rolex and saw that she was due in the conference room in five minutes. Just enough time for a quick walk-through to make sure everything was running smoothly.

The center, situated deep in the *Jean Danjou II* on

deck three, was the size of a baseball diamond. The walls were covered with electronic maps and large-screen HD computer monitors. More than a dozen workstations, dedicated to monitoring the Agency's activities in various territories around the globe, occupied the floor. Each one was manned by an analyst or manager. A tireless and dedicated staff ran the Agency's many concurrent active operations. And it was Jade's job to oversee the control center, as well as serve as personal assistant to one of ICA's top managers.

Jade's professional demeanor, dark leather business suit, patterned stockings, glasses, and the black hair done in a bun might have suggested that she was an executive secretary for a Fortune 500 company. But if one looked past her obvious beauty and noticed her many tattoos—mostly illustrative dragons—and the severe, no-nonsense soul behind her brown eyes, it was apparent that the woman was a formidable and dangerous person.

After making the rounds to each workstation and obtaining status updates from every worker, Jade glanced again at the Rolex. It was time for the meeting with her boss. She informed Julius, her immediate subordinate, where she was going, and then left the command center in his capable hands.

Any ship contained narrow and claustrophobic spaces, but the interior of the *Jean Danjou II* felt more like a high-tech corporate building than a luxury yacht. Each manager, responsible for the various functions that kept the Agency in business, had his or her own private office. Jade knew that one day she would have one. With a promotion to manager, she would gain more responsibility. That meant more money. Working for the Agency was the best job in the world.

Ascending to deck two by a marble and steel staircase, Jade nodded at one of the armed guards who patrolled the ship at all times. She liked to give the guards the perception that she appreciated their protection, when, in fact, Jade could probably take on three of them at once, slit their throats with the stiletto she kept on her person at all times, and then calmly go about her business.

Eventually she reached the conference room and entered.

"Right on time, Jade. My God, you're damned efficient," said the man sitting at a long table in front of a computer monitor. He was finishing his lunch—a po'-boy stuffed with salami, cheese, lettuce, tomatoes, and peppers. "Tell me again where you had combat training?"

"Westerners call it the Golden Triangle," she answered. "Specifically Burma. But I spent a lot of time in Laos."

"Jungle stuff, huh?"

"Yes, sir."

Benjamin Travis allowed his eyes to look her up and down—it was something he did daily, but she didn't mind. All the men on the boat—and some women— thought she was hot. It had its advantages.

Travis said, "Sit down. What have you got for me?"

Jade took a seat and placed her notebook in front of her. "We have a new lead on Agent 47's whereabouts."

Travis raised his eyebrows. "And we've been hearing that every month for a year, Jade."

"This is different, sir. A reliable source informs us that 47 was spotted in Jamaica as recently as two days ago. In fact, the source is one of ours."

Travis swiveled his chair away from the computer. A man in his forties, he always dressed in a gray suit, white shirt, and an Agency tie. He was probably twenty-five pounds overweight; his gut drooped over his belt, and he tended to sweat more than other men. With his thick red-brown mustache, glasses, and communications earpiece, he might have resembled a retired CIA operative who was past his prime. In reality, like Jade, Benjamin Travis was not someone to be underestimated. The epitome of a "company man," Travis was known by his colleagues to have no tolerance for incompetence. Failure was severely punished. As one of the senior managers of the Agency, he was cunning, ruthless, and ambitious. He commanded teams of assassins that operated around the world. He spent just as much time in the control room as did his personal assistant, often doing her job.

It was no wonder that he had quickly risen in the ranks to become one of the Agency's star players.

"Jamaica?" he echoed.

"Yes, sir."

"You don't say. How soon can you verify it?" he asked.

"I have Julius on it. This time it looks promising, Benjamin. Our man in Jamaica is usually reliable on intel but untrustworthy in financial matters."

He merely nodded. Jade knew that Travis never jumped to conclusions before all the i's were dotted and t's crossed.

"What else?"

"That's all, sir. Still no news on Burnwood. I'm afraid that trail has gone quite cold."

Travis nodded again. "That figures. Thank you, Jade. Please keep me informed. The minute you have confirmation on 47, I want to know."

"Yes, sir." She stood and moved toward the door.

"Wait."

Jade stopped and turned. "Yes?"

"Please inform the captain to point the ship toward the Caribbean. If what you say is true, I want to be close enough to intercept the guy." He shrugged. "And if this lead of yours turns out to be another dead end, then we'll stop in Cuba or the Bahamas or somewhere and have an island shore leave. We could use it."

"Yes, sir." She scribbled a note on her pad, pushed her glasses back to the bridge of her nose, and left the room.

Travis turned to the computer monitor and resumed studying the latest report from Chicago. The results had gone beyond expectations. He knew his pet project had the potential to help the Agency evolve into a force with which the entire world would have to reckon. The ICA would possess something that could very well bring governments to their knees.

It represented power. Unimaginable power.

In just a few more months, the project would be completed. As the experiment advanced, the potential was boundless.

Travis could smell the promotion he would receive. It was entirely possible he would be appointed to be the Agency's chairman. And it could have occurred sooner, had Diana Burnwood not betrayed him. The bitch had threatened to make trouble for Travis's project because of some kind of high-and-mighty conscience she suddenly developed. She was a dangerous loose cannon, and she had to be found. His biggest fear was that Agent 47 would beat him to it, make contact with Diana, and then the two would join forces *against* the Agency. Travis didn't put it past Diana to turn the ICA's most valuable asset.

Travis picked up Agent 47's dossier and scanned it again. He knew everything about the assassin, but the manager had never met him. The hitman's exploits were legendary, though. Travis looked forward to the day when he could shake 47's hand and welcome him back to the team. If they could find him. If he would come willingly.

An interesting case, Agent 47. The world's greatest assassin was "created" in a Romanian mental asylum as a clone from the DNA of Dr. Otto Ort-Meyer and four other men. Born on September 5, 1964, Agent 47 was tagged with the identity 640509-040147 by a tattoo on the back of his neck and raised with other "Series IV" clones by the asylum's staff. Along with the other clones, 47 was trained from youth to kill efficiently. Instructed in the use of firearms, military hardware, and more-classic tools of assassination, the clone could wield virtually any weapon with ease.

After thirty years of relentless training, 47 allegedly killed a security guard and escaped from the asylum grounds. Some said that he didn't escape but rather perhaps was allowed to leave, unleashing the world's greatest assassin.

The rest, as they say, was history. At least the parts that were known.

As far as the hitman's personality went, there wasn't much documented. Agent 47 had expensive tastes in clothing, food, and drink, but otherwise he had little interest in material possessions. He took great pride in his personal arsenal: a briefcase containing two customized AMT Hardballers. The assassin said very little, but when he did, he usually spoke in a blunt, informal, and emotionless manner. He wasn't known to have an interest in sex. And while Agent 47 was extremely reliable and a perfectionist in what he did for a living, the man trusted no one. Except, possibly, Diana Burnwood.

Travis wondered if that conviction was still strong, given what had happened to 47 in the Himalayas.

Spotted in Jamaica, was he? Maybe it was true. Did Agent 47 know where Diana was hiding? Had they been in touch? After all, the hitman and his handler had a unique and special relationship. If anyone could get close—personally—to Agent 47, it was Diana.

But the woman hadn't been seen or heard from for a year. Neither had Agent 47, for that matter. He had gone off the grid after their last assignment together. At first the Agency thought the assassin was dead, but 47 unwittingly left bread crumbs indicating he'd survived the disaster in Nepal. The Agency spent months tracking him, but 47 was clever and elusive. He didn't want to be found.

Which was why Travis worried that the hitman and Diana were in cahoots. That could be a deadly combination—for *him*.

He clenched his fists and banged them hard on the table. Jade had to be right about the lead. If the Agency could get its hands on Agent 47 and recruit him back into the organization, Travis had a chance to fulfill his ambition, finish his pet project, and turn 47 against the one person in the world the assassin trusted.

FOUR

Helen McAdams shut down her computer and put away the news clippings in one of the many folders marked "Media Publicity." Her boss wanted everything that was written about him documented and archived. Another assistant, George, duped television appearances. Yet another one scoured the Internet and saved bloggers' and message-board comments—good or bad. Charlie Wilkins, leader of the Church of Will, was a man who documented his life on a daily basis. In the future, he liked to say, someone would have all the material needed for a complete and accurate biography.

Work was finished for the day. Helen gathered her belongings, shut off the lights in her mansion office, stepped out, and locked the door. She had enough time to run to her apartment and whip up some supper before heading to the recruitment center to interview new Church members. While she was paid for her job as one of several personal assistants to Reverend Wilkins, Helen kept busy with other volunteer assignments at Greenhill. For her, recruiting was the most interesting one, for she was able to meet new people. There was always the chance that a suitable man might walk in and join the Church of Will, someone with whom she could become friendly—and perhaps more.

It was good to keep busy. Helen had never liked to be

idle—the "devil's workshop" and all that—but the need to keep her mind occupied was essential ever since the stint in the hospital. It was part of the recovery process. Staying on top of numerous tasks also kept her from dwelling on her situation. Helen rarely admitted to herself that she was lonely, but it was always the elephant in the room. After her parents were killed in a tragic highway accident, and her sister had succumbed to ovarian cancer, Helen sometimes feared she was all alone in the world. That wasn't really true, she had the Church and the friends she had met there. And Charlie, of course. Reverend Charlie Wilkins. He was the light and the hope and the inspiration that kept her going. If she hadn't found the Church of Will . . . Well, she didn't like to think of how she might have ended up.

Before she could go home, there was one other task to do. Helen walked past the other assistants' offices and down the long hall to Wilkins's private sanctuary, where the man worked and prayed. His office door was closed and locked, but she had a key. It made her feel special that she was the only one of his personal assistants whom he trusted with a key to his office. Since he was away on business, one of Helen's duties was to water the many plants he kept inside. She was happy to do so. She felt his presence in the place, and it made her feel good.

Charlie Wilkins's office was a copy of the White House Oval Office in design, but the reverend had decorated it quite differently. For one thing, a wall-sized, curved plate-glass window faced Aquia Lake. The mansion had been erected on the northern shore, for Wilkins loved the view of the water. He claimed it helped him meditate. The moon and stars reflected off its surface at night, which was why he always made it a point to pray in his office at exactly midnight whenever he was on the premises. Helen agreed it was a beautiful, pastoral setting. The Church of Will compound couldn't have been built on a lovelier spot in Virginia. That was why it was called Greenhill.

Other differences from the Oval Office included the abundance of greenery. Wilkins had a green thumb and believed that all plants had souls. There were more than a hundred potted plants in the office, and Helen took the time to water the appropriate ones. They had different schedules—some had to be watered daily, others only once a week or less.

Then there were the many religious artifacts and artworks in the space. In fact, they were displayed all over the mansion. An identical room directly below this one, in the basement, supposedly stored hundreds of such treasures, but Helen had never been in it. It was off-limits to everyone except select personnel.

Wilkins embraced all of the world's religions. The Church of Will laid no claim on any particular one. Christians, Muslims, Jews, Buddhists, Hindus, and even Scientologists—everyone was welcome in the Church of Will. Wilkins had cannily taken aspects from each faith and combined them to create his own. And it worked.

The Church of Will had branches all over America. It had spread like wildfire over a few short decades. And with Charlie Wilkins's charismatic charm, his show-business acumen, and his good looks, he had conquered a sizable percentage of the American population. Some said he should run for president, but Wilkins was happy to let Senator Dana Linder do so. After all, she was a member of the Church. Wilkins did his part to campaign for her and was one of her biggest contributors.

Helen was convinced that the country needed the influence of the Church of Will's doctrines. The past decade had been hard on America. The high rise of unemployment to 23 percent, the unacceptable gasoline prices, the failing of much of the states' infrastructure, and the general dissatisfaction among the people had contributed to the worst depression since the great one of the 1930s. It was no wonder that various militant groups had sprung up all over the nation. Masked, armed militias periodically conducted terrorist attacks on federal and governmental properties. So far, there hadn't been many lives lost—only man-made structures— but the situation was becoming worse. The media usually focused on the New Model Army. Secretive and deadly, the NMA seemed to have the means and ability to strike anywhere at any time. Led by the mysterious outlaw known as "Cromwell," the New Model Army was wanted by the FBI and the police in every state, but on the other hand they had a Robin Hood mystique that ordinary citizens embraced. Helen was certain the American public was protecting the NMA by helping to hide and transport its members from place to place.

When she was done watering the plants, Helen pushed aside the thoughts about the state of the union. It was 5:45. She needed to hurry to her apartment so she could catch Wilkins's television program. She never missed it if she could help it. Helen locked his office door, scampered down the long hallway, and entered the mansion's main rotunda. She said good night to the two security men stationed there and left through the front door.

The mansion was a small palace, separated from the rest of Greenhill by a tall, electrified wire fence. Wilkins was such a celebrity that he needed protection. While most Church members were trustworthy and worshipped the man, there had been a couple of instances in which mentally unbalanced persons had tried to get into the mansion to cause the reverend some harm. Hence, the electric fence, security teams, and extra precautions had been installed. There were also a few other buildings on the inside of the fence—a barn, which was both a storage facility and a garage for Wilkins's personal limousine, and a guardhouse.

The gate was unmanned. Anyone who wanted to open it had to have a keycard, which was issued to only a few select staff members. Helen slipped hers through the magnetic slot, and the mechanism clicked. She pushed open the gate and stepped through. It locked automatically behind her.

She then walked down the paved path to Greenhill's Main Street, where Church members congregated for various activities. There was a general store, a medical facility, a recreation hall, a gym, and other amenities one would find in any subdivision of an American city. Three apartment buildings held over a hundred units for singles and families. As Greenhill was the Church of Will's main headquarters, many members lived in the apartments and worked for the organization. Wilkins owned a private jet and thus had an airstrip built on the premises. The main attraction was the beautiful church, a large sanctuary used for Sunday services and other meetings. It resembled a massive Roman Catholic cathedral, and every side was covered in gorgeous stained-glass windows. When Wilkins was in town, he usually delivered the sermons. Even non-Church members would come to the compound from all over the country to hear him. He was essentially a rock star.

Greenhill was fairly isolated from other communities in Virginia. Located just east of Interstate 95, the compound was south of Coal Landing and west of Arkendale. Around the northwest bend of the lake were other villages, streets, and recreational facilities. Willow Landing Marina wasn't too far. Nevertheless, the area Greenhill occupied on the north shore of Aquia Lake was private and quiet. No member was a prisoner, of course. Anyone could come and go as they pleased. Residents often visited Stafford, Garrisonville, and Garrisonville

Estates, the closest sizable towns. And if one wanted to go to a *big* city, Washington, D.C., and its sprawling suburbs were less than an hour's drive away.

Helen entered her building, inspected her personal mailbox in the lobby—it was always empty, but she checked it daily, anyway—and then climbed the stairs to the second floor. Her one-bedroom apartment was as good as anything one might find in any city, and the rent was nominal since she worked for the Church. It was comfortable and homey, decorated with knick-knacks she'd collected over the years and with Church of Will iconography. Her favorite was a framed, auto-graphed poster of Charlie Wilkins, who pointed at the viewer à la Uncle Sam and asked his signature question in a dialogue bubble: "Will You?" The Church was all about taking control of one's destiny and finding and applying inner strength to get through life on a daily basis. Wilkins believed that each individual should fol-low the "Will" of the common man, collectively bound as a desire to be governed only by the "Supreme One" and not by men or women who made false promises and led people into partisan politics, paths of war, and fi-nancial catastrophe. The Supreme One was not neces-sarily "God" but could be if that was what an individual wanted to believe. The Church of Will allowed its mem-bers to interpret the religion in any way they wanted, as long as certain creeds were followed.

She poured a can of soup into a pot to heat up on the stove, then went to the bathroom to wash her face and hands. As she dried off, she gazed at her features and repeated the mantra Wilkins had drilled into her.

I am pretty. *I am* worthy. *I am* Helen McAdams and I have the *Will.*

Most men found her attractive, she thought. Helen felt them gazing at her. And why not? She was thirty-one years old, thin, and had a pleasant face. She had dated a few of the Church members, but nothing ever came of it. Her shyness and insecurity played a big part in her failure to land a lasting relationship. Her college boyfriend—well, she didn't like to dwell on what happened there. Since then, Helen's love life had been closer to the latter end of the hit-or-miss scale.

They say "loneliness is just a word," she thought to herself.

Six o'clock. Time to turn on the TV.

She returned to the living room, switched on the set, and went back to the kitchen to pour the hot soup into a bowl. She grabbed the open but corked bottle of white wine from the fridge, poured a glass, and then took her supper to the couch in front of the television.

The news was just ending. The top story concerned the New Model Army's attack that morning on an Internal Revenue Service building in Cincinnati, Ohio. Three bombs had gone off simultaneously, destroying an entire side of the structure. Luckily, it was prior to rush hour, so only forty-something people were injured. Two fatalities. If the explosions had occurred during the workday, the death toll would have been disastrous. In many ways, Helen was sympathetic to the NMA's cause, but she was strongly against violence. The fact that innocent people were sometimes "collateral damage," as Cromwell liked to call it, was deplorable. Still, the New Model Army and other splinter militant groups were successful at inciting the unrest that existed in the country. Helen felt that if enough people were unhappy, the government would have to change to accommodate them.

Finally, Wilkins's aptly titled variety show, *Will You?*, came on, with its catchy theme song. *Will You?* was one of the highest-rated TV programs, and it wasn't on a regular network or cable channel. Charlie Wilkins owned his *own* cable network, and he filled it with not only his signature show but also other Church of Will–sponsored dramas and sitcoms, made-for-TV movies, news features, and even cartoons for children. Millions of viewers tuned in. *Will You?* was part talk show, part musical variety acts, part political rhetoric, and part evangelical recruitment. The show was taped in a studio inside the mansion at Greenhill when Wilkins was on the premises (otherwise, reruns were broadcast). Tickets were a hot commodity, and it was said that the show attracted more tourists than the Lincoln and Washington Monuments or the Smithsonian Institute.

At last, the reverend appeared to welcome the studio audience and viewers at home.

Charlie Wilkins was in his sixties; he had a magnificent mane of white hair and sparkling blue eyes that melted the hearts of housewives everywhere. He was terribly handsome, which had a lot to do with his appeal. When he raised one eyebrow and grinned—a signature trait often lampooned by stand-up comics—his eyes sparkled and he exuded goodwill. Mostly it was his charisma and charm that won people over. He was witty, upbeat, and he spoke with the voice of an angel. The smooth timbre of his baritone speech had the power to mesmerize listeners. If he had claimed to be the Second Coming, which he didn't, it was likely that a lot of people would have believed him. There were critics, however. The extremely outspoken ones considered Wilkins just another wacko leading a "cult." Others were more moderate. While they dismissed Wilkins's "godliness," they admitted he was a smart and fascinating personality who had earned and deserved respect. Even Americans unsold on Wilkins thought he was entertaining at the very least.

After the preliminary stand-up monologue and jokes that rivaled anything heard on late-night variety shows, Wilkins announced, "Tonight's guest is none other than presidential candidate Senator Dana Shipley Linder. I know the anticipation is building, so let's get the word from our sponsor over with quickly and get to the main event! We'll be right back."

As always, Wilkins's own companies provided commercials for the network. The reverend's fast-food restaurant chain, Charlie's, had become second only to McDonald's as the go-to eatery for people on the run. The food was more expensive than other chain fare, but Charlie's specialized in guaranteed healthy, organic products. The grass-fed, free-range beef and chicken were from farms owned by the Church of Will, and no artificial chemicals were added to the meat or vegetables. Helen liked it a lot. There was a Charlie's in the Greenhill Town Center, and she ate there several times a week. Everyone in America was familiar with the Charlie's logo—a cartoon depiction of Wilkins's white shock of hair with the word "Charlie's" scribbled where the face would be.

The program resumed and the reverend introduced Dana Linder. As the main challenger to the incumbent president, Mark Burdett, Linder's star had risen rapidly after the creation of a new party to rival the Democrats and Republicans. The America First Party began as a grass-roots movement but quickly grew to a nationwide tidal wave. Blaming the Democrats and Republicans for excessive and endless partisan fighting in Congress, the America First Party promised to end all that. Already, America First Party candidates had taken many seats in the House and Senate in the midterm elections. With the presidential election coming up in just over a month, the pundits were predicting an upset. Burdett would lose out on a second term, and for the first time in recent history, a non-Republican or -Democrat would take the White House. Linder was the woman likely to fulfill that prediction.

Dana Shipley Linder was in her late thirties and had served as a representative from Maryland. She was tall, dark-haired, and attractive. There was no question that she was intelligent and had her finger on the pulse of America. Helen admired her.

"Thank you for coming on the show, Dana."

"Charlie, all you have to do is ask, you know that. I'd do anything for my childhood preacher," she replied, beaming.

Wilkins laughed and rolled his eyes. "Some of you may not know that, but, yes, it's true, when Dana and her brother, Darren, were orphaned as children, I was their pastor and family friend. I looked out for them. I like to think I gave them both the guidance that helped them grow into splendid adults."

"You certainly did, Charlie," she said. "And you were so young then!"

He wagged a finger at her. "Now, now! I'm *still* young! And so are you! And that reminds me, Dana. Happy birthday!"

The audience applauded, and the candidate blushed and waved away the adulation. "Charlie, that was a month ago. You're a little late."

"But I haven't seen you since. I understand you had a spectacular party."

"Oh, we did. John and the children and I threw quite the hootenanny in Towson. I'm so sorry you were away and couldn't make it."

"I am too. You know I would have been there if I could." He took her hands and held them. "Anyway, I hope it was a happy occasion."

"It was. Of course, it would have been better if . . . if Darren had been there."

Wilkins nodded with a sympathetic look on his face,

as the audience applauded again. Many members whistled their appreciation.

Helen considered that much of Linder's popularity was because she had a hero brother. Darren Shipley was a marine who had died in Iraq while on an important mission to sweep insurgents out of a building. There was a massive explosion, and Darren perished in the flames. A savvy media reporter covered Shipley's demise, and the America First Party capitalized on it. The public embraced the story of the handsome marine and his gorgeous sister, he a national hero who sacrificed his life for his country, and she a politician who was destined to change America.

It made good politics.

Wilkins continued the interview. "In another month, Americans will go to the polls to elect our next president. I understand you have a heavy campaign schedule."

Linder nodded. "You know how it is, Charlie. As we approach the finish line, it just gets more intense. But you know, Charlie, I have you to thank for all this."

"Me?"

"It was you who suggested I run for public office when I was younger. Your influence spurred me on. And I'm going to do you proud."

"That's a wonderful thing to hear, Dana. Is there anything you'd like to say to the American people?"

"Yes, there is." She looked straight into the camera. "All of you out there, I know and understand your frustration. President Burdett is completely out of touch with what's happening. His foreign policy is a disaster. He actually tried to make peace with terrorist groups and nations considered to be America's enemies in an effort to influence gasoline prices. That failed. Our economy and unemployment rate are worse than ever. We have militant groups wreaking havoc on government property. President Burdett has turned the National Guard into storm troopers. In an effort to control the militants, the National Guardsmen are hurting innocent civilians. Well, I'm fed up, and I know you are too. I'm fed up with the Democrats and the Republicans and their constant bickering. They never get anything done. Two years ago, the people spoke and placed many America First Party candidates in office. I believe that's going to happen again on Election Day. If I'm elected president, I promise to bring America back to the people and not into the hands of big government, which is squashing you all like insects."

Wilkins raised a finger to attract her attention.

"Yes, Charlie?"

"How do you answer critics who say your candidacy is really an advertisement for the Church of Will? Everyone knows you're a member and you believe in our tenets."

"I'm glad you asked that, Charlie. I just want to point out that more and more people are turning toward these tenets, as you call them, whether they know it or not. But let me make it clear that my following the Church of Will is personal. Past presidents had their religions. I have mine. And while the Church gives me values to follow and practice, it doesn't mean I'll be bringing the Church into the White House. That said, I refuse to be a hypocrite. Much of what the Church teaches can be applied to the running of a country. The Church asks its members to act on our inner Will. Well, I'm asking the country to act on *its* inner Will too!"

Applause. Hoots and hollers.

Helen smiled. She was definitely on the same page as Dana Linder. There was no question that the woman had her vote.

Before the next commercial, Wilkins said, "In the interest of fairness, I invited President Burdett to be on the show next week, and he accepted." The audience greeted this statement with boos and catcalls. Wilkins held up his hands. "Now, now. Let's be respectful, folks. The president has as much right to be on *Will You?* and to speak his mind as Dana Linder does. I look forward to welcoming him."

Helen finished her soup, drank the last sip of wine, and took the bowl and glass into the kitchen. She'd clean up later. The recruitment center opened at seven o'clock. One never knew who might come to Greenhill to sign up, especially after Linder's rousing speech.

She spent a few minutes in the bathroom reapplying her makeup and brushing her long brown hair. Yes, she *was* pretty. There was no reason in the world why she couldn't attract a decent man. Who cared if she'd had some . . . problems in the past? That was exactly what it was. The past.

Helen turned off the television, put on her jacket, and left the apartment. The evening was young.

If it turned out to be uneventful, tomorrow was another day.

FIVE

Roget paid me my fee. One perk was that Roget offered me a ride on his private plane to Rio de Janeiro. I thought that might be a nice place to visit and hunt for work, so I took him up on it. It was also convenient, because I could bring my briefcase on board with me. It contained my handguns. They're AMT Hardballers, but I call them Silverballers because of the pearl handles.

It was a Lear business-class jet, so the cabin was small. It held twelve passengers, but I was the only one aboard. There was no flight attendant. I never saw the pilot, but a voice over the intercom told me to fasten my seat belt and all that. We took off from Montego Bay in the afternoon and I was on my way.

The Jamaican news was full of Corado's death. Emilio Fernandez was taken in for questioning. The States sent an FBI agent down to interrogate him as well. Corado was wanted in a few countries. I guess I saved a lot of taxpayers' money, since the guy would never have a trial. Corado was scum, and I had no problem extracting him from the planet. I wasn't sure exactly what Roget's beef with Corado was. Maybe Corado was muscling in on Roget's territory. Roget didn't seem to be the most up-and-up kind of guy either. For all I knew, his business was human trafficking.

Not that I cared.

As the plane left Caribbean airspace, I reclined the seat and tried to relax. I was hoping to get some sleep on the flight, but I felt a twinge of anxiety. I had taken my pill earlier, but I was starting to wonder if I needed to take two at a time. They said people gain a tolerance for the stuff. So far, that hadn't happened to me. I guess that was because I'm different.

We weren't in the air ten minutes when we hit turbulence. It was bad too. I looked out the window and saw that a storm had appeared out of nowhere. The clouds were dark and threatening. Lightning flashed across the panorama, and the plane lurched violently. It felt like the jet had gone through a cloud of plutonium. I expected the pilot to make an announcement or something, but there was dead silence from the cockpit.

I waited in my seat a few more minutes, but I usually could tell when an airplane was having trouble. We were losing altitude. There was nothing below but ocean. I didn't like the looks of it, so I unbuckled my seat belt and moved up the aisle to the cockpit door, which was closed. I banged on it and shouted, "Hey, in there! What's going on?" Again, dead silence. I banged again.

I went back to my seat to fetch one of the Silverballers. I opened the briefcase, grabbed the handgun, inserted one of the seven-round magazines, a .45 ACP, and returned to the door. One blast was all it took.

Imagine my surprise when I pulled it open. There wasn't anyone in the cockpit. No pilot. No copilot. Nobody.

I've had a little experience with planes, so I jumped into the pilot's seat. If I just leveled the aircraft and kept it from crashing into the sea, I'd be happy. But the control column didn't respond. It was stuck. That's when I noticed the black box with the red lights on it.

It was attached beneath the dash. The plane was controlled by remote.

The Silverballer coughed again. The box shattered to pieces, and at the same time the plane jolted hard. Looking out the window, I saw that one of the engines was out. Great. Flying on one engine in a storm. The aircraft wouldn't respond when I moved the control column.

Time for plan B.

I got up and searched the cockpit for a parachute. If the plane was going down, I wanted to beat it to the water and, hopefully, with a softer landing. But of course there wasn't a parachute in sight, so it was back to the cabin. I searched the overhead compartments. They were all empty. I looked under the seats. At least there was a flotation device. I grabbed it and put it around my chest. I knew I had to blow into the tubes to inflate it. That could wait.

I even did a quick reconnaissance of the lavatory. Nada.

No more ideas.

The plane veered a little but was still losing altitude. There was nothing else to do but buckle myself into my seat. I tried to recall where was the best place to be when a plane crashes. But the Lear was so small, I didn't think it would make any difference where I was.

I was going to die.

Oddly, I wasn't afraid. I was prepared to accept my fate. My whole life, I had expected Death to come calling. The way things had been going the last year, I welcomed his visit.

I closed my eyes. A wave of peace flowed through my body.

But then—that ball of angst bubbled up in my chest. That could mean only one thing, so I opened my eyes and looked out the window.

Rain battered the Plexiglas. In the black clouds—a face. No, not a face. The shape of a face. A familiar one.

Death. The same shadowy faceless figure from my dreams. Watching the plane go down.

I braced myself for the impact. Would the plane survive hitting the water? Would it float or sink?

I was going to die. The last time that thought crossed my mind, I was in Nepal. In the Himalayas.

A year ago . . .

S I X

Agent 47 tapped his earpiece.

"Diana? Are you there?"

If he wasn't mistaken, the line had been cut off. Why would she leave him like that? She gives him some vague instruction, tells him that two hostiles are making their way toward his position on the mountain, and then disappears? Perhaps it was a technical malfunction. Surely she would be back online in a moment.

In the meantime, 47 removed the boomer from his backpack. It was a device that resembled a twelve-inch flashlight, its exterior made of metal. Inside, however, was a complex transmitter that emitted powerful sonic waves. Human ears couldn't hear them, but they would drive any dog within miles completely mad. More important, the sound waves would upset natural faults within rock, ice, or snow. Placed vertically in the snow on the Kangchenjunga cliff where the hitman now crouched, it could cause an avalanche after a minute or two. The trick was to plant it on the precise geological flaw. Only Diana's computer could calculate the right spot.

He had made it to the snow-packed cliff she had indicated, but he had no clue where to stick the boomer. By now the two Chinese bodyguards would be closer. How fast could they move down the face of the mountain? 47

was no expert at mountain climbing, but he could travel ten feet per five minutes. If they were that good or better, it would take them a little while to reach him.

47 dared to lie facedown on the cliff and inch to the edge. It was a long way down, but he could see Nam Vo and his party moving along. They were in the perfect position. He needed to set off the boomer *now*.

Where was Diana?

The assassin rolled to his side so that he could look up. The sun was terribly bright, but the Uvex pocket goggles blocked out the worst of the dangerous rays. Unfortunately, the sun was almost straight above him. The glare prevented him from seeing the two guards that were headed his way.

47 carefully wormed back to the cliff face so they wouldn't see *him*. Once again he tapped the earpiece. It was still working, because he heard static. No, something was definitely wrong on Diana's end.

It had been a perilous mission. The Chinese general known as Nam Vo had come to Nepal so that he would be in close proximity to Tibet. Nam Vo got his kicks by sending a small force of military sadists across the border to terrorize Tibetan villages. They raped women, tortured men, and left children starving. Whether or not Vo was under orders from the Chinese government, or if he had simply gone rogue, was unclear. All 47 knew was that a "concerned party" had hired the Agency to assassinate the monster. Perhaps it was a Tibetan resistance group. Maybe it was a wealthy activist in America or Britain. Perhaps it was the Dalai Lama himself. Unlikely, but 47 didn't really care. Sometimes the Agency told him who the customer was and sometimes they didn't. More often the client was anonymous.

Formulating the plan to assassinate Nam Vo on Kangchenjunga was another dangerous component. Mountain climbing was hazardous enough when it was done for sport. Throw in deadly weapons and a scheme to kill people, and it was madness. Agent 47 wanted to figure out another way to get to Vo, but Diana had insisted the man was unreachable. She had found out he liked to climb, so she kept her eyes and ears to the ground in Nepal and eventually learned about the expedition up the "Kanch," as locals called the peak.

Usually she left the method and means to Agent 47, but this time she worked out the plot. 47 would get a head start up the mountain so that he could be in position to drop tons of snow and ice on the man. Making Nam Vo's death appear to be an accident—better yet, a natural disaster—was the key to the mission's success. Corrupt or not, the Chinese government wouldn't take kindly to one of their top military men being murdered. They would seek revenge. They could take it out on Tibet or even Nepal. 47 hadn't had a problem with it until now.

Where was Diana?

After he set off the boomer, 47 was to move laterally across the mountain face to a designated outcrop of stone. There, a helicopter from Kathmandu would appear, hover above him, and lower a rope ladder. They'd be gone before authorities had time to investigate the avalanche.

Had the chopper left Kathmandu? Surely not. Diana was to give the pilot the green light after 47 had successfully placed the boomer and set off the sonic explosion.

Maybe the satellite failed. That was it. Diana wouldn't abandon him like that. She was the only person on the planet that he almost trusted, and he had a serious problem with trust. He had confidence in only one human being, and that was himself.

His inner clock told him it was nearly a quarter after one. He was late. If he didn't act soon, the mission would have to be aborted. Agent 47 never aborted assignments. The concept was anathema to his soul.

Once more the assassin crawled to the edge of the cliff. Nam Vo was probably a hundred fifty feet below but still in the target range.

Where was Diana?

The sound of rapid gunfire jolted him. A string of powerful kicks punctured the snow six inches from his head. 47 rolled to his side, and this time he saw them. One man was dangling on a rope at such an angle that he had full view of the ice cliff. The other guy was spotting him. The hanging man held an assault rifle, probably a QBZ-95. 47 was a sitting duck.

The assassin scrambled back to the cliff wall, but the Chinese bodyguard still had a bead on him. The man fired again; bullets dotted the rock face as 47 hit the snow and flattened his body as much as he could. There was no question—he had to get out of there.

The assault weapon's noise would surely alert Nam Vo and his party. They would move for cover and 47 would lose his chance. There was only one thing to do. Blindly place the boomer and hope for the best.

Which is exactly what he did.

47 armed the device to start pulsing, and then he plunged it hard into the snow. The tiny beacon resembled a metal stake. How long would it take before the cliff gave way? The hitman didn't want to stay and find out.

More gunshots.

47 froze and backed up. He pulled a Silverballer from his backpack, aimed at the suspended shooter, and fired.

A hit. But not a kill. The sun was simply too strong. It was like trying to aim into a fireball and strike a dot. Nevertheless, 47 heard the man yelp in pain. But the guy held on to the QBZ-95 and started firing again. 47

decided to go in the opposite direction from which he was supposed to climb. It was the only way to avoid getting perforated. He had no idea what the route would be like or where it would take him, but he had to move.

Then he felt a tremor.

Where was Diana?

The cliff rumbled beneath his legs.

Move! Move! Now! Now!

But the Chinese shooter blocked his way with a barrage of death. . . .

SEVEN

. . . just as the Learjet jerked hard, continuing its plummet toward the sea.

Agent 47 broke out of his reverie and returned to the here and now. He was still strapped to the seat in the plane's cabin, utterly helpless. He considered opening the emergency hatch and jumping out right before the aircraft hit the water. Would he survive? Possibly. It was worth a try. He had the life vest. If the fall didn't kill him, he could inflate the vest in the water. Better than sitting there with a useless seat belt across his waist.

He unbuckled it and stood. The assassin clutched the back of the seats as he made his way to the door, located just behind the cockpit. The plane lunged brutally, throwing 47 to the floor. He pulled himself up to continue what might be his final act, but then he remembered the briefcase. If he was going to die, he wanted to perish with his beloved tools of the trade. The hitman retraced his steps, clumsily moving through the cabin as the jet jerked and tilted erratically. When he reached his seat, 47 leaned over and grabbed the case with his adopted insignia, similar to a fleur-de-lis, stamped on the outside.

Back to the door.

He didn't dare look out the window as he moved. How many seconds did he have left? A minute or two? Less?

It took a near-superhuman effort to reach the hatch. The instructions for emergency opening were printed on the interior. It wasn't rocket science. Push this lever and pull that one.

So do it. What are you waiting for?

Push. Pull.

The hatch broke away from the fuselage and soared into space. A huge gush of wet air nearly sucked Agent 47 out with it, but he held on to a safety handle on the side and braced himself with his shoes against the frame.

Now he could see the well of death below. A thousand feet? Less? With the storm battering the doorway, it was difficult to know for certain.

But it was obvious he had only a few seconds left.

Jump!

If he was going to do it, he had to do it now.

Jump!

Agent 47 thrust himself through the hatchway and was hit with a sledgehammer of rain and wind. For a moment he didn't think he was falling; he was aware only of being suspended in the maelstrom. Incongruously, he sensed that he was still clutching the briefcase in one hand. The assassin thought he saw the jet veer off into the darkness above and beyond him, but he wasn't sure. He was blind and deaf from the raging hell around him.

For no logical reason, he started to count to himself.

One . . . two . . .

Was he even moving? Was the frenetic, cold whirlwind spinning him around and around?

Three . . . four . . .

The noise was unbearable. It was as if he were inside the roars of a thousand beasts.

Five . . . six . . . sev—

A wall of *freeze* slammed into his body, and the cacophony abruptly ended. The powerful wind ceased and was replaced by an envelope of frigid liquid.

For a moment he might have lost consciousness. He wasn't sure.

Relax. Don't fight it. Go limp.

Years of training had conditioned Agent 47 to completely surrender to the sea. To fight it would be disastrous. The only way to surface and catch the precious oxygen above was to become a lifeless, weightless particle of ocean trash.

And it worked.

Agent 47's bald head broke the surface, and he gasped for breath. It was only then that he kicked and moved his arms in an effort to tread. The ocean was indeed rough and extremely dangerous.

Incredibly, he still gripped the briefcase. It was as if the thing was in actuality an outgrowth of his arm.

The life jacket!

He had almost forgotten it.

With his free hand, he pulled the tube up and into his mouth. Blowing was extremely difficult. It was hard enough to breathe normally in such conditions, and yet he managed to do it. It took an eternity, but slowly the vest inflated and did its job to keep the assassin afloat.

Completely spent, Agent 47 allowed the roiling waves to carry him wherever they might, yielding to a blanket of black unawareness.

Voices and noises murkily drifted in and out of his brain. As his eyelids blinked open, blurry bright lights pierced his retinas like spears. He felt the urge to cough, but the effort was a gurgling gasp. Hands were on him, pushing, pulling . . .

He heard the distinct words, "He's alive!"

And then he sank back into a cocoon of nothingness.

* * *

When next he opened his eyes, his vision was less blurry. The bright lights were still above him, and he realized he was no longer floating helplessly in the ocean. However, the rocking sensation of being tossed around by the waves was still present.

Agent 47 lay in a bed. He was dressed in a hospital gown and was covered with warm sheets and blankets. An IV was attached to the back of his right hand. A drip on a stand stood next to the bed. Turning his head, he saw a nurse with her back to him.

He coughed, but it came out in an unintelligible croak.

She turned. Dark hair, in her thirties. "Oh, you're awake! I'll get the doctor."

Where am I?

The assassin studied his surroundings. It was no ordinary hospital room. Too small. The windows were round. Portholes.

He was on a boat.

No wonder he still felt the rocking of the sea.

A black man in a white lab coat entered the cabin, followed by the nurse. He was in his fifties, wore glasses, and had a kind face.

"Good morning," he said in a British accent. "I'm Dr. Chalmers. How are you feeling?"

Agent 47 didn't answer.

"You've had a rough time. You were lucky we were nearby. We picked you up out of the water. You'd almost drowned."

Again, the hitman said nothing.

"Don't worry. You're going to be fine. You have a strong constitution."

47 already knew that.

"We're giving you some fluids through an IV. You

were dehydrated. Kind of ironic, isn't it? Being dehydrated in the middle of the ocean?"

The assassin didn't respond.

The doctor indicated the stethoscope around his neck. "May I check your vitals?" Not waiting for an answer, the man leaned in to listen to 47 breathe. The assassin didn't protest.

"Your lungs are clear." The doctor nodded to the nurse, who wrapped a cuff around 47's left arm to take his blood pressure. She pumped it up and then let it deflate.

"One eighteen over seventy-eight," she said.

"That's very good," the doctor commented. "I'll bet you're thirsty and hungry. Nurse Parkins here will get you some juice and something to eat. Get some rest. You've had a rough time."

The nurse quickly left the cabin. The doctor waited for 47 to say something; when the patient didn't, the man turned to leave. He paused at the curved hatch, turned, and replied to the unasked question.

"All will be explained shortly."

And then he left.

It was only then that Agent 47 noticed the embossed insignia on the IV drip bag. It was triangular; a skull and crossbones topped by a crown was inside the pyramid, the Latin phrase *Merces Letifer* scrolled across the bottom.

"Lethal trade."

The emblem of the ICA.

The Agency.

After a meal of scrambled eggs, toast, and orange juice, Agent 47 felt his strength returning. He wanted to jump out of bed and find out what was going on. Given that he was on a ship, he figured it was the *Jean Danjou II*, the Agency's superyacht. What else could it be?

The prospect that the ICA had found him was disturbing. 47 had wanted to remain hidden. The assassin had hoped that, if he ever decided to reconnect with the Agency, it would be on his terms.

The familiar unpleasant fireball of anxiety suddenly grew in his chest. How long had it been since he'd taken an oxycodone pill? The withdrawal symptoms would soon hit him full force. Where was his briefcase? His clothes? His painkillers?

Before he could attempt to get out of bed, an attractive Asian woman, wearing a business suit and carrying a notepad, entered the cabin.

"Good morning, Agent 47," she said without a trace of an accent. "My name is Jade. I'm a senior assistant to the management team of ICA. I take it you've already discerned that's who we are?"

47 stared at her for several seconds and then nodded.

"I suppose you have a lot of questions. Mr. Travis will be here shortly to talk to you. He will be your new handler."

The assassin spoke for the first time since he'd been revived. "I don't work for the Agency anymore."

Jade acknowledged the remark with a bow of her head. "Mr. Travis will speak to you about that. In the meantime, I am authorized to tell you that you are on the *Jean Danjou II*, and we were—"

"I know that."

"—we were sailing in the Atlantic, quite near the Caribbean. We have been searching for you for many months. Your last employer, the man you knew as Roget, alerted us—for a price—that his plane was leaving Jamaica with you on it."

"There was no pilot aboard."

"We had Roget install the remote so we could land the aircraft safely on the water. Unfortunately, the storm hit and an engine failed. Apparently you damaged the remote-control box, and we were unable to help you. Luckily, we were in your vicinity when the jet went down, but it still took us several hours to find you. You are a very lucky man."

Was she telling the truth? Agent 47 supposed that it sounded plausible. He also knew that the Agency was capable of elaborate deceptions.

A middle-aged man in a suit appeared in the hatchway. He wore glasses, had a mustache, and was a bit overweight.

"How's the patient?" he asked.

"Dr. Chalmers says he's doing very well," Jade answered. "Agent 47, this is Benjamin Travis."

The man approached the bed and held out his hand. The hitman ignored it, so Travis shrugged. "I can imagine how you feel. Hiding from the Agency for a year and suddenly finding yourself on our ship. I'll bet you think you were set up."

"Where's Diana?" 47 asked.

Travis and Jade exchanged a look, and then he continued. "I'll get to that. I want to assure you that what Jade told you is true. Yes, we wanted to find you. Yes, we would have paid a lot of money to get you back, and we did. Yes, Roget worked for us, in a way. As an informer and sometimes contractor. I'm sorry the flight didn't go as we planned."

"Where's Diana?" the hitman asked again, with a little more insistence in his voice.

"Very well." Travis took a chair and sat in it. Jade continued to stand. "Diana Burnwood betrayed the Agency. She irreparably damaged the organization by compromising a classified project that top management was working on. And . . . she abandoned you during a crucial mission. The Himalayan assignment would not have gone wrong had she not bailed. She left you in a vulnerable position. I suppose you remember that?"

He did. Agent 47's eyes narrowed as he searched Travis's face for artifice.

"What happened?" he asked.

"I can't go into the classified details, but suffice it to say that she meant for you to die. Diana felt you were the only one who might possibly be sent to come after her when we discovered her betrayal. And she's right. As soon as we find out where she's hiding, we *will* send you after her. After all, you know her better than anyone."

"I don't work for the Agency anymore."

"I was hoping we could discuss that."

"I don't work for the Agency anymore."

"Hear me out, 47. Will you do that?"

The assassin kept silent.

"We know you've been working freelance. We know you're being paid much less than what you're worth. It's beneath you, 47. You were the Agency's greatest asset. We want you back. We're prepared to double your fees."

"I don't care about the money."

"We know you don't. You never have. But you care about your reputation. You care about the quality of your work. You care about what you do best."

"I am nowhere near one hundred percent operational."

"We think you are," Travis said. "The fact that you survived that jump from the plane and the subsequent hours in the sea proves that you are. Did you know you were floating in impossibly rough waters for seven hours before we picked you up? That's extraordinary. Any other human being, even one with your, uh, *special* genetic structure, would never have endured the ordeal. You did, 47. We're all astonished and . . . humbled."

47 didn't respond.

"Look, why don't you rest? Think about it overnight.

You've been through a tough twenty-four hours. But, frankly, we need you. There's a pressing assignment that is quite suited to you. We don't need the verification, but you could prove to yourself that you're, as you call it, one hundred percent operational. And don't you want to get back at Burnwood? She abandoned you, left you like a piece of meat for dogs to devour."

The assassin didn't know what to think about Diana. All the facts weren't in. But Travis was right. If she had indeed intentionally caused the Himalayan task to fail, then she deserved every bit of his . . . *attention*.

"What's the assignment?" he asked.

Travis stood. "It may very well be the most difficult mission of your career. Consider it a challenge. But why don't you rest for a day? We can talk about it tomorrow. It can wait that long." He pointed to two different call buttons on 47's bed. "If you need anything, press one of those buttons. The red one is for the nurse. The blue one is for us."

"Where are my things? Did you recover my briefcase?"

Travis grinned. "It's unbelievable, 47. Even in your unconscious state, being tossed around like flotsam on that rough sea, you held on to that damned briefcase. We have it." He nodded to a locker on the other side of the cabin. "It's all there. Your clothes, everything. We dry-cleaned your suit. It's fresh and like new, hanging right in there. We opened the briefcase to check on your weapons, and they're fine. You'll want to clean them, oil them, do all the things you do to get them back to ship-shape condition, but, miraculously, all of your stuff survived with you. You're one in a million, 47. The Agency will be very grateful, and make it worth your while, if you decide to rejoin us."

With that, the man jerked his head at Jade, and the two left the room.

47 waited a few minutes and then threw back the sheets. He swung his legs around and put his bare feet on the floor. He grabbed the IV pole, which was on wheels, and dragged it across the floor as he unsteadily walked to the locker. He opened it, revealing the black suit hanging in pristine condition. The briefcase sat on the locker bottom. 47 pulled it out and took it back to the bed. He opened it, examined the two Silverballers, and then felt for the hidden latch that unlocked the hidden compartment beneath the handguns. His various passports, currency from several countries, and Fiberwire were all there.

As well as his painkillers.

47 opened the pill bottle, took two tablets, and downed them with the remains of his juice.

He carefully put everything in place, shut the case in the locker, and went back to bed.

Sleep came quickly. The figure of Death mercifully stayed away.

EIGHT

The night passed peacefully, and Agent 47 slept better than he had in months. Perhaps the gentle rocking of the ship helped. By the middle of the second day on the ship, he felt rejuvenated. Travis sent word that they would have dinner together and talk that evening—in the meantime, he was to feel free to make himself at home aboard the *Jean Danjou II*.

Although he was a man of fierce independence, 47 allowed Nurse Parkins to pamper him. It was gratifying to be waited upon. Both Parkins and Dr. Chalmers quickly learned that the assassin spoke very little, so they gave up attempting to engage him in conversation. They did, however, encourage him to get out of bed, dress, and take walks.

The yacht was huge. 47 strolled the deck from bow to stern and back, then explored the ship's bowels. No guards prevented him from entering any restricted areas. He spent time in the control center, observing the various operations and personnel. The hitman figured Travis was attempting to instill confidence. The man wanted 47 to consider himself part of the team again.

The woman known as Jade seemed to be very competent. She managed the control room with admirable patience and efficiency. Travis moved in and out of the space, delivering orders and listening to reports. At one point he acknowledged 47 and asked how he felt. 47 replied that he was fine, and Travis said that he looked forward to their meeting later. Otherwise, everyone on the ship ignored the assassin. He was allowed to stand behind the various workstations and study the computer monitors, maps, and data coming in from all parts of the globe. The Agency was busy. It appeared that the business of killing was in no danger of a recession.

Dinner that evening was served in the yacht's executive dining room, which was designed in luxurious Louis XIV décor, as if the place were a high-end French restaurant. Waiters wore formal uniforms with white gloves. Travis, Jade, and 47 were the only diners.

The food was of exceptional quality. They started with a bottle of Dom Pérignon '57, which the hitman had to admit was smooth on the palate. Never a heavy drinker, Agent 47 did appreciate fine wine and champagne. He had expensive tastes, and over the last year he had not been able to indulge in the kinds of meals to which he was accustomed. He knew full well it was yet another ploy on Travis's part to lure the assassin back to the Agency, so he figured he might as well enjoy it.

A bottle of Château Pétrus, among the priciest and best wine on the planet, was served with dinner, which was a selection of Kobe beef filet mignon, lobster thermidor, and a variety of steamed vegetables. A recently baked challah bread made from an orthodox recipe in Jerusalem was incongruously served with the meal, but it was a surprisingly fitting addition.

Agent 47 declined an after-dinner drink of fino sherry but heartily accepted the crème brûlée.

It was the best meal he'd had in over twelve months.

Travis unsuccessfully attempted to engage 47 in conversation while the trio ate, but the assassin didn't utter much. During the awkward silence, 47 was intent on gauging what Travis had to say and how he said it. The assassin could never fully trust him or his attractive assistant, but at least 47 would give them the benefit of the doubt—for now. The story he'd been told about Diana Burnwood still disturbed him. Could she have really betrayed him and the Agency? 47 thought he knew his former handler better than that. He also accepted the fact that any hitman working for the Agency would be disavowed if anything went wrong during a mission. Could Diana have been compromised in some way? It was possible she didn't have a choice in abandoning him.

The only thing 47 could do was to play out the game. If rejoining the Agency would eventually lead him to Diana—if she was still alive—and to the answers he sought, then so be it.

"I have decided to accept your offer," the assassin unexpectedly announced as Travis lit a cigar.

The man raised his eyebrows. "You have?" Travis exchanged a look with Jade. Then he smiled. "Well! All right, then. I thought Jade and I would have to ply you with promises of Italian sports cars, women, and points in the company's profits!"

"I don't care about any of that. I live for perfection. It appears that you're offering me a fair deal to restore my name to its former glory. I welcome the challenge." 47 thought this was a reasonable explanation that a shallow man like Travis would accept. It had a touch of truth to it, but in reality the assassin felt he could do nothing else but play along.

Travis offered 47 a cigar, but the hitman shook his head. "Upper management will be very pleased to hear that their prized asset is back on board. Thank you, 47. This means a great deal to us." He held out his hand, but 47 didn't take it. Travis awkwardly gave up and gestured for the tall, bald man to follow him into another room. "Let's talk in here. Jade, could you please take notes?"

"Yes, sir."

The three of them moved into a room that was not unlike an English manor study or library, complete with a roaring fireplace. If it hadn't been for the easy rocking, 47 would never have known he was on a boat.

Travis pointed to a leather armchair. "Have a seat." He sat in an identical piece of furniture across from 47, while Jade, notepad in lap, perched on the end of a sofa perpendicular to the men.

"Now, then. The mission," Travis began. "Are you up to date with what's going on with American politics these days?"

Agent 47 shrugged. "I don't pay much attention to it."

"America's economy is in big trouble. They're in the biggest depression since the 1930s, although the government won't admit it. President Burdett has lost the support of the people. A Congress consisting of Democrats and Republicans is ridiculed as being incompetent and petty. In the last few years, a third party has risen to power. The America First Party is conservative, ultra right wing, and anti big government. In the last Congressional election, several AFP members were elected. There's a presidential election coming up in a month. A female senator, Dana Shipley Linder, a member of the America First Party, is poised to be the winner."

"Okay," 47 said.

Jade spoke next. "Thrown into the mix is an uprising of militant terrorist groups around the country. The big one is the New Model Army, led by an individual—"

"A nut, if you ask me," Travis interrupted.

"—called Cromwell. You might recall that Oliver Cromwell, who led a revolt against the English monarchy in the 1640s, called his troops the New Model

Army. We suppose that's where this Cromwell gets the name."

"I've heard about the militant groups," the assassin remarked.

"They've destroyed a lot of federal property. They're inciting violence and urging the American public to rebel against the government. And they're succeeding."

Travis took over. "Now, have you heard of a man named Charlie Wilkins?"

"Yes."

"Big, wealthy celebrity in the United States. Owns a chain of fast-food restaurants, has his own cable TV network, and he's very popular as a television talk-show host. More important, he leads a so-called religion known as the Church of Will. Do you know of it?"

"A little."

"It's widespread, and it's part of the America First Party movement. Dana Linder is a member of the Church of Will and a personal friend of Charlie Wilkins. The U.S. government believes that the Church of Will and the New Model Army are connected in some way. Maybe Wilkins funds them. We don't know. They don't know."

"Wilkins doesn't seem like the militant type," 47 said.

"No, he doesn't," Jade agreed. "He is well loved by much of the American population, and the rest see him as a harmless entertainer who has managed to influence a couple of million people to join his religion."

"Or whatever it is," Travis said. "It's a wacko cult, if you ask me. But that doesn't enter into the assignment. Or maybe it does. You'll have to find out."

"What *is* the assignment?" 47 asked, growing impatient.

"It's really a two-part mission. The first part is set in stone, the fee is very high, and there are special conditions attached to it. The second part is a 'maybe,' the execution of which depends on the fallout from the first hit."

"Could you be more specific?"

Travis cleared his throat. "The first hit is on Dana Linder."

Agent 47 showed no visible reaction. He'd heard and completed more-challenging operations. "A presidential candidate."

"Right."

"Who's the client?" he asked.

"Anonymous," Travis answered. "We don't know who it is, but he's already paid a substantial down payment. That said, we suspect the client is the current U.S. administration. The CIA. Maybe President Burdett himself. Who else would want to eliminate the competition in the election? It makes sense. The America First Party and the Church of Will are in cahoots, so I'm sure the U.S. government doesn't want to see them lead the people in a revolution that could change the face of the country. Washington quite understandably would consider them all dangerous."

"What are the special conditions?"

"The client wants the hit on Linder performed within the week and in a public place, in front of witnesses. And, of course, you can't be seen or caught."

47 pursed his lips. "That's not impossible. Who's the second target?"

"Charlie Wilkins," Travis said. "But you have to wait until the client gives the go-ahead on him. Once Linder is dead, Wilkins may step up and run for president himself. Or he may not. It depends on that. And because of the target's high profile but well-protected status, the client thinks the only way to get to him is from the inside. Undercover."

"You mean within the Church of Will?"

"That's right."

47 wrinkled his brow. "That sounds . . . strange."

"It's so a Church insider would appear to be responsible for the hit," Jade said. "That's important to the client. As you know, sometimes a client's motives are not fully clear. It's not our job to question why."

"You'll have to do your homework on both targets. You're the expert, 47. You'll know best how to play it. Jade and I will be your handlers. The Agency has set up new networks around the world for equipment drop-off and pickup. And while you have your own contacts in the field, we can supply you with new ones if you want. We want you to run the show, 47. That's part of the new way. You'll find the Agency to be a little different now. More accommodating to our contractors."

"I've always 'run the show,' as you put it. Diana gave me full autonomy."

"Then we want to continue that policy." Travis leaned forward. "We want you to trust us, 47. We're forging a new alliance here. The Agency is giving you a second chance. You remember what the ICA's policy is on contractors who go off the grid as you did?"

"I'm supposed to be eliminated," 47 answered with a slight smile.

"That's correct. But that's not how it's going to work this time. We need you. I can't emphasize that enough. *However . . .* " Travis leaned back in his chair. "If you go off the grid again, I can't be responsible for how upper management responds."

Agent 47 stared at Travis with cold, piercing eyes, until the manager looked away and added, "Just saying." There was silence in the room for a full minute. The assassin knew he should say something but didn't.

"All right," he finally announced. "I'm leaving for the States tomorrow."

NINE

Park Slope, Brooklyn. A moderately affluent, relatively upscale neighborhood of New York City. Families. Schools. Brownstones and apartment buildings. Parks where folks walked dogs and watched their children play. Most would say it was an idyllic setting.

Agent 47, who had no reference for what he thought of as a "normal" family life, did not recognize the setting as tranquil. To him, it was just another landscape of conflicting morals, the pretension of happiness, and potential violence. The assassin had learned at a very early age that the world was not his friend. Traditional values and relationships were alien to him. Intellectually, he understood that he was not ordinary, that he was a freak of nature, and that what he practiced was not the standard of society. Despite his striking appearance, Agent 47 had the ability to become a chameleon, blend in with the masses, and play a role. If he had to be a typical American businessman for an hour or two, he could do it. Should he have the need to be a butcher, a baker, or a waiter, he could assume the identity with ease. If he had to exhibit tenderness or compassion, or pretend that he had faith in God, then he could do it. It was part of his tradecraft.

It didn't mean he had to believe it.

The hitman stood at the corner of 3rd Street and 7th

Avenue, watching the townhouse across the street, when the woman opened the door and escorted her two children outside. He figured the boy was probably seven. The little girl was younger, maybe five. They were bundled up for fall morning weather and off to school. First grade for the boy? Preschool or kindergarten for the girl? 47 wasn't sure. He had never experienced that kind of public education or social integration.

The woman, who appeared to be an everyday housewife and mother, thirty-something years old, took each kid's hand and walked them down the block. 47 was patient. He could wait for the woman to return. It wouldn't be long. Drop the children at school, kiss them goodbye, and promise to pick them up later in the day. He figured she'd be back in ten or fifteen minutes.

The assassin turned and stepped inside the café and ordered a large coffee, black. He wondered why so many customers had to have fancy concoctions—a latte this or that, a mocha whatsit, a cuppa-cinno however— when it was just the caffeine anyone wanted. They could be in and out of the shop a lot quicker if they ordered simple coffee. But the whims and desires of the average person meant nothing to 47; if he attempted to fit in, he only found it awkward.

Dressed in his signature black suit, white shirt, and red tie, he sat with his coffee, his briefcase on the floor within reach, and watched through the window as humanity passed by.

No question about it. People were peculiar.

And he was even more so.

The woman returned to the townhouse exactly twelve minutes after she'd left. She fumbled in her purse for her keys, unlocked the front door, and stepped inside. 47 knew that the father of her children lived in Manhattan. The couple was divorced.

She was alone.

The assassin finished his coffee, threw away the cup, and stepped outside with his briefcase.

It was a beautiful, brisk day.

Time for business.

He rang the doorbell as if he were a traveling salesman. After a moment, he noticed the movement in the peephole. She knew he was there. He felt her hesitate, and then she opened the door.

"Holy shit. If it isn't Agent 47," she said.

"Cherry."

"What the hell? I heard you were dead."

"Not yet."

She looked him up and down, not sure if he was a ghost or not. After a moment's silence, she stepped aside and gestured inward. He moved past her and she closed the door behind them.

Cherry Jones was one of the many assets Agent 47 knew around the world. No one suspected that this unassuming, everyday, divorced American mom was a high-level arms dealer, drug distributor, and FBI informant, all rolled into one. She appeared completely harmless, but 47 knew that Cherry was as lethal as they came.

She led him into the living room. "Coffee?"

"I just had some across the street."

She nodded, stepped into the kitchen, and poured herself a cup from a contraption on the counter. When she returned to 47, she held the coffee in her left hand and a Smith & Wesson in the right.

"What brings you here, 47?" she asked.

"Put that away, Cherry. I'm here on business."

"I thought perhaps you'd come to collect on that old debt."

"And I thought perhaps we could talk about that."

"I was going to pay you. Life interfered. I got divorced. I had two kids to raise. You disappeared. Like I said, I thought you were dead."

"Put the gun away and let's talk." He set the briefcase on the floor and held out his empty hands. "I'm not armed."

"Liar. You're always armed. I just can't see your weapons."

He allowed a slight grin to form on his face. "Fair enough."

Cherry set the gun on a table and sat in a chair next to it. The Smith & Wesson was easily within reach, and 47 knew she could grab it and fire a round in the time it took most people's brains to simply initiate the command to do so.

"What do you want?" she asked.

"I gave you a loan of a hundred thousand dollars," he said as he pushed a toy fire truck out of the way with his foot. He then sat on the sofa and crossed his legs. "I'm willing to forgive that loan, but I need some equipment and some information in a hurry."

"I'm low on equipment these days. Business sucks. The information depends on what kind you want."

"You have access to classified material at the FBI. I know that computer of yours in the basement is linked to their secure network. You can pull up any document, any file, any photo, any report. Right?"

"Maybe."

"Let's go to the basement and I'll tell you what I'm looking for. I'd also like to browse what you do have in stock. There's an item I need."

"What item?"

"I'll know it when I see it."

Cherry sipped her coffee. "And you'll forget about the hundred grand? Just for a piece of equipment and some classified FBI info?"

"Yes."

"That's awfully big of you, 47. All right. Let's go."
She picked up the handgun and stood. "You don't mind
if I hold on to this, though, do you?"

"If it makes you more comfortable . . ."

She jerked her head toward a door. Cherry opened it,
revealing a staircase. 47 followed her down to a play-
room full of toys, a flat-screen television, and a tread-
mill. Cherry unlocked another door and led the hitman
into a room that was obviously off-limits to her kids.

It was full of weapons on tables and shelves. High-
tech assault rifles, handguns, bazookas, grenades of all
types and functions, knives, swords, and small bombs.

"Here we are, 47. Mayhem R Us," she said with a
chuckle.

"You make a nice living, Cherry?"

"It's okay. Like I said, business is down. Too much
competition."

The assassin moved between the tables, examining
the various pieces of hardware. He stopped at the table
containing the bombs and grenades. He picked one up
and turned it around in his hand.

"This work?" he asked.

"Of course it works. I mean, it's not going to kill anyone, but it does what it's supposed to do."

He nodded and placed the pear-sized object in his
jacket pocket. "I'll take it."

"All right."

47 continued to browse, paused at the knives, picked
up a few, replaced them, and moved on. He found a
bookshelf filled with Chinese fireworks.

"Why do you have these?" he asked.

"Fireworks are illegal to sell in the city," Cherry explained. "In most states you have to go out of city limits
to buy them." She shrugged. "I make it easier for New
Yorkers when they want to celebrate the Fourth of July
or New Year's Eve. They're not really dangerous."

"But they make a big noise, right?"

"Sure. Some of them do."

"Show me."

She picked out a selection and gave them to him. "On the house. And I won't even ask what you need 'em for."

"Thanks."

"So what about drugs? I got amphetamines, crystal meth, cocaine, heroin, OxyContin, marijuana." She pointed to a cabinet where dozens of bottles and cans were stored. "Oh, wait, I forgot. You don't do any of that stuff."

47 stared at her for a moment, and then he said, "Let's boot up your computer."

"That's all you wanted?"

"Yes."

"You're a funny dude, 47." She walked over to a desk, sat, and switched on a high-end Mac. The hitman stood behind her. "So what do you want to know?"

"Everything the Bureau has on Cromwell and the New Model Army. I'd also like to look at material on Charlie Wilkins. See if there's any evidence of a connection between them."

Cherry laughed. "Charlie Wilkins? Are you kidding?"

"No."

"He's a preacher! What's that religion he runs, the Church of Something . . . ?"

"The Church of Will."

"Right. People love him! Hell, I watch his program on TV every now and then. It's good entertainment. It beats the reality shows that swarm the networks. You're out of your mind, 47. That's like saying Gandhi was a terrorist."

"Just bring up the documents, Cherry."

"Fine."

She went to work on the keyboard, hacked into the Bureau's secure network with a password, and did a search for New Model Army. More than a hundred links popped up.

"Jeez, 47, where do you want to start?"

He scanned the subjects and pointed. "Click that one."

It was everything the FBI knew about Cromwell. Several pages of text.

Cherry stood. "Have a seat and knock yourself out. Looks like that'll keep you busy for an hour or two. I'm going back upstairs. You hungry? Can I make you something to eat?"

"No. Thanks."

"Try not to stay too long on one link. They track stuff like that. You have to be done by noon. That's when I pick up Sally from kindergarten."

"What happens if you don't show up?" he asked.

She shot him a look. "What does that mean?"

"Nothing. This might take a while."

"My ex-husband is on the call list. But he'd have to come in from Manhattan. I'd rather not do that, 47; he's a total asshole. He liked to take it out on me when he got drunk. You didn't know about the two teeth he knocked out a few years back. It was a nasty divorce. He was very greedy and he had a better lawyer. Bill has visitation rights, but I don't have to like it. The kids don't like him much either. And, frankly, I don't want Sally or Billy seeing you here. All right?"

She left him alone but kept the door to her inner sanctum open.

A good assassin always did his homework. 47 made it a point to study his targets, get to know them *personally*, even if he never met them during the course of the operation. He had already researched Dana Linder. She was easy. No skeletons in her closet that 47 could see, other than that she was a member of the Church of Will, for what that was worth. She and her brother,

Darren—twins—had lost their father in a hunting accident in Maryland just before their twelfth birthday. Their mother, 47 learned, was associated with Charlie Wilkins from the beginning. She and her husband were members of Wilkins's "modern" house of worship, a forerunner to the Church of Will. In the 1970s, Wilkins's Church was run out of evangelical touring tent productions. After her husband's death, Mrs. Shipley traveled with Wilkins, dragging the twins along wherever he and his entourage went. She died of cancer when the children were still in high school. Wilkins kept them with his organization and raised them both with the help of other Church followers, even fronting much of the cash for Dana's education.

Interesting, the hitman thought.

By scrutinizing footage of Dana Linder's campaign speeches and appearances, the assassin knew how he would accomplish the hit. A public execution was always difficult, but it was not beyond his ability. He already had a plan in place. Of more interest to him was the background of the second target, should the orders go forward. Wilkins was a fascinating objective; 47 wasn't sure if he'd ever killed someone so famous.

The hitman studied the file and photos. The FBI had no idea who Cromwell really was, but reliable intelligence suggested that he had military training and was of the age to have served in Iraq or Afghanistan. The face he revealed on television was not the one he was born with. Plastic surgery had changed his features considerably. He also had a prosthetic arm, so it was conceivable that the man had seen serious combat. Whoever had performed the plastic surgery had done a remarkable job. Cromwell now had rugged, chiseled features that gave him the appearance of a Roman god. The skin was a bit too shiny and obviously grafted, but he didn't look bad. A bit like an action figure.

The New Model Army had been operative for two years and was supposedly once based in the Pacific Northwest, most likely Oregon or Washington State. It consisted of a battery ranging between fifty and a hundred men, all of whom were either onetime professional soldiers or homegrown military enthusiasts. The FBI and the Pentagon were investigating possible black-market weapons sales between the NMA and the real army and marines. Just as the government had lately become corrupt, so had its military branches.

While everything the NMA was doing was criminal, many of the American people considered Cromwell a folk hero. Whenever the FBI raided a suspected NMA camp, the group had somehow got wind of the impending attack and left in a hurry. It was no longer believed that Cromwell and his men had a permanent base of operations. They moved from town to town, working with local militias and rebels to house and feed them.

And their attacks were moving eastward across the country.

47 scanned the rest of the document and went to another. Titled "The New Model Army and the Church of Will," the folder contained several files. He spent the next half hour going through each one, but they were inconclusive. The only suspicious activity in evidence was that cellphone calls had been made to and from suspected NMA camps and the Church of Will main headquarters in Virginia. The FBI had attempted to legally tap landlines in Wilkins's compound, but more than one judge had denied permission. 47 was surprised that the Bureau hadn't gone ahead and done it anyway. Apparently Wilkins held more power and influence than the hitman had imagined, but there was no sub-

stantiation that the reverend himself was involved with the NMA.

One file contained a satellite image and corresponding map of Greenhill, the Church of Will's compound in Virginia. Blueprints revealed the layout of Wilkins's mansion. 47 found it interesting that the man's home was so well protected. A bulletproof wall-sized picture window facing a lake? Surely the man wasn't afraid of being attacked by an amphibious landing force. Nevertheless, the hitman thought the file might come in handy, especially if he had to go through with an undercover operation. A spindle of blank CD-Rs sat on the desk, so he took one, inserted it into the computer, and copied the ground plan onto the disk.

"Are you done yet?" Cherry called from the top of the stairs.

He ejected the disk and took it. "Yes."

She came down and looked at the screen. "Get what you needed?"

"I suppose."

She took over the mouse and keyboard and closed the software.

"Cherry, you down there?" a male voice called from the top of the stairs. They both heard footsteps descending.

"Shit!" Cherry whispered. "My ex! We have to—"

Before she or 47 could move, a man appeared, wide-eyed and mouth gaping. He was a little older than Cherry and was dressed in a suit.

"What the hell is this? Since when did we have *this* extra room in our house?" Then he saw the guns and other weapons. "What the—" He turned to 47. "Who the hell are you?" Back to Cherry. "You will tell me what the *fuck* is going on here now."

"Bill, calm down; it's *my* house now, and this is not what you think," Cherry said, but 47 noted she was obviously distressed. She had also left the Smith & Wesson upstairs. "And how the hell did you get in? The judge said you weren't allowed to have a key."

"Yes, let's call the judge!" the man said, moving toward his ex-wife. "You've got *my* kids living in a house with goddamned weapons? Wait until my lawyer hears *this*! You'll never see those brats again."

Agent 47 did have the presence of mind, despite the commotion, to slip to the foot of the stairs and stand there, blocking Bill's exit.

The former couple continued to yell at each other. Clearly, the man couldn't leave the house with knowledge of Cherry's extracurricular activities. Too many people would be hurt, and the assassin would lose a valuable asset. And didn't she say the man used to beat her? Sure, the kids might miss having a father, but there was no question that the husband was going the wrong direction on a one-way street.

Over Bill's shoulder, 47 saw Cherry give him a barely perceptible nod. It was a signal, a green light.

Agent 47 spoke. "Bill."

The man whirled around, furious. "What?"

The killer grabbed the man's head in his gloved hands, wrenching it sharply to the right. With a sickening *pop,* the third cervical vertebra snapped and a shard was driven through Bill's spinal cord.

Bill's mouth gaped as he fell. He died before he hit the floor, his body slumped in an unnatural position.

A moment of silence passed.

"Thanks, 47," Cherry said, exhaling deeply. "If he had gotten out of here alive, I'd be in deep shit."

"What about the body? Won't the police suspect you?"

"I know an excellent cleanup crew. They'll destroy every bit of evidence. He was never here."

47 gazed at the corpse.

"You did me a favor, 47," she said. "It's something I've wanted to do for a long time. He was a sick bastard."

"I didn't do it because of your domestic situation," 47 replied. "I did it because I had no choice. He knew too much."

Cherry eventually nodded. "Is there anything else you want? Anything?"

The assassin considered her words for a moment and then gestured to the "medicine cabinet." She snickered a bit, went over, and unlocked it. "Help yourself," she said.

He found several bottles of oxycodone and stuffed them in his jacket pocket.

Back upstairs, he asked to use the washroom while Cherry made the call to her crew. He popped a pill and swallowed it with water in a cupped hand. Then he simply and quietly left the townhouse without saying good-bye and grabbed a taxi on 7th Avenue.

Next stop, the airport.

TEN

I'd just landed at O'Hare. Chicago. Dana Linder's next campaign stop was a rally at the Jay Pritzker Pavilion in Millennium Park. Facing the Great Lawn. Tomorrow.

I'd be there.

I rented a car and drove to Des Plaines, not far from the airport. The storage facility was easy to find. I already had the key; I didn't even have to check in at the front desk. Just parked at the storage building, climbed the stairs to the second floor, and unlocked door 210. My briefcase and other equipment, including a custom-made U.S. military M40A3 sniper rifle with a removable stock, were waiting there for me. The drop-off had worked like a charm.

I drove in to the city and parked in one of the garages in the Loop. The weather was turning cooler. Chicago was the Windy City, so the temperature was lower than in New York.

Millennium Park was packed with people no matter what time of day. They expected a few thousand people at Linder's rally tomorrow. Police had already put up those wooden sawhorse blockades around the area for crowd control. Volunteers were at work putting up banners and signs. The pavilion was a beehive.

Time to get to work.

Planning an operation usually consisted of three things.

One, research. You had to get to know your target. I'd studied everything I could about Linder. I knew she was married and had two teenage boys. I knew she was smart and employed even smarter people to be around her. She'd be well protected.

Two, know the scene. If possible, you had to visit the place where the hit was going to take place. That's what I was doing today. I wanted to get a sense of the light during the day, the location of various man-made and natural obstacles, and the possible escape routes. Where were the danger spots? What was the safest spot from which to operate?

Three, plan the hit. I had to know what weapon I was going to use and how I'd use it. Ideally, it was always good to make a kill appear as if it were accidental. This time, however, the client wanted a public assassination. Why, I didn't know. I didn't care. A job was a job. If the client was really the U.S. government, as the Agency suspected, then killing a politician in front of TV cameras seemed very odd to me. You'd think they'd want to do it surreptitiously, make it look like an accident. I was supplied the M40A3 sniper rifle by the client. It was a fine weapon. I'd test it tonight. The ammunition looked sound. I was supposed to leave the rifle behind after the kill. Maybe it could be traced to someone else. Maybe they were trying to frame another killer, which could be done by identifying the serial number. Fine with me; I'd be long gone before the police realized what had happened.

I did sometimes get special requests from a client. For example, I've had to show the client's photograph to the target right before he died. So he'd know who ordered the hit. His last dying thought. Made sense. It was some kind of justice for the client. There was no right or wrong when it came to what I did for a living, no matter who was doing it. I couldn't feel bad for Dana Linder. Sure, her family would be upset. Her death would make international news. I didn't know if she was a good person or a bad person. I didn't care. I suppose in some way it helped me when I knew the target was a bad person, but it usually didn't make much difference to me.

I just did the job as professionally and perfectly as I could.

For the next hour, I walked around the park and found the best spot from which to shoot Dana Linder. The rifle had a range of a thousand yards. That was plenty. The big, curvy silver-steel bridge at the southeastern edge of the park was promising. I spent a half hour pacing the distance from the highest point of the bridge to the stage. I then checked my calculation with a handheld laser the size of a pen. My pacing was off by only three yards. It would do. The items I picked up at Cherry's place would also play big parts in the undertaking. I found a suitable container for one of them in the middle of the expansive lawn in front of the pavilion. I examined the sky and noted the cloud formations. I'm pretty good at predicting the weather. At any rate, I'd monitor the local meteorologists' reports. It was definitely windy that close to Lake Michigan, so I would have to adjust my aim. There were flagpoles on the west side of the park. The flags would give me a good indication of wind velocity before I took the shot. Perfect.

Knowing my escape route in detail had saved me several times; it was often the key to making the hit appear to be magic. So I spent another hour walking the streets around the park. Although it was getting colder, I took the time to mentally map out the best spots for cover. If a firefight broke out, I needed to know what offered adequate protection—for me or an opponent. I knew I could rely on being faster and more precise than a normal person, but nothing really beat being smart and planning ahead.

There was one more thing to do—I just had to pick up a couple of items I'd need. That included a disguise.

As I left the park, a double-decker bus drove by on Michigan Avenue. It was full of tourists, both on the top level and inside. They waved at people on the street. For a second, I could swear I saw that shadowy figure sitting up top. Death. Faceless and cold. Looking right at me.

I felt that edge of anxiety again, and I realized I hadn't taken a painkiller in a while. Was I hallucinating? Possibly.

The moment passed and the bus was gone.

I could quit those pills anytime. I knew I could.

I just didn't want to. Not right now.

ELEVEN

Police estimated that nine thousand people attended the noon rally for Dana Linder in Chicago's Millennium Park. Located between Michigan Avenue and Columbus Drive and sitting just north of the famed Art Institute, the park was the city's star attraction.

Architect Frank Gehry's Jay Pritzker Pavilion was the focal point. Linder was due to deliver her campaign speech from its stage. The 120-foot-high pavilion sported an unusual flowerlike, billowing crown made of brushed stainless-steel ribbons that framed the stage's proscenium arch, all connecting to an overhead trellis of crisscrossing steel pipes that extended over the four thousand fixed seats. The Great Lawn, which faced the stage, could hold another seven thousand people. For the rally, two giant TV screens were erected on either side of the proscenium so that the audience could get up close and personal with Dana Linder.

Another Gehry creation, the 925-foot BP Bridge, spanned Columbus Drive by connecting the park with Daley Bicentennial Plaza, situated east of the park and bordering Lake Michigan. The long, winding bridge, adorned with brushed stainless-steel panels, complemented the pavilion in function as well as design by creating an acoustic barrier from the traffic noise below. The structure was used by walkers and runners alike.

From atop the bridge, pedestrians could view the impressive Chicago skyline and overlook the entire park. The bridge was crowded, of course, not only with the usual patrons who used the structure for exercise but also with rally attendees.

From the bridge's southern tip, one had an excellent view of the pavilion stage, albeit from some distance.

It was close enough, though.

Political rallies could be peaceful events that were pulled off without a hitch. On the other hand, they might be tinderboxes ignited by an inadvertent, unanticipated spark. When a gathering of that size assembled in the city, it was best to have a strong police presence; thus, the men and women in blue were out in droves. Most of them were on the lawn and around the pavilion, but one officer stood on the bridge's apex, his eyes on the multitude to the south. Another three patrolmen were positioned at the southern end, where the bridge emptied onto the lawn. Their backs were to the bridge as they also faced the throng.

The woman pushing the baby stroller onto the BP Bridge from the Daley Plaza side was tall and thin, but not so much that she attracted undue attention. She wore a gray and blue pantsuit that was otherwise nondescript. A full head of gray hair topped by a Chicago Cubs baseball cap and the pair of sunglasses hid her facial features well enough from anyone who happened to afford her a second glance. Otherwise, she appeared to be a grandmother out for a stroll with her grandchild on a beautiful early October day.

At the highest point of the curving bridge, the woman surveyed the park and the mass of humanity that spread across the Great Lawn. All eyes were focused on the pavilion stage, where the festivities had begun with a local high school band performing patriotic tunes such as "Yankee Doodle Dandy" and "Stars and Stripes Forever" as a prelude to the presidential candidate's appearance.

When the music finished, the woman bent over the stroller, cooed, and held a bottle of formula to the bundle inside. No one paid any attention to her.

One of the America First Party's House representatives from Illinois took the stage and warmed up the audience. He spoke about national values and their importance in the grand scheme of democracy. He pointed out various goals of the party. And then he announced a surprise satellite telecast from someone the people all knew and loved.

Charlie Wilkins.

The woman with the baby stroller finished feeding the bottle to the package of joy inside the carriage, stood, and focused her attention on the big TV screens.

The crowd cheered exuberantly when Wilkins's face appeared.

"Greetings to you all!" he said. "I'm sorry I can't be there in person to join my good friend Dana in Chicago. But I want you to know she has my endorsement, my support, and my love! I've known Dana since she was a child. She and her brother, Darren, God bless his soul, were parishioners under my tutelage and guidance back in Maryland when the Church of Will was just a fledgling organization. I knew then as I know now that Dana has the brains and the leadership qualities to take this great nation back to its former glory. With Dana Linder at the top, I assure you the United States will be number one again. So let me now get out of your face, 'cause that's enough of me. Allow me to introduce the person who will lead the people of America to meet the values and goals of the America First Party—Senator Dana Shipley Linder!"

The horde erupted with noise. If there was any doubt that the candidate had support, that notion quickly dissipated. Even the boos and catcalls from a group of Democrats and a bunch of Republicans who had staked out separate territories on the Great Lawn were drowned out and rendered ineffective.

Wilkins's broadcast disappeared from the TV screens as Dana Linder took the stage. She was dressed in a smart business suit of muted colors. Her face took over the giant monitors and beamed at the multitude. It took a full minute for the audience to quiet down and let her speak. Her voice echoed through the park with exuberance.

"My fellow Americans!"

More cheers.

"And good afternoon, Chicago!"

Even bigger shouts.

"You aren't sports fans, are you?"

The crowd went wild.

"Well, how about this for sport? Come this November fourth, the people will put an America First Party candidate in the White House!"

Tumultuous rejoicing.

Linder continued with a carefully prepared, pep-rallying speech designed to incite enthusiasm and excitement among her listeners.

The woman with the stroller looked around the bridge and confirmed that all eyes were on the pavilion stage.

The moment had come. It was when time slowed down and every thought, every action, seemed to last an eternity, and yet only a partial second elapsed with each effort.

The woman noted the flags waving on the poles and determined wind velocity and direction. Perfect.

The noise of Linder speaking ceased. The sound of the *air* became a vacuum.

As she'd rehearsed faultlessly, the woman reached into the carriage and picked up a cellphone. She quickly dialed a number and dropped the mobile back inside. An instant later, surprisingly loud, popping explosions went off in a trash barrel in the middle of the park. The crowd around it screamed in fright, reacting to the sudden clamor. This diverted everyone's attention, including Linder's.

The woman on the bridge swung the weapon to position, resting the barrel on top of the carriage in lieu of a tripod base. She bent her knees slightly and aimed. Even through the sunglasses, she got a clear bead on Linder through the Schmidt & Bender telescopic sight.

Linder's forehead appeared in the crosshairs. Her mouth was opening and closing, uttering silent words blocked by the sniper's sensitive discipline.

The woman's index finger touched the trigger. All it would take was a simple squeeze. She took a split second to breathe, and then she instinctively and efficiently applied the appropriate amount of pressure.

The shot rang out over the bridge.

Without looking to see if the target was hit—the woman knew she was—she reached into her pocket and removed the smoke grenade obtained from Cherry Jones's arsenal. The woman pulled the pin and tossed it a few feet away from the baby carriage. With a loud, thudding *boom*, a thick cloud of violet-colored smoke immediately filled that section of the BP Bridge. Pedestrians screamed.

Time resumed its normal pace.

Visibility was reduced to zero. Then came the vocal reactions from the crowd near the stage. Something had happened. Something bad.

Police whistles. Shouts. Pandemonium.

It took several minutes for the smoke to thin. By then, a large host of onlookers had congregated at the foot of the bridge as uniformed officers desperately tried to keep them back. They all shouted at once:

"Someone shot Dana!"

"The killer was on the bridge!"

"It was a woman!"

"Where'd she go?"

"What happened?"

With handgun drawn, one officer cautiously approached the stroller, which still stood where the woman had abandoned it. He looked inside and found no infant—just an M40A3 sniper rifle, a gray wig, a baseball cap, and a gray and blue woman's pantsuit that had literally been ripped off a body.

Agent 47, naturally bald-headed and now wearing his black suit—revealed after tearing away the woman's clothing—stood among the agitated crowd, participating in the shouting and clamor. He was just another one of the herd, deftly blending in with the chaos around him.

As the police joined arms to force the crowd off the bridge, 47 slipped farther south and onto the Great Lawn. The audience was straining to see the stage and yearning for news of what had happened. The assassin slowly moved through them as he also pretended to be a concerned supporter. The TV screens by the stage had gone blank, and a group of campaign workers and police were huddled around the fallen body of Dana Linder.

It took nearly twenty minutes for 47 to make his way to the south side of the lawn. He spied the trash barrel that police were now inspecting. The fireworks the hitman had procured from Cherry had done the trick once he had hooked up a firing cap with a cellphone detonator. They had supplied the appropriate amount of diversion. Pleased with himself, 47 moved on to AT&T Plaza, which contained the famed Cloud Gate stainless-steel sculpture—commonly called by its nick-name, the "bean." As Agent 47 looked up into its silver surface and adjusted his tie, he saw a distorted, fun-house-like reflection of the mayhem going on behind him in the park.

He then calmly walked past the McCormick Tribune Plaza and Ice Rink, which was not yet open for the win-ter, and onto the sidewalk of Michigan Avenue. From there, he went to the Art Institute and spent the next two hours admiring the world-class exhibits and killing time, seemingly oblivious to the horror that had oc-curred in the park that day.

He'd catch it on the evening news.

TWELVE

Helen McAdams sat alone in her office in the Green-hill mansion, just down a long hall and around the corner from Charlie Wilkins's private space. She knew the boss was extremely upset, as was everyone in the compound. Dana Linder had been like a daughter to Wilkins. Helen felt terrible for the man.

The killing had profoundly affected every member of the Church of Will. A gloomy pall had settled on the compound in Virginia. It didn't help that October brought continuous rain, as heavy black clouds stubbornly hovered over Aquia Lake.

Worldwide reaction was one of shock and disbelief. In the three days since the incident in Chicago, conspiracy theories and rumors dominated the Internet, newspapers, and television talk shows. The killer, of course, was not caught, and she—or he—left little behind in the way of clues. There were no fingerprints or telltale evidence on the baby stroller. The clothing and wig were useless—they could have been purchased at any Target or Walmart in the country. The only significant finding was that the M40A3 rifle at the scene was registered to a soldier stationed at Fort Hood, Texas, although he had reported, and the military confirmed, that the weapon was stolen a month earlier. This development ignited the most popular conspiracy theory—

that the current administration was somehow responsible. The president ordered it. The CIA executed it. Plenty of people believed that the government was so afraid of the America First Party that they had utilized the last resort to win the election. The White House categorically denied any involvement in Dana Linder's death.

Police and FBI investigators had no leads. Witness testimonies were wildly contradictory. A majority claimed that the shooter was a woman who vanished in a cloud of smoke. Cooler heads suggested that the assassin was a man disguised as a woman. Surveillance videos caught the killer in action, but analysts were still not certain of the gender. After the smoke grenade detonated, all bets were off. The huge crowd of people that swarmed the bridge made it impossible for face-recognition software to do its job. The murderer had indeed disappeared into thin air.

Helen sighed forlornly as she read yet another incendiary blog on her computer. It had been an emotional day. That morning, Wilkins had presided over a memorial service in the Greenhill sanctuary. Dignitaries from all over the country, including President Burdett, had attended. A poignant but loaded moment occurred when the president expressed his deepest sympathy to Linder's husband and teenage boys, who were devastated with grief. Television cameras were not allowed inside. After the service, the VIPs rushed away from the site, the family went home to Maryland, and Wilkins blockaded himself in his office to pray and reflect on the terrible occurrence.

Usually, Helen was very busy when she was at work, but today there was nothing to do. She thought about leaving the mansion and going back to her apartment. During the sermon, Wilkins had told Church members they didn't have to work and could go home to grieve if they wished, but Helen wouldn't budge from her desk. She wanted to be there if Charlie needed her.

As if Wilkins had read her thoughts, the intercom buzzed. Helen pressed the button and asked, "Yes, sir?"

"Helen, oh, you're still there."

"Yes, sir. I'm here."

"Could you come down to my office? Are you busy?"

"No, sir. I'll be right there."

Glad she hadn't gone home, Helen stood and walked out of her office. Since the building was mostly empty, few lights were on. She went ten feet to a T-intersection in the hallway, turned left, and proceeded down the dark twenty-five-foot corridor, which was lined with religious artwork of diverse cultures and beliefs. Thin beams of flickering illumination shone from the slightly ajar door to Wilkins's executive space.

When she reached the entrance, Helen knocked.

"Helen? Come on in."

She pushed open the door. The spacious office was lit only by candles. Wilkins sat at his broad oak desk, which faced the large wall-sized picture window over-looking Aquia. He stared at the storm raging outside as lightning struck over the water.

"Four o'clock in the afternoon and it's darker than dusk," he said as she approached. "It means something, Helen."

"Sir?"

He turned to her. "Have a seat." He gestured to one of the chairs normally used by the assistants. Helen dutifully sat and folded her hands in her lap.

He was quiet. Distracted.

"Are you all right, sir?" she asked.

"Huh? Oh, yes, yes, I'm sorry. I asked you in here for a reason, Helen," Wilkins said. He turned his throne-like swivel chair away from the window and faced her. "Have you heard the latest news?"

"Not today, sir."

"The New Model Army attacked two federal buildings, one in Pittsburgh and one in Philadelphia. One is completely destroyed and seven people were killed. The other sustained extensive structural damage and one person died. Many others were injured. It's deplorable. Cromwell released a statement that it's in retaliation for Dana Linder's murder by the government of the United States."

"But, sir, that's not true, is it?" she asked.

"Helen, you don't have to call me 'sir.' Please, call me Charlie."

"I can't help it, sir, I'll always think of you as a 'sir.' " She let out a nervous laugh. "Sorry. Okay, Charlie. I'll try."

"Thank you."

"So is it true? About the conspiracy?"

"It's all speculation stoked by the media, Helen. There's no proof. That rifle could have come from anywhere, if it was really stolen from that base. What disturbs me is there are some who believe I am somehow connected to Cromwell. And that's just not true."

"I believe you, si—Charlie."

"I want you to start working with George about coming up with a PR campaign to dispel that myth."

Helen nodded. George, one of the other assistants, was a competent copywriter.

"All right."

"And there's another task I'd like you to start on tomorrow."

"What's that, sir?"

"I want you to be the liaison between my presidential campaign team and everyone here at Greenhill."

At first she didn't catch what he'd said. "Yes, sir, I'd be glad to." Then she blinked. "Wait. Presidential campaign?"

"Yes, Helen. I've decided to throw my hat into the ring. It's a little late, the election is next month, but someone in the America First Party has to step up to the plate. It's essential. And I suppose I'm the guy that needs to do it."

Helen put her hands to her mouth. "I'm sure that's what Dana—" She stopped herself. Perhaps that wasn't an appropriate thing to say.

"What, you think that's what Dana would have wanted me to do?" he asked.

"Yes, sir."

"Well, so do I. And I think I'm obligated to do it. Get George on the phone and ask him if he'll come up to the house. Tell him to bring his umbrella. I'm going to announce my candidacy tonight on national television. We need to get a speech ready, pronto." He rubbed his hands together.

"Will do, sir." She stood and moved quickly toward the door, then paused and turned to him. "Sir? Charlie?"

"Yes?"

"I think you'll win, sir. I really do."

Wilkins raised an eyebrow and grinned at her. His signature pose for the media.

"So do I, my dear," he said.

When he was alone again, Charlie Wilkins picked up the secure landline phone and made a call.

A man answered. "Charlie."

"My, my, you've been busy," Wilkins said.

"I told you so. It was for Dana, sir. You know that."

"Cromwell, I can't condone violence. People died today."

"I know, and I'm sorry for the collateral damage, but that's what it is. We're at war with the United States government, sir, and they're going to pay for this terrible crime. I *know* Burdett and his sycophants were behind it."

"You don't know that."

"Yeah, but admit it, sir. You know in your heart that it's true. Look inside; look in your Will. It's what you always tell me, and that's what the Will tells me."

"I'm afraid I agree with you," Wilkins said. "I do believe it. I'm not so sure it's wise of me to say so. I'm going to announce my candidacy for president tonight. I'm going to step into Dana's spot."

"I was hoping you would do that, sir."

"You don't need to call me 'sir.'"

"I know." There was a pause. "I can't believe she's dead, sir."

"It's a terrible tragedy. But maybe I can turn this around into something positive."

"You know we'll be behind you, sir. Oh, and just a heads-up. We're on our way to Virginia. Expect some noise."

"Cromwell, I repeat, I don't condone violence." Wilkins peered through the picture window once again at the dark, wet storm. "But a man's got to follow the Will. You need to do what you need to do."

THIRTEEN

Agent 47 found the dilapidated school bus in a bad neighborhood on the western edge of Chicago's city limits. If there was any doubt that the Windy City had its fair share of poverty, ghettos, and gangbangers, all one had to do was travel to that miserable section of town.

Birdie's bus sat on Lake Street, right on the northern edge of Garfield Park. As expected, the spot was inundated with pigeons. The birds seemed to have a natural attraction to Birdie, who also kept cages of various types of *Aves* inside the bus. As for the man himself, Birdie lounged on a lawn chair in front of his mobile home and arsenal. While the underworld black-market dealer did travel about the country, he tended to make Chicago more or less a permanent base of operations.

Agent 47 figured Birdie to be around forty years old. He was very thin and bony, had shifty eyes, and needed a shave, not to mention a shower. Birdie always wore a faded Hawaiian shirt and brown leather jacket, opened to reveal a gold chain. Every bit of his clothing was covered in bird droppings. There was even some in Birdie's slicked-back, oily black hair. 47 couldn't understand why anyone would want to live the way Birdie did. The guy had plenty of money; the man just liked to perpetuate the notion that he was poor, dirty, and homeless.

47 had done business with Birdie before, but that didn't mean they were friends. In fact, there was some kind of unspoken animosity between the two. Birdie always enjoyed taunting Agent 47 to the point of annoyance. Since Birdie had also worked in the past as a killer for the Agency, 47 figured the thin man was jealous of the superior assassin's reputation and skill. There was no question which one of them was the master of his craft. Still, 47 acknowledged that Birdie was a formidable hitman and could be a very dangerous enemy if one became careless. The contact was a necessary evil 47 had to endure in order to obtain something he needed.

"Well, if it isn't Agent 47," the weasely operative said as the assassin slowly approached the bus in plain sight. "I heard you was in town."

"How is it that you still work for the Agency, Birdie?" the assassin asked. "You go rogue, you do what you want, but then you continue to do jobs for ICA. The Agency's policy is to eliminate former contractors that go off the grid. Why aren't you dead?"

"Ah, but you see, 'former' is the operative word here, 47. I never was 'former.' The Agency and I, well, let's just say we have an understanding. I never really left. I have something of a 'nonexclusive' deal with ICA."

The hitman surveyed the surroundings. As it was midday, the block was relatively quiet. A group of teenagers played basketball on the court in the park. A few mothers were out with younger children and strollers. No sign of any gangs. It was said, though, that a crime was committed every few minutes in this part of town.

"Where's your pal? Fei Zhu?"

"Fat Pig?" Birdie jerked his head toward the skyline. "He's in Chinatown on business." Birdie was almost never without his sleazy—and cruel—sidekick. Fei Zhu did most of Birdie's dirty work for him. Agent 47 was pleased that he didn't have to set eyes on the overweight, cocky thug.

"So to what do I owe this surprise visit, 47?" Birdie asked.

"I need some equipment. I understand you might have it."

"Oh? And what'll that be? I see you've got your beloved briefcase. Still using those fancy Hardballers? What else could you want?"

"You have explosives."

"Explosives? My, my, what are we up to, 47? You planning to join the New Model Army or something? I hear they're taking volunteers. Gonna blow up a federal building or two?"

"Are you going to sell me something or not, Birdie? I don't have time for your games."

Birdie sniffed and wiped his nose, leaving a gooey mess on his jacket sleeve. A pigeon must have sensed the treat, for it fluttered its wings, hopped up on Birdie's lap, and immediately began pecking at the spot on the man's clothing.

"Can you be more specific?" Birdie asked as he pulled a cigarette from a pack in his shirt pocket.

47 nodded at the bus. "You keep everything in there, don't you?"

"Oh, you want to browse? I normally charge a browsing fee, you know."

The hitman's patience was coming to an end. "Birdie—"

"*But* seeing it's you, 47, I'll waive that browsing fee." The thin man stood, flinging the pigeon to the pavement. He took a moment to brush feathers off his pants and jacket, then he stepped toward the bus door. He opened it and went inside. 47 took that as an invitation to follow.

The stench was unbearable. Birds in cages squawked

and flapped as the two men passed down the aisle. Feathers flew, and 47 had to use his free hand to wave them out of his face. At last they came to the back of the bus, where Birdie stored several trunks full of goods.

"Explosives, explosives . . . ah, here they are." Birdie lifted one case and threw it on top of another to get to the trunk he wanted. He stooped, swirled the knob on the combination lock, and opened it. 47 moved closer to peer inside. "I'm out of TNT," Birdie said. "But there should be something in there that'll work for you." Like Cherry Jones, Birdie stocked a variety of grenades and small bombs, sticks of dynamite, and limpet mines. 47 was interested only in the bricklike white packages.

The hitman reached in and removed one. "C4."

"That's right."

"I assume you have all the accessories? Blasting caps, a timer?"

"Sure. I throw in all that stuff with the purchase. Each of these bricks has a detonation velocity much higher than your average military C4. Let's say you want to blow up this bus. A quarter of a brick would do the trick. A whole brick would blow a hole in a concrete wall. Three or four bricks . . . well, if placed correctly at key structural points, you could bring down a building."

47 examined the brick and determined it was sound. "I'll take three, and I'll need a remote detonator."

"Cellphones or stopwatches are always best for that." Birdie moved forward in the bus and rummaged through some cardboard boxes in the seats. "Here we go. What do you prefer?" He pulled out two old Nokias. "That's one thing nice about outdated cellphones. They can always be used for *something*."

"I'd rather have a stopwatch."

Birdie shrugged, dug out one, and showed it to 47. "Fine."

"Need any knives? Garrotes? Oh, wait, you have that wire thing you like to use. Never mind. Poisons? How about some plastic zip ties? Excellent tools for securing someone's wrists behind his back."

"They're breakable, Birdie. If you know how."

"True. Still, most people don't know how."

47 thought about the contents of his briefcase and asked, "What kinds of poisons do you have?"

Birdie raised his eyebrows, moved to another seat on the bus, and unlocked a strongbox. He pulled out a vial and said, "Here you go. Clear, odorless, and undetectable in an autopsy. Victim looks like he had a heart attack. Comes in both fast-acting and slow-acting formulas."

The hitman recognized the label, nodded, and said he'd take a vial of each.

Birdie packed the goods in a brown paper bag from Trader Joe's grocery store. The two men discussed terms, haggled without malice, and then Agent 47 paid in cash. Business completed, they climbed out of the bus together. The hitman did his best to avoid stepping in bird feces.

"Want something to eat, 47? I have some chicken left over from last night."

The thought repulsed the assassin. "I don't think so." 47 started to walk away.

"Aren't you gonna say 'thanks'?" Agent 47 stopped and turned but didn't say anything. "Oh, I forgot. You have the personality of a fire hydrant. Say, I heard your handler flew the coop. What happened? She got tired of your shiny bald head?"

47 narrowed his eyes at the shifty criminal. "What do you know about her?"

Birdie returned to his seat, reached into his jacket pocket, and tossed some bird feed on the pavement around him. The act initiated a feeding frenzy among the pigeons.

"Nothing, 47. Only that she left the Agency under a cloud. I never met Diana, but I heard she was a looker. A real swan."

47 took a deep breath to control his temper. There was something about Birdie that made the hitman want to punch the guy. "If you hear anything about her, especially where she might be hiding, see if you can get word to me. All right?"

"Sure, 47. Does this mean we're buddies now? We can go out drinking together? Chase women? Share our innermost secrets? Join a club and play golf?"

The assassin waited a beat before replying, "No."

The thin man laughed, but it came out more like a snivel. "You're a strange bird, 47. See you later."

47 walked away, briefcase in one hand and brown bag in the other.

He didn't look back.

FOURTEEN

The Church of Will's recruitment center was busy.

Ever since Dana Linder's assassination, Helen McAdams had noticed an increase in membership applications. Ten to twenty people from all over the country showed up at Greenhill daily wanting to join, asking how they could volunteer, if there were any openings for Church jobs . . . but Helen and the other recruitment staff had to reject them, because all of the on-site apartments were taken. While many applicants could live away from the compound, come and go, and still join the Church, those who wanted to live on the premises were placed on waiting lists or sent to Church branches in other states.

Sundays were particularly popular, not only for applicants but for tourists and the curious. When Wilkins wasn't available or was traveling, morning services in the sanctuary were conducted by various assistant pastors called "adherents." These men and women took turns at the pulpit, and most of them were eloquent, captivating speakers. But no one was like Charlie. When it was known that he was present at the compound, visitors flooded the gates to hear him speak. Hundreds always had to be turned away. Helen considered it a treat when Charlie was present. She supposed it was similar to when lucky Roman Catholics visited the Vatican and the pope was in town to preside over Mass.

Even so, Helen barely had time to work at the recruitment center. Ever since Charlie Wilkins had announced his candidacy for president, all the personal assistants were putting in extra hours per week. Wilkins had hired a completely independent campaign-managing committee, and the key players had moved into the mansion's guest rooms. Helen's new responsibilities included conveying orders and requests between the committee and Greenhill administration. Thus, the past several days had been nonstop. Normally all Church members had the day off on Sunday, except for those involved in sanctuary services. However, with the new political developments, Helen and the others were expected to be available at any time.

After that morning's service, Wilkins had told her she wouldn't be needed in the afternoon, as he had business with his guests. So, having nothing better to do and not wanting to be by herself in her apartment, Helen decided to work at the recruitment center. Staying active was always a good thing. She found that if she spent too much time alone, unpleasant thoughts crept inside her heart.

For some, memories were cherished. For Helen, the past needed to stay where it belonged.

"Daydreaming again?"

The voice startled her. Helen turned to see Mitch Carson standing by the desk.

"Oh, hi, Mitch," she said. "No, I was just thinking: Where are all these people going to go?" She indicated the long line of applicants straggling out the center's front door.

"We'll find places for them—if not here, then in other branches. But we can always use the volunteer work if they're willing to keep their homes where they are."

Mitch Carson was the general manager of Greenhill. That meant he was technically Helen's boss, but of course any orders by Wilkins superseded what Carson instructed her to do. In his sixties, single, and efficient to the nth degree, Carson was not well liked by most members. Slightly effeminate and possessing a somewhat high-and-mighty demeanor in his dealings with others, Carson was definitely a yes-man to Wilkins and a no-man to everyone else. Because he had been with Wilkins since the Church's inception in the 1970s, Carson wielded a lot of power at Greenhill on the administrative side.

"By the way," he said. "We have space for a grounds-keeper slash maintenance man."

"Oh?"

"Yeah. Philip died last night. Heart attack."

"Oh, no! I'm so sorry to hear that. I liked Philip."

Carson shrugged. "He was old and he'd already had, what, two or three bypasses? We knew he wasn't long for this world."

"He was good at his job."

"Until he got ill and could hardly work."

Helen thought Carson was being insensitive. "Will there be a memorial service?"

"I haven't been able to talk to Charlie about it yet. In the meantime, though, if you have any applicants who could fill the bill, Philip's job is open, as is his apartment."

"Okay. How soon will it be cleaned out?"

"I have a crew working on that right now. It'll be ready for someone to move in this evening." Carson looked at his watch. "I'm supposed to meet Charlie and the Colonel here. They're a few minutes late."

"Charlie's coming here?" she asked. The man rarely appeared in front of recruits.

"The Colonel wants to evaluate all the security measures we have in place at Greenhill."

Carson stood for a moment in silence. Helen guessed what was bothering him.

"You knew Dana Linder, didn't you?" she asked.

"I watched her grow up. Her brother Darren too."

"Did you know their mother?"

"I did. Wendy. I also knew their father, Eric. They were both early and very loyal members of the Church of Will when we were first starting."

"What happened to them?"

"Eric was out hunting and was accidentally shot. If I remember correctly, it happened just before the kids' twelfth birthday."

"Oh, my, how awful!"

"Charlie never liked hunting and always cautioned Eric against it. We all wish Eric had listened."

"What was Wendy like?"

"Very sweet. Quiet. Poor woman got cancer and passed away some years after her husband. Charlie took that hard. They became close after Wendy lost her husband."

A murmur of excitement grew among the applicants in line until it peaked with cheers. Carson perked up. "There they are."

Charlie Wilkins was outside the door, shaking hands and signing autographs. His guest, "Colonel" Bruce Ashton, stood at attention behind the reverend. Ashton's hand cautiously cradled the ivory-handled, nickel-plated Colt Single-Action Army .45 "Peacemaker" on his belt, allegedly chosen because it was the same revolver carried by famed World War II general George S. Patton.

Ashton had arrived from overseas and accepted the job as director of campaign security for the candidate. Everyone always called Ashton "the Colonel," although he wasn't currently an enlisted officer. Helen had met the man on the few occasions when he visited Green-

hill, but she knew very little about him. In her time at
the compound, he had appeared only twice. He lived in
the Middle East somewhere. A mysterious character,
Ashton was in his fifties, always wore military garb,
and conducted himself as if he was giving orders to enlisted men. The truth was that he was once in the U.S.
Armed Forces, served in the first Gulf War and some in
Iraq, and then retired. Afterward he set up a security
business for Americans on business in the Mediterranean area. Apparently he and Wilkins were longtime
friends, so when the post became available, the reverend made the call to Ashton.

Several tourists and applicants wanted photographs
with Wilkins, and the candidate warmly obliged. It
took nearly fifteen minutes before Wilkins and Ashton
were able to get inside the center.

". . . not so safe, in my opinion," Ashton was saying.
"You can't just expose yourself like that from now on."

"Colonel, that's hogwash," Wilkins replied. "These
people are here to see me, they're here to volunteer for
the Church, and they're the folks who will elect me to
office. Of course I'm going to greet them and sign autographs and pose for pictures. That's what presidential
candidates do, Colonel."

"Well, we'll have to be more careful when we're outside the compound, that's all I'm saying."

Wilkins looked at Carson. "Mitch, we need you in
the conference room up at the house in one hour."

"Yes, sir."

"Helen, you know the Colonel, don't you?"

Ashton squinted at her and held out his hand.

"Yes, we've met before," Helen said as she shook his
palm.

"I remember," Ashton said. "How are you?"

"Fine."

"Helen is one of my personal assistants in the mansion," Wilkins said. "She's also the liaison between the campaign committee and the Greenhill administration. Anything you need, talk to Helen here, or to Mitch."

Ashton nodded at both of them.

Wilkins led him away. "Are you hungry? We could get a bite to eat in the cafeteria before the meeting. . . ."

When they were gone, Carson shot Helen a look and said, "I don't like that man. Why would Charlie hire a mercenary to be his head of security?" Then he walked away too, following Wilkins and Ashton.

Helen paid no attention to Carson's rhetorical question. He always seemed to be cranky about something. She tolerated her boss as much as anyone could. Helen figured he resented her being appointed liaison to the campaign committee over him. Wilkins had quite correctly informed Carson that his knowledge and experience running Greenhill was invaluable and that he couldn't be pulled away from that responsibility.

"Helen? Could you come here, please?" She got up from the intake desk and went over to Gordy, who was interviewing applicants. "Can you help do interviews? Unless you're busy doing something else?"

"No, no, I can do that." She addressed the next person in line and said, "Follow me, please." She went across the room to an empty desk and sat, gesturing to a chair in front of her. A woman handed over her paperwork and told Helen that she came all the way from California to join Wilkins's group in Virginia.

"There are two branches in California," Helen said. "One near San Francisco, and one near L.A."

"I know, but I understand Reverend Wilkins spends most of his time here. After all, this is where his mansion is. It was so exciting to see him outside just now!" the woman gushed.

Helen had to disappoint the woman and tell her there were no openings for apartments, but if she'd like to find a place to live in one of the neighboring villages, she was welcome to become a member.

It was like that for the next hour. One by one, they entered and sat at her desk, mostly women of all ages, but also a few men who were more interested in the sexier job of working on Wilkins's television program.

It was nearly five in the afternoon when a tall, bald-headed man approached Helen's desk. She was immediately struck by his presence, for he emitted a powerful charisma and intangible sense of high intelligence. He wore blue jeans, a plaid flannel shirt, and a backpack. Incongruously, he carried a leather briefcase with an odd flowery symbol embossed on the side.

"Hello," she said. "How can I help you?"

The man spoke with a shyness that she found endearing. "Um, I'd like to join the Church of Will. They said I should talk to you." He handed her the paperwork.

"Have a seat, Mr. . . ."

"Stan Johnson."

"I'm glad to meet you, Mr. Johnson." She held out a hand and he shook it. His skin was warm and coarse, but, more significant, his touch sent a spark of excitement up her arm and into her chest. She blinked and for a moment was dumbstruck.

"Ma'am?" he asked, releasing her hand. "Are you all right?"

"Oh, yes, I'm sorry. I've been distracted today; there's a lot going on here, as you can imagine. My name is Helen McAdams. Where are you from, Mr. Johnson?"

"Iowa."

She scanned the application and noticed that for "Skills" he had written: "Good with hands, tools, gardening, fixing things."

"Oh," she said. "Mr. Johnson, I think you might be in luck. It just so happens we have an opening for a groundskeeper and maintenance man. I see here that you do that sort of thing. Is that something that would interest you?"

The bald-headed man's dark-blue eyes pierced her, almost as if he could see and study her very soul.

Then he smiled warmly.

"Yes. It would."

FIFTEEN

Benjamin Travis and Jade told me they'd get word to me if and when the second hit—the one on Wilkins—was given the go-ahead. In the meantime, I knew I had to get close to the target. Now that he was running for president, there could be opportunities to accomplish the hit in a public place. The same way I did with Linder. But the client wanted it to appear to be an "inside job." In order to get close enough to Wilkins to kill him, I had to join the Church of Will.

So I did as much research on the Church's compound in Virginia as I could. The place called Greenhill. It's where Wilkins had a mansion and where he lived when he wasn't traveling. It's where I could integrate myself into the Church society, become one of them, and execute the assignment within hours of the green light.

I phoned the facility to inquire about jobs and housing at the compound. I told the person on the end that I desperately wanted to join the Church of Will. She replied that there were no openings at this time. So I had to figure out another way to place myself inside their community.

I drove a rental car from Chicago to Pittsburgh and then down into Virginia. Instead of going out of my way to Washington, D.C., and Alexandria, I took side roads and state highways to Leesburg and Manassas and finally to Greenhill. Miles from civilization. If the place hadn't been next to Aquia Lake, it would be nowhere. I parked at the side of the road, where I could see the comings and goings through the arch that was the entrance to the compound. But it was after sundown, so I figured I'd find a hotel in a nearby town and wait until the next day—Sunday—to make my move. It was at that moment that I saw a pickup truck leave the place. An old guy was driving it. The side of the truck had words painted on it: GREENHILL MAINTENANCE.

Interesting.

I followed him to nearby Stafford, a nothing of a town. He pulled in to Dougherty's Tavern on Jefferson Davis Highway. He got out and went inside. I estimated his age to be seventy or older. Walked with a limp. Wore overalls.

Interesting.

He looked like a maintenance man from Greenhill who liked to have a few rounds on Saturday night before the Church services the next morning.

I went inside the tavern, which was relatively empty. My man had hauled up on a bar stool and was addressing the bartender. I went over there and took a seat two down from him. I saw that Old Man Maintenance had ordered a beer, so I told the bartender I'd have what that guy had.

The maintenance guy looked at me and said, "You have good taste in beer, sir."

"I was going to say the same about you."

"You're not from around here, are you?"

"No. Just passing through. Been driving all day. Think I'll find a hotel room for the night."

"Where you headed?"

Small talk like that. Pretty dull. Said his name was Phil.

He complained about his "ticker." He'd had some

bypasses but he couldn't stop his craving for beer. He kept coughing into a handkerchief. I could tell his time was nearly up; perhaps I could save him from a painful, protracted death.

When the guy was done with his drink, I offered to buy another. He accepted. I ordered one for me as well. When the bartender delivered them, I went over and sat beside the fellow. We clinked our glass mugs and said, "Cheers."

People have many strange rituals.

We drank those down, then both lifted our mugs. Waved them at the bartender and asked for refills. I had palmed one of the vials Birdie sold me and emptied it into the dregs of the guy's beer before it was filled again.

After one more round, which the maintenance man bought, I left. Found a cheap motel, got a room, and slept soundly with no bad dreams. The painkillers did their job for the night.

I went to Greenhill the next day. It was Sunday, and the compound was crowded with tourists and other membership applicants. A sign out front indicated that Reverend Charlie Wilkins was on the premises and was preaching that day. I had already missed the morning service. That was all right; I didn't particularly want to hear it anyway. I'd get plenty of chances.

I dressed down for the role I'd be playing. For some reason, when I assumed a phony identity, the clothes helped me get in character. I became a farm boy from Iowa, so I wore farm clothes. I couldn't do much about my bald head, so I left it alone. I didn't want to have to fuss with a toupee for however many days I'd be there.

There were a couple of people at desks doing intake. A man and a woman. I chose to get in the woman's queue. I knew who she was from my research. Helen McAdams. One of Wilkins's personal assistants.

Perfect.

I supposed she was attractive, not that something like that mattered to me. But I sensed she was a bird with a wing down. There was something in her eyes and mannerisms. She was a troubled person. Vulnerable. Lonely. Unhappy. Someone I could manipulate.

When it was my turn, I introduced myself as Stan Johnson. It was as good a name as any. I did my best to appear shy and nervous. I said I was currently unemployed but had experience on a farm. I told her I was seeking more spirituality in my life and thought the Church of Will could help me.

I'd put on the application form that I was good with my hands, and she immediately offered me the job of groundskeeper and maintenance man—the position at the compound that became vacant that very day. She said I was lucky. I'd even get an apartment of my own, the rent for which would come out of my pay.

Fancy that.

I think she must have taken to me, for she told her colleague she was going to give me a tour of the compound. She made a call to Mitch Carson. I knew him to be the manager of the facility, but I feigned ignorance. When she hung up, Helen said we were to meet him in the cafeteria. Apparently my apartment wouldn't be ready for an hour or two. Helen let me store my backpack full of clothes and my briefcase in a locker for the time being.

I met Carson in the cafeteria. He was awfully officious and treated me as an inferior human being because of my newfound lowly janitorial job, but I was polite and shook his clammy hand. He took my paperwork from Helen and said he had to go to a meeting "up at the house." We said goodbye and Helen asked if I was hungry. I told her no, but she explained how the cafeteria was available for breakfast, lunch, and din-

ner. A snack room with vending machines was open twenty-four hours a day. Church employees were issued a meal ticket that was swiped each time we had a meal. A small fee was once again taken out of our pay. For the most part, it turned out that Church employees worked in exchange for room and board. Not a bad deal.

Helen showed me the huge sanctuary. I appreciated the artwork. I'd spent time in Rome and befriended a Catholic priest at one time, so I knew what I was looking at.

I suppose there was some kind of beauty there.

There was a Main Street at Greenhill. It had a convenience store, a small medical office, a bank, a florist, a clothing shop, and a grocery store with fresh produce, a bakery, and a butcher. It was like a small village. The staff got around in little golf-cart-like vehicles, as if it was some kind of country club.

Then she pointed out the section of Greenhill I was most interested in. The off-limits area. Where the mansion was located.

"Only authorized personnel are allowed inside the gate," Helen said as she indicated the high fence surrounding the space. I knew it was electrified. Why would a supposedly peace-loving reverend of a religious group have an electrified fence around his property? Helen had a keycard to swipe at the gate, because her office was in the mansion. Someday, she said, maybe she'd get permission to bring me inside and show it to me. As a groundskeeper and maintenance man, however, I would be allowed inside the fence during work hours. There was a team of workers and I'd be supervised. Helen pointed out the extensive gardens on the right side of the house. I told her that was my specialty, and she hinted that she'd see what she could do about that. On the left side of the house was a small building. She said it was the guardhouse. Next to that was a large barn.

Helen also pointed out the section of the mansion that fronted the lake. She said Wilkins's office had a large plate-glass window that faced it, and when he was on the premises he always made it a point to pray in that spot at midnight.

Of course, I knew that window was bulletproof. Again, why would Wilkins bulletproof his office? He must be pretty paranoid. Especially now that he was running for president.

Finally, we entered one of the three housing buildings. My room was on the first floor. It was a studio apartment, complete with a kitchenette and my own bathroom. I asked Helen where she lived. Next building over, second floor.

Convenient.

By now it was almost six o'clock. Helen's cellphone rang. She spoke to "Charlie" and said she'd be right there. Wilkins.

Apparently there was going to be an impromptu memorial service for a Church member who had died, and Wilkins was going to lead it. She had to get to the sanctuary. She told me that in a moment the compound loudspeaker system would make the announcement. She encouraged me to go and that perhaps she'd see me there.

I said I wouldn't miss it.

Helen left me alone in my apartment. I unpacked and gave the room a once-over to make sure it wasn't bugged. I didn't expect it to be, but one can't be too careful. After taking one of the oxycodone pills, I reflected on what I was doing at Greenhill.

Helen McAdams was a nice person. Too bad she felt she had to cover the scars on the inside of her forearms *with the long sleeves of her blouse. Yes, I detected a susceptible personality there, and she would suit my purposes.*

The closer I could get to her, the closer I'd be to Charlie Wilkins.

SIXTEEN

More than three hundred people gathered in the sanctuary after the announcement was made throughout the compound that Wilkins was going to speak again that day. Agent 47 dutifully followed the crowd and sat in a pew near the back. He saw Helen McAdams sitting in the front row. Mitch Carson paced the sanctuary foyer and greeted members that he knew personally.

When Wilkins got up to address the congregation, Agent 47 was immediately struck by the man's charisma and charm. On television, the reverend was extremely engaging; in person, he was magnetic. His voice was smooth and rich in timbre. The shock of white hair caught the overhead lights just right, providing a subliminal divine illusion. The assassin figured the reverend had personally spent some time with his lighting designers to achieve the effect.

"My friends and fellow followers of the Will," he began. "This evening we're holding an impromptu memorial service for Philip McHenry, who went to his maker during the night after a long illness. Many of you probably knew him as a quiet groundskeeper and maintenance man who always had a twinkle in his eye."

He went on for two or three more minutes, performing a eulogy for someone to whom he had most likely never spoken except for an occasional "Hello, how are you?"

Agent 47 tuned out the details of the fallen maintenance man. They weren't anything he particularly wanted
to hear. He spent the time looking around the room,
studying the members. They were of all ages, including
several families with children. There were more women
than men. Harmless, friendly people, except for the man
standing at the exit looking more like a guard than a
church usher. Several bodies down from Helen sat a
man wearing a military uniform. He was a colonel in
the U.S. Army.

Maybe.

The hitman was jolted out of his musings when he
heard the reverend say his name.

". . . and a Mr. Stan Johnson joined the Church of
Will today, and he'll be taking over for Philip. Mr.
Johnson? Where is Mr. Stan Johnson?"

47 hesitantly raised his hand.

"Oh, Mr. Johnson, there you are. Please stand up!
Don't be shy. We're all friends here."

The bald-headed man stood awkwardly and waved
reticently. He caught Helen smiling at him.

"Welcome, Stan. I'm sure everyone will introduce
him or herself to you in the next few days. Good luck
remembering everybody's name!"

Laughs. Applause.

47 quickly sat down.

Wilkins took a sip from a glass of water that was sitting on the podium. "Now, my friends, as you know,
I'm running for president."

Cheers. Hoots and hollers.

"I'm holding a big campaign rally in D.C. a few days
before the election. I'm looking for Church volunteers
to ride in some buses from here to the rally. I know
some of you have been looking for a way to protest
against the current administration and show your support for me, so here's your chance."

The congregation erupted in bigger applause.

Wilkins quieted them down with his hands. "Now, unfortunately, there won't be enough seats to fill every request. So it'll be a lottery. If you want to go, there's a little form to fill out. Mitch Carson will have a drop box in the cafeteria. Names will be drawn until all the seats are filled, okay?"

Everyone thought that was fair.

He then changed the subject and went back to Philip the maintenance man for a benediction and final word. Wilkins spoke about the importance of the community's spirit and its ability to coexist as one big, happy family.

"We all have the Will," he said. "That's why we're here."

That made sense to everyone but Agent 47.

The ceremony ended with a prayer. After that, the congregation stood and made their way out, 47 among them. With respect for the service's purpose, people spoke in low voices. Once they were outside, several men stepped up to the assassin and shook his hand.

"Welcome to Greenhill, Mr. Johnson."

"Glad to have you aboard, Mr. Johnson."

Although Agent 47 had expected some degree of non-anonymity during his stay at the compound, he hadn't anticipated this. Nevertheless, he played the introverted farmer and smoothly deflected earnest attempts at conversation. 47 wasn't worried. The more well known he was at Greenhill, the more people would trust him.

"Stan!"

He turned to see Helen moving toward him.

"Well, what did you think? Charlie's great, isn't he?"

47 nodded. "Even more charismatic than he is on TV."

"Sorry he put you on the spot. He tends to do that with new people." She laughed a little. "You looked kind of uncomfortable."

"I'm a bit timid. You've probably noticed."

"That's all right. I'm pretty quiet too. In high school I was always the girl that no one would ask to dance." She forced another laugh. There was a moment of awkward silence. "Are you going to put your name in the hat to go on the buses to Washington?"

The hitman shuffled his feet. "Oh, I don't know."

She squeezed his arm and leaned in conspiratorially. "Well, I *have* to go. I get a seat no matter what."

"I won't tell anyone."

"It's all right. Everybody'll know anyway."

"Well, then maybe I will put my name in the hat." He had no intention of doing so.

"Great!" She looked at her watch. "Hey, you know, I just realized how hungry I am. How about you? Want to come with me?" When he hesitated, she added, "I mean, if you want to. I didn't mean—"

Smiling, he raised his hand to stop her excuses. "I could eat."

"Oh! Okay, then, uh . . . let's go to the cafeteria! It's dinnertime."

He sensed that she was taken aback that he'd accepted.

The food was surprisingly good. Agent 47 had expected it to be the kind of fare served in high school cafeterias, but it was several steps above that.

"We have a couple of gourmet chefs on the premises," Helen explained as they sat at a table by themselves at one end of the gymnasium-sized dining hall. "They make it a point to bring in fresh ingredients and prepare healthy choices for the members. Some of us are vegetarians. The carnivores get the best beef and chicken, all grass-fed, no chemicals or preservatives added."

"I'm impressed," the assassin said. He had chosen

spaghetti, meat sauce, and meatballs, with a Caesar salad and a Coke. Helen had baked salmon topped with horseradish and bread crumbs, and steamed vegetables.

"So tell me why you're here, Stan. Why the Church of Will?"

Agent 47 had prepared his cover story well and effortlessly launched into it, with the appropriate character traits he had rehearsed. "Well, it's not much of a story, really. My dad had a farm in Iowa. I grew up on it, so I knew how to be a farmer from an early age. No brothers or sisters. I think my parents wanted more children after me, but for some reason my mom couldn't conceive. Anyway, I went to an agricultural college after high school. Both of my parents died in a fire while I was there. I went back to manage the family farm. It did okay for a while, but it went belly-up two years ago."

"You poor thing. I'm sorry about your parents."

"Yeah."

"What happened with the farm?"

"You know, the bad economy and everything. And the winters were awful. A lot of crops were destroyed. The government didn't help the farmers. Like most people in the country, I started to get fed up. I went to a few protests in Des Moines and one in Chicago. And then I started watching *Will You?* on television, and that did the trick. I realized I was feeling sort of lost in the world. I knew I needed a jump start in the spirituality department."

"I know what you mean. *Will You?* is a great show, isn't it?"

"I enjoy it a lot."

They continued to eat in silence for a few moments, and then she asked, "Stan, what about a family of your own? No wife or children?"

He shook his head. "No."

"Girlfriend?"

47 took another sip of Coke and looked directly at

her. "I'm afraid not. I've never been very good at that sort of thing."

Helen smiled. "You know what?"

"What?"

"Neither have I." She chuckled nervously and continued to eat.

After another pause, Agent 47 found that she was studying his face. "What?" he asked.

"Nothing." She took a breath. "Well, there's something about your eyes that seems so familiar to me. They're very intense."

He shrugged and laughed self-consciously. "They're just the eyes that came with me." The killer then looked at his plate to avoid more unnecessary eye contact. He had noticed that Helen had the same well of loneliness in her own eyes that he did, and 47 did not care for the conversation to linger on the subject. A shyness act would cover his discomfort.

At that point, Colonel Ashton marched through the cafeteria, tray in hand, followed by two or three other men and Mitch Carson.

The assassin whispered, "Who's he?"

"Oh, that's the Colonel. We *call* him the Colonel. His real name is Bruce Ashton. He's not a real colonel. In fact, he's not in the military, but he acts like he is. I think he *was* a colonel in the army but he's retired. I don't know his whole story."

"Is he a member of the Church?"

"He is. But he's also just been appointed Charlie's director of security for his campaign travels. That's what the Colonel does for a living. Some kind of security business overseas in the Middle East."

"I see."

"I don't have many dealings with him."

47 nodded. "So tell me more about you, Helen. Why are *you* here?"

It was her turn to be diffident. "I don't know. Like you, I was feeling lost, I guess. My parents are gone, no brothers or sisters. So I suppose I'm all alone in the world too. I also had—"

She hesitated and looked away.

"What?"

"Never mind." She unconsciously pulled at the sleeves of her blouse, hiding the angry red marks.

47 did his best to appear sympathetic. "It's all right, Helen. You can tell me."

"Oh, I just had some, um, medical problems, that's all."

He waited for her to elaborate. When she didn't, the hitman said, "Well, I hope you're better now."

"I am." She smiled at him, but 47 didn't believe it. Helen McAdams was definitely a vulnerable soul.

After yet another beat of awkward stillness, she asked, "Would you excuse me? I'm going to run to the ladies' room."

"Sure."

She got up and walked away. Agent 47 finished his meal and studied the cafeteria crowd. How many of them were lost souls too? Did they all have unhappy pasts? Were they all looking for that "eureka" moment when their lives suddenly became meaningful? Did they really think they'd find it *here*?

Colonel Ashton and his entourage had finished their meals and stood. Agent 47 watched them as they left the dining hall. The assassin grabbed his tray and took it over to the conveyor belt below the sign that read: PLACE TRAYS AND DISHES HERE. He then followed Ashton and stood outside the door, watching the mercenary get into a Jeep with the other men. They drove away toward the restricted area.

Secrets, 47 thought.

Greenhill had a lot of secrets.

SEVENTEEN

It was my first night in the studio apartment at Greenhill. The middle of the night, actually. Usually I had no problem sleeping, but tonight I couldn't. Not sure why.

Everything had gone according to plan. I'd established a believable cover. I'd made friends with someone on the inside. Now I had to wait until the Agency told me I could go ahead and kill Charlie Wilkins.

How long would I have to wait? The election was in less than a month.

A window in my apartment faced the Main Street area of the compound. I parted the drapes and looked outside. All was dark. Streetlamps cast a dull glow on the "street." Not a soul was about. Did everyone go to sleep at night? Was the place that disciplined? I'd never known of any area occupied by people who followed routine hours. It's a fact that some humans are night people, others are morning people. Surely somewhere in the compound there was someone who was awake like me. I wondered if that person might be Helen. My friend.

It was ironic that I'd had a "dinner date" with her. Me. A dinner date.

It was strange, this feeling of having a friend. Even though it was all deceit, there was something genuine *in the attraction between us. Of course, the person I presented to her was not really me.*

I wasn't sure who the real me was. I was never sure.

I suppose I'd always thought of myself as a kind of machine. A "thing" that does what I do without any feeling. But I did have flesh and blood. I did have nerve endings on my skin. I did have internal organs and a brain and a heart. I may have been created in a laboratory, but I was a human—I supposed.

So why didn't I have the feelings that other humans had? I didn't know.

Sometimes, though, I did feel as if feelings were straining to get out. As if some kind of barrier prevented them from bubbling to the surface.

Take the hit on Dana Linder. She was not a bad person, from what I could tell. Shouldn't I have felt some kind of remorse or guilt for that hit? "Normal" people would. Sometimes I wondered if there was a way I could allow myself to feel those things. Was there a button I could push? A trigger?

Today I felt something when I talked to Helen. I'd never really spoken to a woman as a friend before. Diana was the closest I'd ever come to having a female friend. That didn't turn out so well.

How long could I keep up the subterfuge with Helen? Where was this all going?

I didn't know, but I would do whatever I had to do.

I was in Millennium Park in Chicago.

The baby stroller. Dressed as a woman. Sniper rifle in hand. Dana Linder was onstage. I was about to raise the gun, put her within the crosshairs, and squeeze the trigger.

But there was no one else in the park. It was just her and me. Dead silence. Not even wind or birds.

I put my eye to the scope. And the figure wasn't Dana

Linder at all. It was the shadow. The Faceless One. Death.

And suddenly I was not in Chicago. I was no longer pointing the rifle at Death on the stage of the pavilion.

I was back on that mountain in the Himalayas. The snow and ice beneath my feet were crumbling.

Death was watching me with anticipation.

I woke up in a sweat. Another nightmare. Hadn't had one for a while. Odd that it would happen now. I wondered what it meant.

The clock said it was nearly five in the morning. I must have eventually fallen asleep.

I shook the remains of the dream from my head and got out of bed. Went to the bathroom, found my bottle of pills, and took two.

And my thoughts went back to that fateful day in Nepal. . . .

EIGHTEEN

The cliff edge trembled violently as rock and ice debris showered around him. Agent 47 couldn't move forward because of the hail of gunfire from the Chinese man's QBZ-95. Going backward would mean falling with the imminent avalanche and being buried alive beneath tons of ice and snow.

Once again, the assassin aimed the Silverballer at the dangling bodyguard, exposing himself in the man's line of fire. But the turbulence was too strong. The entire mountainside acted as if it was about to topple like a house of cards. The ice beneath his feet lurched and threw 47 sideways, just as he felt a searing stab of fire penetrate his left side. As he fell hard on the craggy surface, he had the presence of mind to realize that the shaking ground had saved his life. The Chinese man's round had indeed pierced the fleshy part at the edge of his waist, but had 47 been standing upright, the bullet would have gone through his abdomen.

The shock waves traveled up the side of the cliff to Nam Vo's men. The one spotting the dangling man lost his balance and slipped. He slid off the cliff edge but managed to grab hold of the rope that suspended his partner. Agent 47 heard them shout to each other in their language. The rope wouldn't hold them both. The rock ledge cracked, and the two men bounced with the hemp. One of them screamed in terror, for there was nothing below them but thousands of feet of air.

Agent 47 crawled forward. Blood trailed on the white snow behind him. The tremors grew more intense as the boomer did its job. If only he could get far enough away in time. . . .

The rope holding the Chinese men finally gave way. They both shouted a death call.

Agent 47 watched them plummet until they were mere dots against the gray misty mountainside.

He kept moving. The outward edge of the cliff was just a few feet to his right. Still intent on the success of his mission, the hitman dared to peer down to see what Nam Vo and his party were doing.

They were still in place, not really sure what all the commotion above them was about and oblivious to the oncoming holocaust.

Then the sky and earth opened and the ice cliff completely collapsed, carrying Agent 47 with it through blinding lights and into deep and total darkness.

Morphological experts and the news media recorded the catastrophe as a large "slab avalanche" that measured 4,600 meters in length and 18,000 meters in volume, making it one of the biggest in the Himalayan region. It was blamed on a natural trigger. Nam Vo and his expeditionary team were wiped away, and their bodies were never recovered.

Although he didn't know it at the time, Agent 47 was very, very lucky.

He had fallen with the bulk of the sliding snow and ice for about eight hundred feet when his body struck an upward incline of rock upon which was packed new, soft snow. The impact caused the assassin to bounce toward the mountain face instead of away from it. Unconscious, Agent 47 rolled like a log into a rock-solid crevice from which the ledge protruded. He would have plummeted deep into the fissure had its walls not been so narrow. Instead, his body wedged inside a bottle-neck, several feet from the opening at the top. He was cut off and protected from the deadly maelstrom that lasted nearly thirty minutes.

When his eyes fluttered open, the first thing he noticed was the cold. Then, almost immediately, he felt the excruciating pain in his back. He didn't know if it was broken or not. He couldn't move, although he knew his legs dangled freely. He was stuck in the crevice, his torso pinned in place by the tapered walls of ice.

Trapped. Like a cork in a bottle.

The only thing that brought him any comfort was that the sun shone above him through the opening. He could climb out if he made the effort. The agony in his back was the biggest obstacle to doing so.

47 couldn't see his legs, since the rock walls squeezed tightly against his chest and waist, but he could kick them. He wasn't paralyzed, which meant his back was miraculously unbroken. It just hurt like the devil. He had most likely ruptured a disc or two. The cleft in the mountain had saved his life, but it had brutally wrenched his torso as if it were made of clay.

It was also difficult to breathe. The pressure of the stone against his chest prevented him from inhaling deeply. That realization was enough for 47 to attempt the escape. He'd known pain in his lifetime, but this was going to be severe. Luckily, his arms were caught above his shoulder line, allowing him to gain some leverage. The mere act of pressing down with his forearms and hands brought intense jolts of misery to his muscles.

Take it a little at a time.

Push down, wiggle up. Push down, wiggle up.

Agent 47 felt like a worm struggling to slip through a hole lined with sharp spikes.

His clothing ripped as the rocks dug into the skin on his chest and belly. The bullet wound was minor compared to what his back was going through.

The assassin nearly blacked out from the pain and effort, but he willed himself to keep at it. If he didn't get out of that hole *now*, he'd never do it. He would die there, a fly caught in a web of ice and stone.

Push down, wiggle up.

He didn't know how long it took, but once his hip bones cleared the craggy bottleneck, he was home free. It was then only partially painful to use his legs and boots to support his weight. Five minutes later, he was standing on top, looking down at the abyss that might have been his grave.

There was snow everywhere—so much bright whiteness that it was difficult to discern where the edge of the cliff dropped off.

47 took stock of what he had on him.

His beloved briefcase was gone. The Silverballer he'd had in his hand—vanished. The backpack containing his supplies—obliterated and buried somewhere thousands of feet below. He had no climbing equipment. All he could account for was a wad of currency in his pocket and a fake passport.

Except for the ripped clothing and his boots, he was unprotected from the elements. He pulled off one of the shreds of his jacket, lifted his shirt, and tied it around his waist to hopefully stop the bleeding from the gunshot wound.

Perhaps he would die on Kangchenjunga after all.

There didn't seem to be an easy path down, but the mountain face going upward appeared to be climbable with only hands and feet. Agent 47 thought he could make out a level rim some fifty feet above his head. Perhaps that led to another, more agreeable route that he could traverse without climbing equipment. He knew it was unlikely, since reaching any sort of altitude on the Kanch required gear and more expertise than he possessed. But he had to try.

The icy wind grew stronger as he scaled the rocky face. His gloves helped with handholds, and at least the boots were still strong and sturdy. Every few inches he ascended were painful. He felt as if he had been tortured on a medieval rack, his vertebrae pulled apart or crushed together and permanently fixed in that position.

When he reached the level ledge, 47 collapsed and lay on his stomach. He rarely cursed, but for once he allowed a few epithets to spill from his mouth.

It was then that he thought angrily about Diana.

What had happened? Where had she gone? Why had she left him stranded? The mission was a success—he was certain that Nam Vo was dead—but who else might have perished in the avalanche? The boomer had obviously caused a very destructive landslide, but, without Diana's exact pinpoint on the cliff, it turned out sloppily.

He must have fallen asleep from the exertion and the pain, for the next thing he knew, the sun was low on the horizon, the temperature was dozens of degrees colder, and the wind was biting. 47 had lost his bivouac tent with his backpack. Could he survive a night on the mountain? Perhaps he'd been better off stuck in that crevice after all!

47 rolled over on his side and winced. There was no position that was comfortable. No matter what he did, the nerves in his back screamed bloody murder.

And then he heard voices.

Was he hallucinating?

The assassin reached for a flare that he had in his

jacket pocket—but it was gone. If only he could attract some attention. Would anyone see him?

The voices grew louder.

Someone was near!

He tried to call out, but his voice cracked. 47 couldn't seem to make his vocal cords operate.

Then two shadows appeared on the rim. People.

The hitman was unable to determine how far away they were. He was delirious from the pain. He did, though, manage to raise an arm and wave it back and forth. In the dim light, the fading sun cast a glint off his wristwatch and acted as a beacon.

The two travelers saw him and rushed forward.

When he awoke, Agent 47 saw a flickering light dancing across a stony ceiling. Icy stalactites hung like daggers but were in no danger of falling on him.

He was in a cave of some sort.

The assassin turned his head.

A campfire. A man and a woman, bundled up, sitting close to the warmth. They weren't Caucasian. Nepalese, most likely. Maybe Tibetan.

The woman glanced at him and muttered something. They both got up and moved closer to him. They spoke a language 47 didn't understand.

He tried to raise himself, but the pain shot through his back and he nearly cried out. The woman spoke comforting words and gently pushed him down. He was lying on a fur blanket. She said something else, crawled away, and then returned with a bowl of hot liquid.

Yak butter soup with grain barley on the side.

Although it tasted absolutely horrible, Agent 47 consumed it voraciously, as if it was his final meal on earth.

* * *

The Nepalese nomads sewed up the bullet wound and nursed the assassin for two weeks in their private ice cave on the side of Kangchenjunga. From what Agent 47 could fathom, the couple had left civilization quite some time ago. Perhaps they were hiding from the Chinese in Tibet. The husband made monthly trips down to one of the villages to stock up on food and supplies. Their home was well furnished and comfortable—for a cavern. Agent 47 thought the couple might be a little crazy from the seclusion, but at least they knew how to care for him.

At last, 47 was well enough to leave. The Nepalese man accompanied the hitman down Kangchenjunga. Using the couple's climbing equipment, a seven-hour trip took twice as long due to 47's discomfort. At the end, though, Agent 47 found himself on solid, flat ground. He paid the man from the money he had in his pocket. At first the hermit refused, but the assassin insisted. They parted ways with a handshake.

The pain was still severe. Simply walking was a chore.

He checked in to a hospital in Kathmandu and discovered that he was suffering from a spinal disc herniation. His sciatic nerve was under constant bombardment from the pressure. The doctor told him that anti-inflammatory drugs and painkillers were the best approach but that 47 should get plenty of bed rest for about six weeks. The hitman took the man's advice, checked into a fleabag hotel, and dosed himself with oxycodone and naproxen sodium tablets.

After two weeks, he limped like a cripple to an Internet café and tried to contact Diana. Every line of communication to her was broken. He checked the secure server where he picked up messages from the Agency. There were several for him, asking him to contact ICA if he received them. They most likely assumed he was dead. Tellingly, there was no mention of Diana.

It took fourteen weeks before Agent 47 was finally pain free. He thanked the doctor and left Nepal with a three-month supply of the painkillers. The hitman had found that he liked the effects, which had nothing to do with managing discomfort. He had begun to have strange dreams, even nightmares, and the oxycodone tended to control them. For some reason, the pills didn't dope him up but rather made him clearheaded and confident. It was only if he tapered down the dosage or stopped altogether that he experienced a nervous, anxiety-producing reaction. Best to continue taking them.

Agent 47 made his way to Mexico and holed up in Guadalajara. He knew an arms dealer there who replaced his ATM Hardballers, complete with the pearl handles, just like his long-lost Silverballers. It took a month to re-create the leather briefcase with the fleur-de-lis insignia on it.

All that time, the hitman periodically attempted to find Diana. There was still no trace of his former handler. He ignored all messages from the Agency. He had no desire to go back to them. He'd had enough of the ICA. Six months after the avalanche, the Agency stopped sending him missives.

Although damaged and not up to the high standard Agent 47 liked to maintain, he was free to do what he wanted.

NINETEEN

Benjamin Travis drummed his fingertips on the desk in his office and once again played the message from the Agency's client.

"Stand by."

That was it. No further instruction, no explanation, or no indication that the second hit—the one on Charlie Wilkins—would still be ordered.

Travis had come to the conclusion that it wasn't the U.S. government that had ordered the hit on Dana Linder. If that were true, why would they purposefully instruct the assassin to leave a weapon at the scene that incriminated the American military? The gun's serial number had been traced to a soldier in Texas who had reported the rifle stolen. Television and newspapers were full of accusations that President Burdett and the CIA were behind the murder. Wilkins himself had been quick to point a finger. The most vocal proponent of the current administration's involvement in the tragedy was the man known as Cromwell. "It's time for a new revolution in America," the mercenary announced on national television. Since the Linder killing, the New Model Army had stepped up the frequency of strikes at various targets and delivering the message to the public: *Rebel.*

Sitting safely aboard the *Jean Danjou II*, back in the

waters of the Mediterranean near the Costa del Sol, Travis wasn't too concerned about the fate of his home country. He had turned his back on the United States long ago. He'd been watching the political developments in America with detached amusement until Jade reminded him that, should America fall, so would the world economy. And if that happened, there would be fewer clients for the Agency. Travis didn't think that would be the case—perhaps there would be even *more* clients—but a global financial meltdown would be bad for everyone. Nevertheless, he fully expected Cromwell and the NMA to succeed. The state of the union was a powder keg. Most recently, the National Guard and U.S. Army were called out to control militia attacks. A full-out firefight had erupted in Virginia at the Civil War battlefield site of Manassas. Seven civilians were killed. More than half of the population staged protests all over the country, and twelve thousand people marched on Washington. Just one or two more incendiary events allegedly perpetrated by the government would be all it would take to bring the crisis to a head. The assassination of Charlie Wilkins, if orchestrated by the CIA, would certainly push the country over the edge into civil war.

So if the current administration wasn't the client, then who was?

Travis had ordered Jade to utilize every intelligence apparatus the Agency possessed to uncover the speaker's identity. When he communicated, it was always by phone. An electronic scrambler disguised his voice. The number from which he called was never traceable. It didn't help that the Agency's own encryption process for accepting email and phone calls was extremely complicated and unshakable. Satellites bounced signals between several countries before a client could deal with the ICA. This was also true for reverse traffic.

From the analysis that he, Jade, and the team had performed thus far, Travis suspected the client might be
Cromwell himself. Who else wanted to see a rebellion,
and what more could cause that rebellion than the as-
sassinations of Dana Linder and Charlie Wilkins?

Travis considered the state of the operation. Agent 47
was now ensconced at Greenhill, supposedly infiltrating the community to get closer to the proposed target.
The client promised that the orders for the second hit
would come within a couple of weeks. Travis didn't
think the client would renege; he had thus far acted in
good faith. The money for the Linder killing came
through, and the Agency had received a nonrefundable
down payment for the Wilkins part of the job. Travis
fully expected to go through with the second phase of
the mission.

But the manager wasn't sure what to make of Agent
47. The hitman had a sparkling reputation, to be sure,
but he was unpredictable. Given the fact that the assassin was a clone and a warrior constructed from various
DNA strains and bloodlines, 47 was no doubt a *machine* of a man—and machines could break down or
malfunction. Travis had never met Agent 47 prior to
their face-to-face encounter aboard the yacht a week
earlier, but Travis knew everything about him. He had
thoroughly studied the assassin's history, and the hitman was completely unaware he had been used.

It was vitally important that 47 never find out. Hence,
finding Diana was a top priority. Jade had a lead in the
midwestern United States. Perhaps that would prove to
be fruitful. The Agency's operatives just might be successful in locating the traitorous woman. And once
that was done, Travis would send Agent 47 to be her
assassin.

Luring the hitman back into the fold had not been
easy. After a year of searching for the killer, the Agen-

cy's operative Roget reported that he had employed "freelancer" Agent 47 in Jamaica. So Travis set the plan in motion. They paid Roget a substantial fee to deliver the wayward killer to them via the remote-controlled plane. It wasn't Travis's fault that 47 shot up the remote so the Agency couldn't land the aircraft safely. At least the hitman's ordeal in the Caribbean was a good test to see if he was up to snuff.

The assassin's performance had impressed Travis and upper management enough to decide that 47 could be reinstated. The masquerade aboard the yacht—allowing 47 to wander freely into restricted areas under the pretext of the "new honesty and trustworthiness" of the Agency—was icing on the cake. Jade wasn't convinced 47 had fallen for it, but apparently something worked. The hitman had agreed to rejoin. The current job—the Linder hit and the possible Wilkins one—was to be a further assessment of 47's loyalty and present skill level. Travis had no doubt that, if 47 succeeded in this very difficult assignment, he could cope with going after his former handler. The hitman was the only one who *could* kill Diana.

If only she hadn't managed to escape that hotel in Paris before Travis's team burst into her room, guns blazing. She should be in a grave. Instead, the woman got away with too much of Travis's classified material. She had threatened to expose the project to the world, and he believed she could—and would—do it. So why hadn't she? That was a year ago. What was she waiting for?

Travis figured that she still needed some sort of physical evidence. All she had at the moment was the knowledge in her head. It would take more than that to convince the world that Travis and the Agency were up to no good. Diana was a dead woman as soon as she was found.

Now Travis had to convince Agent 47 that his former handler had betrayed him on that fateful day in the Himalayas. He had to plant the seeds of doubt and mistrust in the assassin's already suspicious mind.

And it was working.

TWENTY

The days passed into mid-October.

Agent 47 dutifully worked as groundskeeper and maintenance man, although most of his jobs had nothing to do with that description. His supervisor was a young man named Stuart Chambers. The hitman developed an immediate dislike for him. Chambers took his managerial role much too seriously. For the first few days on the job, "Stan" was given the most menial and disgusting tasks, such as scrubbing out the men's and women's toilets in all the restroom facilities at Greenhill. When that was done, Chambers ordered 47 to clean out the grease trap in the cafeteria kitchen. It was a revolting, dirty job that put the assassin in a foul mood. After a week, 47 had still not been given any tasks within the restricted area.

The only positive things about being at Greenhill, he decided, were the evenings he spent with Helen. Since his cover required him to flirt with a more "human" identity, he made the effort to talk more and be more personable. The shyness act played well, for it encouraged Helen to "draw him out," bringing them closer to a kind of friendship that, surprisingly, 47 enjoyed. He was uncommonly comfortable with the platonic relationship they had built in the short time they'd known each other. He sensed, however, that she wanted to take their friendship to another level. Sometimes she referred to their get-togethers as "dates," and one night he was certain that she wanted him to kiss her good night after he'd walked her to her building. But 47 couldn't do it. Something prevented him from crossing that line with her.

One evening after dinner, they took a walk outside the compound along the two-lane road toward Coal Landing. The sun was rapidly sinking and the weather had turned autumn-cool, so Helen bundled up in a sweater and light jacket. Agent 47 simply wore his work shirt and overalls with a windbreaker. At one point, she shivered and complained of being chilled. 47 recognized the hint, so he placed his arm around her and held her closer. It was all part of acting the role, even though it felt completely foreign to him.

"Mmm, that's better," she said.

The hitman felt awkward but used that in his characterization of timorous Stan Johnson.

"I told Mitch Carson that you wanted to work in the mansion gardens. He said he'd speak to Stuart about it."

47 allowed a wry laugh. "I don't think Stuart Chambers likes me very much."

"Why do you say that?"

"Have you noticed he gives me all the ugly jobs? I have yet to do any real maintenance work. He's not very nice to me. Why is he such an . . . such an—"

"Asshole?"

He looked at her and smiled. "Yeah, I guess that's what I was trying to say."

"I don't know, but I agree. He's actually kind of sweet on me. About a year ago he asked me out. We dated a few times, but he wanted . . . er, he wanted more from me than I was willing to give at the time. I also thought he was disrespectful and insensitive. I broke it off with him." She looked up at 47 and squeezed his arm. "Maybe he's jealous."

"Of me?"

"Of you and *me*."

"Oh."

Did that mean the rest of the compound was already viewing Helen and Stan as a *couple*? 47 didn't know if that was a good or a bad thing.

"People are talking, you know," she said mischievously.

"About us?"

"Yep. Hey, we've been together every night since you got here. There may be a couple hundred people living at Greenhill, but it's really a little place. It's like small-town gossip. Whenever someone hooks up with somebody, it becomes news."

"I didn't know." 47 found that disturbing. "Why would anyone care?"

"People are people."

He had never thought of that. This relationship stuff was very new to him and he said so.

She squeezed his arm again, stood on her tiptoes because of his height, and kissed his cheek. 47 was flustered.

"I'm new at it too, Stan," she said.

This was all very bizarre.

Helen was acting like I was her boyfriend or something.

I knew I had to get close to her when I came here. The plan was that I would integrate myself into a "normal" human social life, and I'd been able to do it. I was surprised by my success, although I couldn't say I found it particularly comfortable. It was very alien to me. It made me feel like even more of a freak, because no matter how hard I tried, even if I meant it, I would never be "normal."

Every morning Helen used her keycard to go through the gate to the restricted area. She was in the mansion all day working for Charlie Wilkins. Helen was my means of getting inside that mansion, so I had to keep up the illusion that we were a couple. What was strange about it all—and I wasn't sure how to handle it—was that I was truly enjoying her company. I'd never had a friend of that sort. Diana Burnwood was the closest thing, and she was my Agency handler. I rarely saw her in person. I could count the number of times on one hand. Helen was very different. She was just an innocent, regular person, except there was something in her past that she wasn't proud of, something that wounded her. I aimed to find out what that was.

Wilkins had left the compound and was traveling with his campaign committee. The man had a lot of work to do before the election, which was in three weeks. There had been no word from the Agency regarding the hit on him. I didn't expect the orders to come too soon. Helen told me some interesting things about Wilkins. I had already done due diligence and researched the man thoroughly. I knew how he had started the Church back in the 1970s and worked his way up. He became a millionaire when he opened his fast-food chain restaurants, so that gave him the means to expand his Church. Helen told me he was close with Dana Shipley Linder's mother and that her father had died in a hunting accident.

Interesting.

Fatal hunting accidents are actually quite rare.

In the meantime, I resolved to continue my so-called "work" at Greenhill and keep seeing Helen. I dared myself to say it. I liked her. And what a curious and *unfamiliar sensation that was. For the first time in my life I was feeling what others call an emotion.*

With one hand carrying a bouquet of flowers from Sam's Florist on Greenhill's Main Street, 47 knocked on the apartment door with the other. It opened swiftly, and Helen stood wearing a daringly low-cut evening dress. He wore his signature black suit and red tie.

"Stan, come in. Oh, flowers! Are these for me?"

"Of course." He handed them to her and stepped inside. She closed the door and smelled the mixed bouquet. "How lovely! Let me get a vase to put these in. Come on in and make yourself at home. Dinner's almost ready."

While he had been in her apartment a couple of times, this was the first for an honest-to-goodness dinner date. A one-bedroom space, Helen's home was decidedly feminine and tastefully furnished. A card table, covered by a white tablecloth, sat in the middle of the living room. Two large lit candles provided flickering illumination. In fact, Helen had placed several candles around the room.

Was this what they called a "romantic" dinner? 47 wondered. In preparation for what might be an unpredictable situation, he had chosen not to take any oxycodone that day. So far, he felt fine.

She reentered the room with the flowers in a glass vase. "I'll put these on the coffee table, since the vase is too big to go on our table. How do you like it? I borrowed the tablecloth from the cafeteria."

"It's very nice."

She laughed. "Stan, you really are a man of few words." She pointed to a bottle of champagne sitting in an ice bucket. "Could you open that? I just have to check on the chicken."

47 took the bottle, examined the label, and didn't recognize the name. He figured it was one of the inexpen-
sive brands sold in the convenience store at Greenhill. It
didn't matter. He wasn't planning to drink much of it.
47 tore off the foil top, worked the cork, and pointed
the bottle at the ceiling. After the *pop*, sudsy liquid
spilled onto the rug. Helen came back in to witness it.

"Sorry," he said.

She laughed again. "Don't be silly. That's what's supposed to happen with champagne." She picked up two
glasses from the table and held them out to him. "Fill
'em up, sir."

He did, then placed the bottle back in the bucket.
"Are we celebrating something?"

"Not really. Who says you have to be celebrating
something to have champagne?"

He took his glass. She held hers up and said, "To
Charlie winning president, to the Church of Will, and
to our friendship." 47 clinked her glass and took a sip.
She nearly downed hers. It wasn't the best champagne
he'd ever had, nor was it the worst.

Dinner was a roasted chicken covered with a mustard-
based rubbing that 47 found delicious. Helen had also
prepared baked potatoes and a dish of broccoli roasted
with garlic cloves. She broke out a bottle of red wine
and filled yet another glass. 47 watched her consume
too much during the meal, and she became giddy and
talkative. She was obviously nervous, as if she expected
something to happen between them that night.

47 recognized that if he were perhaps a bit more like
other men, something *would* happen. Fortunately, he
wasn't.

When they were done with the meal, the assassin
helped her with the dishes. She washed and he dried. At
one point, though, his hands began to shake. The
dreaded anxiety had returned. When she handed him a

wet plate, it slipped right out of his trembling fingers and shattered on the floor.

"Helen, I'm sorry. How clumsy of me."

"It's okay, it's okay. Let me get a dustpan and broom."

He stooped and picked up shards. She brought him a paper bag to throw them in. "Be careful; don't cut yourself," she said.

47 helped her with the dustpan, and soon the mess was cleared. Then he asked to use the washroom. When he was alone, he dug the pill bottle out of his pocket and opened it—but it slipped from his shaking hands, spilling tablets all over the floor.

"You all right in there?" he heard her call.

"Fine."

He managed to collect the pills, swallowed two, and replaced the rest in the bottle. When he returned to the living room, Helen stood and said, "You had a good idea. It's my turn now—excuse me."

"Sure," he said.

While she was out of the room, he took the time to examine some of her things. There was a collection of paperbacks on a shelf, mostly romantic novels and a few self-help books. Especially striking was the absence of photographs. No family pictures. No high school graduation shot.

Was that a symptom of loneliness?

Helen reappeared with a concerned expression on her face.

"Everything all right?" 47 asked.

"Stan? What are these?" She held out her palm. There were three oxycodone pills in her hand. "I saw these on the floor behind the door. They're yours, aren't they?"

47 had missed them during his cleanup. Now that he was caught, he figured he might as well be honest. "Yes, they're mine. They're pills I take. For pain."

"Pain? Really?"

He shrugged. "No. Not really."

"Stan. I know these pills. They're OxyContin, aren't they?"

He nodded.

Helen took his hand and led him to the couch. As they sat, she asked, "Stan, why are you taking them?"

"I had an injury about a year ago. I was on them for pain management, but I guess I never stopped."

"Stan, you're addicted. You know that, don't you?"

He shook his head. "I can quit anytime I want. I just don't want to yet."

"That means you're addicted. Stan, listen to me. *I* was addicted to OxyContin too. For a long time. I haven't told anyone at Greenhill this, not even Charlie. But—I don't know, I trust you. I think we're kindred souls, Stan. There's a sadness in you that I can relate to. Do you . . . do you know what I'm talking about?"

He hesitated but then nodded.

She turned her head and didn't look at him as she spoke. 47 could see this was very difficult for her. "Stan, I was very lost a few years ago. I was into drugs, a lot of them. I did everything. I was hooked on heroin. The OxyContin came later, and I got hooked on that. I did . . . I did some pretty awful things to support my habit. I'm not proud of it. Stan, it's still a struggle for me. Every day I go through a few moments in which I crave those awful drugs. That's the reason I joined the Church of Will. I needed the strength to fight my addiction. Stan, if you knew the things I've done . . ."

47 thought, *If you knew the things* I've *done!*

She turned to him and said, "I can help you, Stan. You need to kick it. You know you do. You may not want to admit it, but deep down you have the Will. It's what Charlie teaches us. You have the Will to quit those pills and throw them away. You might need some medical help, but some people can quit cold turkey. It messes you up for a few weeks, but you can get through it. I'll help you, Stan. Will you let me help you?"

"Helen . . ."

"If I can do it, I know you can do it. I'm not a very strong person, Stan. I'm pretty weak. I guess that's something you should understand about me if we're going to continue to be . . . friends." Then she looked at him. "Or more." She leaned in close, looking into his eyes, her mouth parted.

She wanted Stan Johnson to kiss her.

"Helen, I . . ."

She reached up and placed a hand on his cheek.

But Agent 47 couldn't do that.

"Helen, I'm . . . I'm just not wired for that kind of relationship."

She blinked but didn't remove her hand. "Are you . . . ?"

"No, I'm not gay. But I've never had a relationship that worked the way it's supposed to. I guess you can say I'm jaded. It's difficult for me to trust anyone."

"You can trust me, Stan."

"I'm sure I can. I think the world of you. I believe we can be very close, but I was hoping we could just be . . . friends."

He saw the disappointment in her eyes. She removed her hand and then took a big sip of champagne. "Sure. We can do that."

"Helen. You really don't know me—"

She held up a hand. "Stop. It's all right. I know you've got your own set of secrets. Perhaps you'll tell me about them someday. And, about us, I'm not pressuring you, Stan. I like you. I like you more than anyone I've known here at Greenhill. So if you want to be friends, then I can accept that. I'm a damaged person too. Yes, I can see that you're damaged. Your wounds are deep and permanent. I know."

He took one of her hands and gently slid her sleeve up, revealing the red welts.

"Just like mine," she added.

"What happened?" he asked gently.

"I thought I was at the bottom. The lowest of the low. I was selling my body for drugs. I was stealing. I was even homeless for a time. So I tried to end it." She snorted. "It didn't work, obviously."

He lightly ran his fingers over the disfigured flesh.

"After that, I resolved to change my life. It was a wake-up call. I turned to the Church of Will and things started getting better. I had something to believe in. I gained a purpose beyond sticking a needle in my vein or popping a pill. Stan, you can do that too. I'll help you, if you let me."

A long silence passed, after which 47 replied, "I'll consider it."

An hour later, she was asleep on the couch. They had continued to talk, but she drank nearly all the champagne and wine by herself. She cuddled next to him, put her head on his shoulder, and drifted off.

47, however, was wide awake. The pills had kicked in, and his thoughts were clear and focused. He couldn't think of a moment in his life in which a woman had fallen asleep next to him in this fashion. It was indeed a totally new and somewhat uncomfortable experience for him. Or maybe it was the other way around.

Could it be that the uncomfortable feeling he had was actually a *comfortable* one, which was so unreal to him that it seemed foreign?

Of one thing he was certain: He admired Helen. Not for any sexual attraction he might have for her but for what she was able to accomplish.

She had combated Death and won.

TWENTY-ONE

Jade frowned as she took off her headset and checked the time. She muttered an epithet and quickly left her workstation. She moved across the Agency command center toward Travis, where he stood looking over the shoulder of the Middle East analyst.

". . . and the handler is in place in Tel Aviv?"

"Yes, sir. We should be good to go," the analyst answered.

"Excellent. Good work."

Jade stepped up. "Sir."

"What is it?"

She jerked her head slightly, indicating that he should follow her. "Client 432 will call in two minutes. I just received the transmission to alert us."

"He doesn't give us much notice, does he? All right, let's go to my office."

Travis led the way out of the central hub, down a corridor, and into the cabin that served as both his quarters and workspace, separated by a bulkhead. He sat at his desk and turned the computer monitor so they both could see it. Jade sat in one of the chairs in front of the desk, her notepad and laptop ready. Travis typed on his keypad, and the communications screen appeared. He then handed Jade a headset and they waited.

At exactly the appointed time, the call came through.

The monitor displayed the caller's voice as visual sound waves, which were recorded and analyzed in an attempt to decipher not only the client's identity but his location and means of transmission.

Travis spoke. "This is the Agency, Manager Three."

"Good afternoon." The voice was electronically garbled as usual.

"Are you ready to proceed with phase two of your operation, sir?"

"Not yet. All the pieces are not quite in place. But I can assure you that it's going to happen. It's only a question of timing."

Travis grimaced at Jade. "Well, sir, our operative *is* in place and awaiting the order. You realize that for every day that goes by, it is costing you?"

"Of course. I have already wired a second down payment—a retainer, so to speak—to the numbered bank account I was provided."

Travis nodded at Jade. She immediately set to work typing on her laptop. "Then what can we do for you today, sir?"

"I need to know the identity and description of your assassin."

Jade wrinkled her brow as she and Travis shared a look.

"And why do you need to know that?" Travis asked.

"I have my reasons."

Jade studied her laptop screen and whispered, "I can verify a payment of two million was received this morning."

Travis nodded and then spoke. "I'm sorry, I can't give you that information. I'm sure you understand. I can't reveal any details that might compromise our operative. But I assure you the hit will be accomplished with professionalism and secrecy."

"Is he one of your best?"

Travis hesitated. "What makes you think the operative is a 'he'?"

"Come now. I'm losing patience. I have paid the Agency a lot of money already. I have powerful friends in high places. And I know more about the International Contract Agency than you can imagine. In fact, I know that you are at this moment sitting aboard a yacht in the Mediterranean."

Travis blinked. How was that possible? Again he looked at Jade, this time with concern. "Sir, I'm not sure I understand why you need to know who the operative is. Wouldn't that endanger his security and anonymity? It could jeopardize the operation."

"I'm the goddamned client. I'm orchestrating the goddamned hit. I can control the goddamned flow of information. Do you think I'm stupid?"

"No, sir."

"Then tell me what I need to know. I would hate to expose the Agency to law-enforcement authorities."

Travis sighed. He would have to report this to upper management. There was a security breach somewhere. It was also obvious that this client was turning into what could be a formidable enemy. Still, a contract was a contract.

"Very well," he said. "The assassin assigned to your operation is the legendary Agent 47. If you indeed travel in the circles you claim, then I'm sure you've heard of him."

There was a pause. "Yes. I have heard of Agent 47. I thought he was dead."

"You are mistaken. Agent 47 is very much alive. So perhaps the name alone will give you everything you need to get a description of his appearance from other sources."

"Yes. I can do that. And he is at the Church of Will compound in Virginia now? The hit must appear—"

"As an inside job, we know that. I told you, he is in place and ready to act on your orders."

"Thank you."

"Is that all, sir?"

"For now. I'll be in touch."

The communications link was abruptly broken. Travis slammed a fist on the desk. "Damn it! Who the hell is this son of a bitch? How in blazes does he have the ability to find out where we are?"

Jade shrugged. "I honestly don't know, sir, but I will put someone on it right away."

He pointed a finger at her. "Pull out all the stops. We have to find out who this is and act now. I don't care if he's a top-paying client. He's a threat." He narrowed his eyes at his assistant. "This has got to be that nutcase Cromwell. He bumps off Dana Linder and then kills Wilkins and he's got all of America gunning for the government. He's got that nationwide militia and who knows what kind of technical expertise behind him. He manages to lead small armies across America, and the ineffective government can't find him. I'm going to make a call to upper management. And I want you to get a message to Agent 47. Tell him Cromwell is suspected of being the client and that he should be aware that the operation is starting to smell."

Jade stood. "I'll get right on it."

"For God's sake, can't our analysts do more with that voice capture? We've got some of the best engineers on the planet and they can't trace that call? Tell them heads will roll if they don't get cracking."

"Yes, sir."

She quickly left the cabin as Travis sat there and steamed.

Was Agent 47 in danger? Perhaps it was risky after all to place such a *singular* person undercover in a tightly knit religious community like Greenhill. While 47 was a man of complexity, it was a hard truth that the assassin wasn't "normal." For such a lengthy undercover job, it was essential that one appear to be ordinary.

And yet, so far, the hitman was doing fine. He had been at Greenhill for two weeks and made much progress infiltrating the Wilkins inner circle. For a moment Travis considered recalling the hitman and aborting the assignment. After all, the manager wanted 47 alive, willing, and able to do the next job the Agency had in store for him.

Especially since a very important piece of his pet project was missing from the laboratory in Chicago. The *most* important piece.

That was what was really pissing him off.

And it had to be Diana Burnwood who was responsible. She was the only one who'd known what the package was and how to get to it.

Travis had to get it back. If Jade's latest report was correct, then it was likely that Diana had hidden the package somewhere in the Midwest.

During the nerve-racking months since Diana's defection, Travis had covered up what had happened. Upper management didn't know about it. Travis had managed to convince them there was a scientific problem that was stalling his project's advancement. He counted on finding Diana soon and retrieving the specimen before anyone was the wiser.

If he didn't, his ass was on the line.

TWENTY-TWO

Agent 47 used the secure call-in number on his cellphone to check for messages from the Agency. Jade's message was interesting. If Cromwell was indeed the client, then it wouldn't make sense that he was connected to the Church of Will. There was still no concrete evidence of that, though.

He popped an oxycodone pill and met Helen in the cafeteria for breakfast as he always did before they both reported to their jobs for the day. She wore the same simple blouse and skirt to work but managed to look fresh and pretty on a daily basis. In contrast to her, he had on dirty, greasy blue jeans and a flannel shirt. They were indeed an odd couple.

"I spoke to Mitch about your situation," she said as they dug in to an all-American morning meal—eggs, bacon, hash browns, and pancakes. "I think he had a word with Stuart, so hopefully things will change for you soon."

"Really? You didn't have to do that."

"I know. But I could see you weren't being treated fairly. Stuart can be . . . difficult."

47 shrugged and took a sip of hot coffee. "I appreciate it."

"Listen," she said. "I'm leaving tonight with Charlie."

He looked up.

"He's coming back this afternoon and apparently we're flying in his jet a little later. It's for the campaign. He asked me to come along."

"Where are you going?"

"I don't know, he didn't say! But he told me to bring clothes for warm weather and that I need my passport."

The hitman found that odd. Why would Charlie Wilkins leave the country if he were doing campaign business? At that moment, 47 decided that wherever Wilkins and his team were headed, he must follow. But it would be problematic. Greenhill's airstrip was private. The only planes allowed in and out were Wilkins's Learjet 85, a business-class aircraft capable of transcontinental flights, and guest VIPs with their own vessels.

"Do you know when you'll be back?" he asked.

"It's only for a couple of days, I think. Two or three nights."

"When do you leave?"

"I'm supposed to be ready at the end of the workday. I don't know if I'll see you at dinner."

Stan Johnson placed a hand on her shoulder and said, "That's all right. I'll see you when you return."

She looked down at her plate. "I'll miss you."

"I'll miss you too."

When they finished their meals, 47 escorted Helen to the path leading up the hill, said an awkward goodbye, and then reported to the toolshed.

Chambers told him that he'd be working in the mansion gardens for the day. Apparently Helen's word to Carson had done the trick.

"Winter's coming, so you'll need to clean up any of the already dead and fallen flowers," Chambers outlined. "You'll have a couple of hours in the restricted area. The other two guys will be mowing the lawn and raking leaves. You are not to venture anywhere near the house, do you understand? There are hidden security cameras, and I guarantee they'll catch you if you try anything."

The man issued the instructions and warning as if 47 had a mental disability. The assassin said nothing. Inside, though, he was fuming, and he would have liked nothing better than to throttle the supervisor. Instead, the hitman merely nodded submissively and gathered his materials needed for the day.

The toolshed was located behind and south of the apartment buildings, near a warehouse where large pieces of equipment such as the riding mowers were kept. 47 had been pleased to find the shed well stocked. Aside from the usual assortment of hammers, screwdrivers, and wrenches, there was a table saw, jigsaw, metal cutter, and lathe. A healthy supply of lumber was stored in the barn. But when 47 first started his job, the shed was a mess. One of his earliest duties at Greenhill was to reorganize the space and create outlined placeholders on the walls for every tool. He painstakingly arranged an improved, categorized bin-and-container system for holding nails, screws, electrical switches, and other hardware. He cleaned out excess rubbish and faulty equipment. When he took the initiative to repair some broken-down machinery, even Chambers was impressed. Thus, every day since he'd begun his job, 47 spent a little time in the shed perfecting what was becoming known as "Stan's Place."

Now, finally, after two weeks, he was being allowed inside the electrified fence. With garden tools in hand, he marched south up the hill alongside his two mower-riding colleagues until they came to the gate. Chambers swiped his keycard, which produced a hard *click*, and then held the door open for the men to pass through. 47 noted that a couple of security guards stood in front of the guardhouse, watching them. They were armed and also carried batons on their belts.

The gardens spread from the west side of the mansion to the back, where Wilkins's office with the wall-sized window faced the lake. The first thing 47 did was perform a reconnaissance of the area. On the exterior mansion wall was an employee entrance and a paved path that led to the front of the building. There were a few windows. No security cameras that he could see. Perhaps the warning was bogus, just to intimidate workers. 47 was especially interested in the southern edge of the garden, where he could see and study the back of the mansion. There were plenty of manicured hedges on the garden perimeter that could serve as useful cover should he need it.

The hitman set to work, mostly cutting away dead foliage and clearing leaves that had blown in from the trees. 47 found it relaxing. It also reminded him of the time he had spent in Italy, gardening for a priest who became a friend for a short time. At one point, the hitman found a rabbit hole, which he probably should have plugged, but 47 chose to leave it alone. He recalled his early-childhood pet rabbit that he'd nurtured at the asylum. The only time 47 had ever cried as a boy was when the animal died.

"Johnson!"

47 looked up. Chambers stood at the northern edge of the gardens with the two security guards he'd seen earlier.

"Yeah?"

"Come here! Now!"

47's senses prickled. Something was up.

"Sure. Let me get my tools."

"Leave 'em! Just come here!"

The assassin stepped out of the garden and walked

alongside the mansion to where Chambers and the men waited.

"The Colonel wants to see you."

47 played dumb. "Who's he?"

"You haven't seen the Colonel? The military guy. Wears army clothes."

"Why does he want to see me?"

"He wants to talk to you. These men will escort you."

The assassin looked at the two beefy guards. One of them jerked his head toward the guardhouse.

"Is there a problem?" 47 asked.

"Let's go, bud," one of them said.

"Nothing to worry about, fella," the other added.

As they walked away, 47 looked back at Chambers. The man had a smirk on his face.

There was no reason to believe he was in trouble, but 47's instinct was to ready a weapon. Unfortunately, he had none on his person. If need be, he'd improvise.

The guardhouse was a small, nondescript one-story ranch. When the trio walked inside, 47 was confronted with another uniformed man, who sat behind a desk. A door marked AUTHORIZED PERSONNEL ONLY and a security camera were the only features on the wall behind him. A few chairs in the space constituted a waiting area.

One of the guards pointed to a chair and said, "Have a seat. The Colonel will be with you in a minute." He swiped a keycard and went through the door, leaving the other guard standing next to the desk, watching 47. The hitman shrugged and sat.

"You have any magazines?" 47 asked the guard behind the desk. The man shook his head but said nothing.

The place was awfully quiet. A clock ticked somewhere.

47 considered what he could use for a weapon. In his

hands, even a magazine could be a deadly instrument. So could his fists, for that matter.

Five minutes passed and the first guard returned. He held the door open and said, "Johnson. Come this way." 47 stood and obeyed. The second guard stepped in behind the hitman and followed him through. On the other side of the door was a small hallway with two doors on one side and a single one at the end. The guards marched 47 to the end and knocked.

"Come in," barked a voice.

The lead guard opened the door and let the assassin inside. The place looked more like a police interrogation room. Bare concrete walls and a single desk against the wall. Colonel Ashton sat behind it, a closed file folder and a notepad in front of him. The two guards stood in back of 47 after closing the door. There were no extra chairs.

Ashton squinted at him. "Stan Johnson?"

"Yes, sir?"

"Sorry to take you away from your duties. It's my job to have a chat with all new personnel, especially ones working in the restricted area. This is your first time in the restricted area?"

47 nodded. "Yes."

"Where exactly are you from, Johnson?"

"Iowa. Just outside Davenport."

"I understand you have—or had—a farm there?"

"Yes, sir."

"Please tell me its location."

47 told him and Ashton jotted it down. There was, in fact, a closed farm at the address, and anyone who was curious enough to look into its ownership history would discover Stan Johnson's name. Such was the efficiency of the Agency.

"May I see your identification?" Ashton asked.

The hitman patted his pockets. "I'm sorry. I don't

have it on me. It's in my room. I normally don't carry a wallet to work."

"You need to keep your ID on you at all times while you're at Greenhill, Johnson. Understand?"

"Yes, sir."

"Especially since you're not who you say you are."

A shot of adrenaline burst through 47's veins. "Sir?"

Ashton slowly stood and added, "I said, especially since you're not who you say you are, *Agent 47*."

Before the assassin could react, one of the guards clubbed him hard on the back of the head with his baton.

By the time 47 collapsed onto the floor, he had lost all consciousness.

TWENTY-THREE

The first thing I was aware of was that it was dark. Night.

The second thing was the rumbling, the vibration. I was in a moving vehicle, lying on a metal floor with my hands tied behind my back.

I peeked through slitted eyes. My head was splitting with pain. I was careful not to move, though. If I was being watched, I wanted my captors to think I was still unconscious.

It was a van. I was in the back of a van.

The back of my head felt like it'd been chopped into two pieces. Did I have a concussion? Even though I had genetic superiority over my captors, I wasn't infallible. I felt nauseated, but I fought the urge to vomit.

My hands were tied—with what? Not rope. Not cuffs. Something thin and plastic but strong. Zip ties. Heavy-duty zip ties. Killers often used them to restrain their victims. Cheap and easy to find at the local hardware store. Even Birdie carried them.

Two men in the van. A driver and a passenger. The two guards from Ashton's office. Where were they taking me? I must have been out for hours, since it was now night. How long had we been driving? How far away from Greenhill were we?

A flood of anxiety almost made me grunt aloud. But I held it in.

The pills. They caused this. I never would have fallen for such an obvious trap before . . . before last year.

Helen was right. I had to stop. They affected my brain after all. Made me slower. Made me dumber. I had to quit them. Throw them away. Go cold turkey.

But I'd worry about that later. I had to deal with the current situation first.

The van made a turn, and the feel of the road changed. The driver had exited a highway. I could see a little of the surroundings through the back window. Dark sky. Streetlights every now and then. We weren't in a city, though.

I thought about Helen. She was on her way somewhere in an airplane with Wilkins. What was going on at Greenhill? Was the client Cromwell, as the Agency now suspected? Who ratted me out? Did Wilkins know?

The van slowed. We moved past a tall freestanding sign. I recognized the logo: A man's white hair. The word CHARLIE'S beneath it. The message read: ANOTHER CHARLIE'S COMING SOON TO THIS LOCATION!

The passenger said something to the driver I couldn't understand. The driver responded, "Is he still out?" I closed my eyes. I heard the passenger reply, "Looks like it. You sure you didn't crack his skull?"

"What does it matter?" the driver said. "Dead is dead."

The vehicle pulled to a stop. Both men got out of the van, went around to the back doors, and opened them. I stayed motionless.

"Hey, Mac! Start her up!" one of them shouted.

Some twenty or thirty feet away, I heard the sound of a vehicle rev up. Some kind of big industrial thing, like a semi truck.

"Sleeping Beauty's still out."

"Come on, let's grab his legs."

I felt their hands grip my ankles and pull. With my hands tied behind my back, I couldn't do much but let them. I needed to assess the situation before I attempted anything.

They didn't bother to grab my shoulders to carry me. My upper body fell to the ground, which was covered with gravel. Then they started to drag me by the legs, faceup. It wasn't pleasant. The rocks and debris dug into my forearms and hands. I managed to peer out the slit of an open eye.

It was a construction site at a rest stop on an interstate highway. The foundation for the restaurant had already been laid, but nothing else had been built on top. It was only a big pit in the ground, maybe eight or ten feet deep, with utility pipes and stuff in it. The truck noise I heard was a concrete-mixer transport. The big drum was rotating. Its chute was aimed at the pit, ready to fill it with cement. A third guy was sitting in the driver's seat. A couple of floodlights were trained on the area so they could see what they were doing. From the road, I'm sure, nothing appeared suspicious. Just looked like workers doing night construction.

They dropped my legs when I was at the edge of the foundation. Then one guy kicked my shoulders hard and I rolled off into the pit. I landed like a ton of bricks on the concrete floor. It took tremendous effort not to make a sound, even though it hurt—really hurt.

"Frank, I think he is dead," I heard the driver say.

Frank called to the truck guy, "Okay, Mac, let her rip!"

The concrete mixer made a gurgling sound and started to sputter. Wet cement began to pour out of the drum, down the chute, and into the foundation.

* * *

*They were going to bury me in concrete underneath
a Charlie's restaurant.*

*So how was I going to play it? If I got up now, which
I could do, it would still take some time to get out of
the restraints and climb up to ground level. By then the
guards could simply shoot me. They still had their side-
arms on their belts. Then there was the third guy, Mac.
I didn't know if he was armed too.*

*The best course of action was surprise. I just hoped
my improvised plan would work.*

*The concrete dumped out fast. Already I felt the stuff
inching up around my body. In seconds I'd be covered
with the thick muck. I waited . . . waited . . . until exactly the right moment . . . when the cement was about
to cover my face . . . and I took a deep, deep breath.*

*A minute later, I was completely covered. The wet
concrete was heavy. They'd keep filling the foundation
until the cement was level with the ground. How much
time would it take? Could I hold my breath that long?*

Concentrate . . .

*I allowed my mind to drift back. Back through the
decades . . .*

*I was eight years old. At the asylum. Training. Learn-
ing how to be a killer.*

*Dr. Ort-Meyer supervised my athletic exercises. He
pushed me to extremes that no ordinary child of that
age could endure. Sometimes he took me to a tall cliff
and made me climb it. Other instances involved crawl-
ing through an artificial jungle environment complete
with bugs and snakes. This time, it was winter and I
was forced to drop into a hole in the ice that covered a
pond on the asylum grounds. My task was to jump in
at one end, swim under the ice to the other end, retrieve a baton that had been placed there before the surface froze, and then swim back and climb out of the*

hole. Holding my breath the entire time. The exercise would have taken an Olympic athlete four minutes, maybe more. A very small percentage of the human race could hold its breath for that amount of time.

I was only eight years old, and I was no Olympian.

I wore only swim trunks. It was probably around ten below zero Celsius outside. My skin was turning blue and I wasn't even in the water yet.

Ort-Meyer held a stopwatch. "Take a deep breath," he ordered. I did what I was told. "Ready . . . set . . . GO!"

I jumped into the frigid water. It felt as if dozens of needles assaulted my skin. I wanted to shout from the shock of the cold. But I didn't. I kept my mouth closed. I kept the precious breath inside me. And I started to swim. Under the ice. Opening my eyes, I could see the whitish crusty ceiling above my head. What was the length of the pond? Maybe forty yards? Not too bad. Not even half the size of an American football field.

But I had never done it before. I was frightened. My lungs already hurt, probably more from the punishment my heart was taking by subjecting my body to such dangerous temperatures than from any lack of air.

Still, I swam. I swam as if my life depended on it, which it did. If I failed the task, it was unlikely that Ort-Meyer would make any attempt to save me. He would chalk it up to another experiment that didn't quite measure up. He'd go back to the drawing board and try a different cloning recipe.

Before I knew it, I had reached the other side. The baton stuck out of a holder embedded in the rock, just under the ice surface. I grabbed it and kicked off the side of the pond, back toward the hole and to safety.

I lost myself in the memory of the event. It helped me hold my breath as the cement continued to pour on top of me. Concrete, ice—what was the difference?

There was a moment before I reached the hole when I panicked. I remembered it clearly. I didn't particularly want to relive that part of the exercise, because it was very unpleasant at the time. I thought I had veered off course and couldn't see the hole on the other side. There I was, back in my eight-year-old body, as I frantically searched for the proper route. I wanted to skip that part of the film in my head, edit it right out, and jump to the part where I finally found the hole and climbed out to gulp some precious air. But my reminiscence wouldn't censor that scene. I found myself trapped under the ice, terrified that I was about to drown. And I suddenly felt the familiar anxiety that had been plaguing me since Nepal.

As my younger self struggled in that dark, glacial netherworld, I beat on the ice above me, hoping I could break it.

That was impossible.

And then I saw him. Swimming toward me.

This wasn't how it happened! He wasn't there then! My memory was lying to me!

The shadow man. The faceless figure. Death. Swimming right at me. Reaching out. Ready to take me.

I tried to swim away, but my hands were tied behind my back and I was no longer in water. I was submerged in thick, wet cement, and it was more difficult to maneuver in that substance than in quicksand.

The dark black arms embraced me. They were strong and viselike. I struggled against him, but I couldn't move. I desperately wanted to see his face, though, so I turned my head to look.

Nothing there. Just a blank spot where eyes, nose, and a mouth should be.

Death had me.

No!

I was aware that I was no longer lying on my side on

the foundation floor. I was squatting. I didn't recall moving into that position, but I had done it. Summoning every ounce of strength in my legs, I pushed off and upward. Death's arms released me. I was free! But it was like swimming through molasses. The surface was close, yet so very far away. With my wrists bound, it was a near hopeless dream.

But I kicked my feet like a machine and slowly ascended, inches at a time.

I sensed I was nearing the top.

Harder! I had to kick harder!

And then . . . at last . . . my head broke the surface and I gasped the lovely, valuable oxygen. A surge of power coursed through my veins as I filled my lungs with the warmth of . . .

Life.

I climbed out of the pool of wet concrete and stood at the edge. I was covered in the stuff. I must have looked like a monster. I was a walking gray thing.

First—I had to get out of the restraints. As I'd told Birdie back in Chicago, they're breakable if you know how. They had a weakness, no matter if you were tied in front or back. In this case, since my hands were behind me, I simply had to bend forward at the waist so that my tailbone jutted out a bit. Then, I made sure the little cubelike "lock" on the tie was positioned in the center, between my wrists, on the inside of my arms. I had to rub my tied hands against the back of my belt a few times in order to slide the lock around to the appropriate spot. Then, even though it was somewhat awkward, I raised my arms behind me as far as they would go—and I slammed them down against my tailbone. The square lock was breakable if the right amount of force was applied in just the right place.

I was successful. My hands were free.

I then wiped the mucky concrete off my eyes so I could see, but otherwise the stuff was caked on.

The van and cement truck were still there. The men were not in sight, but I heard them laughing on the other side of the truck. Probably having a smoke or a drink and celebrating. I trudged over to an area where stacks of lumber and bricks were covered by plastic tarps. I found a two-by-four the length of a baseball bat.

That would do.

I couldn't move very quickly because of the goop all over me. It was already starting to settle and dry. Nevertheless, I plodded over to the truck and listened.

"Pass me that bottle."

"Who was this guy we buried, anyway?"

"I don't know. Ashton just told us to do the job and not to tell anyone, especially not Reverend Wilkins."

"What time did the Colonel leave?"

"Seven, I think. Won't be back for a couple of days."

"So we don't have to be back till morning?"

"Let's get out of here. I know a good titty bar in Alexandria."

They were getting out of there, all right. Permanently.

I stepped out in front of them. I must have been an awful sight. One man screamed, and another yelled the F-word. I raised the two-by-four and brought it down hard on the guy called Frank, who had the sense and reflexes to go for his gun.

The sound of his skull cracking was very, very loud.

The guy they called Mac tried to bolt. I stuck my leg out and tripped him. By then I was already swinging the two-by-four at the third man. He tried to duck, but he wasn't quick enough. The wooden club glanced off the top of his head but didn't do much damage. Mac started to crawl away, but I slammed my boot on top of his back, pinning him down. At the same time, the face of the guy who'd ducked was even with my elbow, so I jabbed it into his nose. He yelped and fell back against the cement truck, giving me ample time to level the two-by-four and swing it at him as if his head were a curveball.

Finally, I directed my full attention to Mac, the truck driver. He didn't seem to be a guard; he had no weapon. Just a worker assigned the wrong duty at the wrong place and at the wrong time.

That wasn't an excuse.

I raised the club as if I were chopping wood. Brought it down. He stopped squirming soon enough.

With that task completed, I scanned the construction site for something else I needed and saw it near the piles of lumber. I clumped over to the hose, turned on the water, and set about washing away the concrete that covered my body and clothes. It took nearly ten minutes; in the end I was sopping wet but completely clean.

All the while, cars zoomed by on the expressway. There wasn't much for them to see. The bodies were behind the truck and I probably looked like an ordinary construction worker. I figured I must be near Alexandria, since Tomato-Face had mentioned it.

I went back to the three dead men. One of them was the van driver, but I couldn't remember which one, so I searched their pockets until I came up with the keys, and also took some money from a wallet. Then, one at a time, I picked them up in my arms and carried them over to the rapidly drying pool of concrete. I dropped them in. Plop, plop, plop. They sank to the bottom.

The side of the van bore the legend GREENHILL SECURITY. *I'd have to take it where I wanted to go and then abandon the vehicle as soon as possible. I was still puzzled by the turn of events. How did Colonel Ashton know who I was? From what the guard said, it sounded like Wilkins wasn't involved and didn't know. Could I be sure? Was Helen aware of it?*

I knew one thing, though. Well, two.

First—I had to find out where Wilkins, Helen, Ashton, and his party flew. I had a score to settle with the Colonel.

And second—I wasn't going to take any more oxycodone.

I needed to be at my best.

TWENTY-FOUR

Once he hit the road, Agent 47 found that he was in Pennsylvania, all the way up near Harrisburg. He wanted to get back to the compound as quickly as possible, but it was a long drive and he didn't want to speed and risk being stopped by law enforcement. The two guards would not be missed until the following day. 47 wasn't worried. He just didn't feel well. His head still hurt, and he had the shakes. The withdrawal from the painkillers was already kicking in, with gusto. 47 stopped at a roadside Quik Mart to pick up a bottle of Advil, which did little to alleviate the throbbing hell in the back of his skull. He was more concerned about his reflexes, judgment, and effectiveness as he fought the withdrawal symptoms. He knew that some people went mad for a few days when kicking powerful addictive drugs. With his genetic advantage, would his experience be as bad? Worse?

He drove to Frederick, Maryland, got on I-270, and headed for the Washington, D.C., metro area. It would be the fastest route, especially at that time of night. Eventually, he merged onto I-95 and shot south toward Greenhill. At two in the morning he arrived in Stafford, the same small town where 47 had poisoned the old maintenance man. 47 thought it best to wait until daylight before attempting to get inside the compound. A

visitor in the middle of the night would attract too much
attention. There were no guards at the entrance—
Greenhill was open to the public and was something of
a tourist destination—but to visit his apartment was
another matter. From what he'd heard at the restaurant
site, it sounded as if only Ashton and the two guards
knew about him. But he couldn't be too careful. Whatever the case, 47 wanted his briefcase and clothes and
was willing to risk being caught in order to retrieve
them.

The assassin checked in to a roadside motel, hung up
his still-damp clothes, and took a long hot shower. 47
thought that if there was a paradise, then that was it.
After drying off, he crawled into bed. He knew that
sleeping with a concussion—which he feared he might
have—was dangerous. Nevertheless, he was dead tired
and didn't care. He turned out the light and was asleep
within minutes.

The dreams and nightmares were vivid and disturbing. At various times Agent 47 thought he was being
chased by various entities. Death, as usual, Colonel
Ashton, and, oddly, Diana Burnwood. He relived the
incident in Nepal, this time with Helen bizarrely by his
side. When the Chinese bodyguard started to shoot at
him, Helen was hit. Instead of bloody bullet holes punc-
turing her body, crimson-red roses sprouted there in the
manner of time-lapse photography. Before he could
reach out to her, 47 found himself running through the
Church of Will compound. He kept colliding with
Charlie Wilkins, who smiled and raised his eyebrow at
him. The man held out his hand, palm upward, as if to
offer solace to a poor sinner. 47 was inexplicably repelled by Wilkins, so he turned and ran in another
direction—until he bumped into the reverend again.
This sequence looped several times, as if 47 were in a
maze without an exit. Finally, though, he discovered a

clear pathway between the apartment buildings. But when he got to the end, the faceless figure of Death was waiting for him.

47 awoke in a sweat. The shakes were worse than ever. He felt nauseated and disoriented.

And yet it was morning, 7:15 A.M., and he had a job to do. It was exactly when he'd hoped to awaken. At least his internal clock still functioned.

The clothes were more or less dry, so he put them on, checked out of the hotel, and got back in the van. It had been untouched. 47 found it ironic that Stafford was awfully close to Quantico, the headquarters of the FBI. Had anyone in that organization known that the legendary Agent 47 from the International Contract Agency was within miles of their buildings, there would have been a scramble to see who could catch the hitman first.

47 left Stafford and boldly drove the van along the two-lane blacktop that ended at Greenhill. As he approached the site, he noticed a turnoff onto a dirt road just wide enough for the vehicle to traverse. Surprisingly, it was a back entrance to Greenhill's private airstrip. Wilkins and his team normally got there by using a paved road that connected the compound with the area, which was comprised of a hangar, small control tower, and runway. Apparently the dirt road was a not-often-used rear entrance that snaked west through a dense forest until it emptied onto the main road. 47 parked the van there, hidden among the trees, and walked back. It wasn't far to the compound.

It was a normal, active morning at Greenhill, with Church members bustling about and starting their day. Agent 47 calmly walked through Main Street, said hello to a few familiar faces, and headed for his apartment building. All the while he kept a lookout for security guards. The first one he came upon was patrolling the front of the three housing units.

Now was as good a time as any to test the waters.

The hitman nonchalantly strolled toward his building, nodded at the guard, and entered. The man did nothing. 47 stalled for a moment inside the building foyer and watched the guard. The man didn't reach for his walkie-talkie to report a sighting. He didn't draw his gun. He simply continued the slow pacing along the three buildings.

Good.

Agent 47 went to his room on the first floor, unlocked it with the key that had amazingly remained in his pocket during his ordeal in the concrete pool, and entered.

The place had been ransacked.

His clothes were thrown about, all the drawers in the dressers were open, and the closet was emptied.

That figured.

He changed into a clean set of work clothes, gathered the rest of his clothing, folded it as neatly as possible, and packed it in the backpack. The black suit was crumpled, but he could eventually get it pressed. After claiming his belongings, 47 left the room and returned outside. The guard was down at the third housing unit, so the hitman acted as if it was business as usual and headed for the toolshed—Stan's Place. He used a key entrusted to him to get inside and locked the door behind him.

Nothing appeared disturbed. All the tools were in the proper places.

47 took a Phillips-head screwdriver, stooped beside the lathe, and unscrewed a side panel on the base. The briefcase sat among the wires, next to the motor, right where the hitman had stashed it.

He replaced the panel and looked out the dirty win-

dow. The coast was clear. 47 moved to the door, reached
to open it, and froze.

Voices outside. Coming nearer.

"Stuart, I'm glad I ran into you. Can you do me a
favor?"

47 recognized the speaker. It was Mitch Carson.

"Sure, what's up?" Stuart Chambers. 47's new nemesis.

"Charlie called, and there's a change in his flight plan.
Can you run this envelope over to the airstrip and give
it to Louis? He should be there in the tower. I have to be
at a meeting in five minutes. You're not too busy, are
you?"

"No, I can do it."

"Thanks. Oh, and tell him to come see me. I need to
go over some things with him about the upcoming campaign trip."

47 couldn't believe his luck. He could kill two birds
with one stone, so to speak.

He waited a few moments, looked out the window
again, and saw Carson walking toward the hill. As for
Chambers, he climbed aboard one of the golf carts the
staff used to get around Greenhill. The man took off
and headed for the paved road to the airstrip.

47 stepped out of the shed, locked it, and jumped into
one of the extra carts. The key was in it. The hitman
didn't follow Chambers, though. He took the long way
out, through Main Street and out the front gate to the
main road. No one paid any attention to him.

He reached the dirt turnoff within minutes. 47 passed
the van and kept going until he drove out of the woods
and onto the tarmac surrounding the control tower.
The hangar that usually contained Wilkins's plane was
fifty yards away. The runway lay perpendicular to the
buildings, running north and south.

Chambers's cart was parked next to a Ford pickup,

the only other vehicle in front of the tower. 47 stopped his buggy around the back, got out of the cart, and crept silently toward the building. He heard voices and peered around the corner.

A man 47 recognized but didn't know stood smoking a cigarette and talking to Chambers. Louis. Probably the air-traffic controller and manager of the tower and hangar.

". . . see you too. Mitch asked if you'd come up to the house when you have a chance," Chambers said.

"Sure, I could go now. Go on in. You can put the plan update there and I'll take a look when I get back." Louis dropped the cigarette, stepped on it, and looked at his watch. "See you later."

Louis hurried to his truck and drove off toward the compound. Chambers went inside the control tower, carrying the envelope.

47 opened the briefcase and removed one handgun. He then stepped around to the front door and listened.

Footsteps climbing a set of stairs.

The hitman quietly went inside and waited until Chambers was all the way up the three flights. He then calmly and silently followed his prey.

The assassin peeked into the control room. A lone flight-control workstation faced a window looking out at the runway. Chambers was there with his back to him, searching through papers.

When Chambers spun around, a Silverballer was pointed directly at his face.

"What the fuck!?" Chambers blurted.

"Quiet," 47 said.

"What the hell are you doing, Johnson?"

"I said quiet. And raise your hands."

Chambers did as he was told, his eyes wide with fear.

"Where is Wilkins?"

Chambers couldn't speak.

"*Where is Wilkins?*"

The supervisor shook his head. "I . . . I don't know. They flew somewhere yesterday."

47 nodded at the envelope on the station. "Open that and read it to me."

Chambers did so. "Uh, it's, uh, a flight plan. Looks like they were going to come back tomorrow, but they're not coming back until the next day."

"From where?"

"Uh, Larnaca? I don't know where that is."

Agent 47 did. Larnaca was the main airport in southern Cyprus. In the Mediterranean. A long way from the United States.

That was a very strange campaign stop for a presidential candidate.

"Why would Wilkins fly to Cyprus?"

Chambers shrugged, his hands still raised. "*I* don't know! That kind of stuff is above my pay grade. Johnson, what are you—"

"Shut up and answer my questions. What do you know about yesterday? When those guards came to get me?"

Chambers swallowed. "Nothing! I mean it. They just came to me and said the Colonel wanted to talk to you."

"You're lying."

"No! No, I'm not!"

"You found it funny. You were glad to see me summoned to the guardhouse."

"Look, Stan, I don't have any idea why he wanted to talk to you. I figured you were in some kind of trouble."

"And you were glad about that. You don't like me, do you, Stuart?"

Chambers blinked and swallowed again. "It's not that. It's—"

"Never mind. I know why." 47 knew there was nothing else worthwhile he could get from Chambers. "Come with me."

"Are you . . . are you going . . . are you going to shoot me?"

"No. But come with me. Keep your hands up." Chambers walked toward 47. The assassin moved aside, the gun still trained on the man. "Out." He stepped in behind Chambers, the Silverballer nudging his back. "To the stairs. Walk."

"You're not going to shoot me?"

"I said no."

They moved the twenty feet to the top of the staircase. "Stop," 47 ordered. He stuck the Silverballer into the pocket of his overalls. Then he reached out with both hands and grabbed Chambers's head from behind.

A sharp jerk to the right—and *snap!*

Followed by a shove.

The man with the broken neck tumbled down the stairs and hit the landing, bounced, and then lay still, facedown.

The hitman had told the truth. He didn't shoot the guy.

Agent 47 coolly descended the three flights and went outside. He grabbed his briefcase from the cart and walked back to the van.

As he drove away, he figured they probably wouldn't miss the van for a few more hours.

TWENTY-FIVE

After removing a few items that he kept in the secret compartment of his briefcase, Agent 47 locked it and the weapons in a public storage facility in the Baltimore/ Washington Airport and boarded a flight to Paris.

The trip to Cyprus was pure hell.

Even in first class, he was uncomfortable. The withdrawal symptoms had increased tenfold. The flight attendant took one look at him and asked if he was all right. It was a small miracle they allowed him to board.

"Just getting over the flu," he explained. "Don't worry, I'm not contagious."

Still, his skin was pale and he sweated profusely. The passenger in the next seat requested to move. At one point the hitman thought he was going to be sick and spent ten minutes in the lavatory. He attempted to sleep during the voyage and did so fitfully. Dreams and nightmares plagued him with images from his childhood at the asylum. Much of the anger he felt back then manifested itself in ghostly apparitions of enemies from his past, all of whom had returned to kill him. Diana Burnwood appeared, this time in the person of a game-show host. She asked 47 if he wanted door number one, two, or three. There were no doors to be seen, but the assassin answered, "Three." A hatch materialized in the space beside her. Suddenly Diana was a flight attendant, he was inside an airplane, and she pulled the emergency lever. The hatch disengaged from the aircraft and shot away. 47 looked out to see the Caribbean below. The wind and rain pelted him.

"This is your stop, sir," Diana said.

"I'm not getting out here."

"Yes, you are." With that, she pushed him out of the plane.

47 plummeted toward the sea but then abruptly slowed, as if he had just opened a parachute. He looked up and, sure enough, a canopy was attached to a pack on his back. As with all dreams, he accepted the turn of events and went with the flow without question. At least he wasn't going to die in the water.

But then the sea was gone. A landscape of fire had taken its place. 47 felt the intense heat, even from such a high altitude. It was as if he were descending toward a blazing sun. He knew he shouldn't look directly into it—the rays would burn through his retinas—and yet he couldn't tear his eyes away. Something was moving on the sun's surface; the flames and molten lava were forming a shape.

A face.

No, a *blank* face. No eyes, no nose, no mouth.

Death.

47 was falling into the jaws of Death.

"Sir, wake up, sir!"

Gentle nudging startled him, and he was back on the flight to Paris. The flight attendant stood over him.

"What?"

"You were . . . you were having a bad dream, I think. You kept shouting. I'm sorry to wake you, but you were . . . well, it looked like you *needed* to be woken up."

He nodded. "I'm sorry. Thank you. You're right. My apologies."

She handed him a cup of water. "We're about to land. Here, drink this."

"Thank you."

47 felt so weak he could barely walk off the plane.
There was a three-hour layover. The flight to Cyprus
would get him into Larnaca roughly a day after Wilkins
and his party had arrived. He used the time at Orly to
freshen up. He washed the sweat off his body and
changed shirts in the men's room. After getting a bite to
eat, he called the Agency's secure number with his cellphone. Following the usual coded verifications, he was
routed to none other than Jade.

"Where are you, 47?" she asked.

"Paris. I'm about to board a flight to Cyprus."

"Cyprus? Whatever for?"

"That's where Wilkins is. You were right, Jade. Something about this job stinks." He told her what had happened to him at Greenhill.

"Is your cover blown?"

"I'm not sure. I don't think so. I think only Ashton
and a couple of guards know who I am. We won't be
hearing from the guards. Ashton's in Cyprus with
Wilkins. I don't know what he's told the reverend, if
anything, but I intend to find out. Listen, can you find
out where Wilkins is and why he's halfway across the
world when he should be campaigning in American cit-
ies?"

She told him to call her back when he was on the island.

"Oh, and one other thing. Can you find the police
report on the accidental death of Eric Shipley? It happened in Maryland in the 1970s. Shipley was Dana
Linder's father."

"Why do you want that?"

"I have my reasons." His last question to her was, "Is
there any word about Diana?"

"We're pursuing a lead in the States. It looks promising."

"Good to know."

He hung up, took three ibuprofen tablets for the massive headache that had never left him, and waited to board the flight to Cyprus.

Cyprus had been a divided country since 1974. The southern two-thirds of the island was occupied by Greek Cypriots. This section of the country, the Republic of Cyprus, was recognized by the United Nations and the rest of the world as a sovereign nation. The other third, in the north, was known as the Turkish Republic of Northern Cyprus and, according to most everyone except the Turks, was there illegally. Turkey had invaded the island nearly four decades earlier and started a bloody conflict that ultimately ended in a tentative, uneasy peace. The Greek-side capital, Nicosia, was divided by a no-man's-land that still contained remnants of that 1974 dispute: overturned cars, burned-out and empty storefronts, and rubble. On the other side of the barrier was the Turkish half of the capital, Lefkosia.

Wilkins and his party were in the Hilton Cyprus, Nicosia's only five-star hotel. 47 was happy to learn that they were in the Greek portion. There was less red tape to maneuver through, and it was more tourist-friendly.

He checked into the hotel wearing a cloth poncho over blue jeans and a flannel shirt, sunglasses, and a bandanna on his bald head. He might have been a gypsy traveler from any part of the globe, albeit a wealthy one. Among the supplies he had taken from his briefcase was a set of makeup tools. He had brought along eyeliners, pencils, skin-coloring pancake base, and even crepe hair and spirit gum. These were handy for creating a quick disguise, and they were undetectable going through airport security. The masquerades he developed in this fashion were akin to what actors might do for stage appearances. They were sufficient for brief appearances but wouldn't hold up under close scrutiny. Therefore he had to be careful not to be seen except in transitory instances.

47 was careful to scope out the lobby before entering, just in case Ashton—or Helen—was there. He was confident, though, that no one would recognize him in this guise.

Before venturing out, he contacted the Agency. Jade told him that several "VIPs" from Europe and the Middle East were also registered at the hotel. They included members of OPEC, banking executives, and independent financiers. It was unclear if they were connected to Wilkins's visit. She also said that the Agency's top analysts were working on tracing the client's calls to pinpoint where they were coming from. It was difficult and time-consuming, because both parties used sophisticated encryption. Last, Jade provided a copy of the police report from the hunting accident involving Eric Shipley. Apparently he and some friends had been hunting in the Maryland woods in 1976. Shipley's shotgun went off when he was cleaning it. His face was in the way. Several hunters had witnessed the event and supplied testimony at the inquest. The case was closed. The ruling: accidental death.

Interesting.

"Who were the witnesses?"

"According to the court record, three men: two Church of Will adherents and a friend of Charlie Wilkins. Malcolm James Woodworth, Thomas Strome, and Bruce Ashton."

Ashton. Very *interesting.*

"Do any photographs exist of Wilkins prior to 1976?" he asked.

He heard her sigh with slight irritation. "Would you like me to look?"

"Please." He hung up, ignoring her request to explain.

47 spent the afternoon in the hotel lobby, drinking coffee, reading newspapers, and keeping his eyes and ears open. Finally, Wilkins and his entourage walked through. Helen was with them, looking harried and busy with a notepad in hand, as if she was taking down every word the reverend uttered. Colonel Ashton marched alongside Wilkins and exuded such menace that anyone would think twice before approaching the famous Church of Will leader. Two other bodyguards walked behind the trio. 47 didn't recognize them. There were certainly people in the hotel that identified Wilkins and wanted to meet him. The reverend graciously obliged, shook hands, and signed autographs, all the while displaying his trademark smile and raised eyebrow. Ashton kept close by and vetted every person who came near.

During this ritual, 47 stood and walked across the lobby, intentionally passing next to Helen. She did glance at him but then went back to her notepad as she scribbled something. She paid him no mind.

Good.

47 loitered as Wilkins finished with his fans. The reverend turned to Helen and said, "My dear, I won't need you at the meeting tomorrow. Feel free to take the day off. Go to the pool. Go shopping. I understand the old town in Nicosia has many nice stores."

She seemed surprised. "Really? You don't want me there?"

"No, it's not necessary. Just be available for dinner tomorrow evening."

"Thank you, sir—er, Charlie."

One of the bodyguards said, "Sir, the car is here."

"Fine," Wilkins said. "We can't keep the ambassador waiting."

The entire party left the hotel and got into a limousine.

47 watched from the front doors, considered following them, and decided to check out the bar instead. They'd be back. It was what they were doing at the hotel that interested him.

The Paddock Bar wasn't open until five o'clock, so 47 went to the Lobby Lounge. Many guests were having afternoon tea. The assassin thought that sounded good; a hot drink would help ease the nasty withdrawal symptoms. He sat in a comfortable armchair overlooking the long room, ordered the drink, and eyed the crowd. His attention settled on three men sitting at a nearby table. They spoke Russian and were dressed a little too smartly for the teatime clientele. 47 was almost positive they were gangsters. He wasn't exactly fluent in their language, but he knew enough to catch the gist of the conversation. One man complained that they shouldn't have to be in a long meeting the following day. A second man asked if they knew where it was being held. The third guy answered that it was obviously in the hotel's business center, probably in a conference room the reverend had reserved. The first man commented that the "food better be good." The second Russian joked, "It'll probably be Charlie's chicken!" That evoked laughter.

Interesting.

47 decided he needed to learn more about that meeting. He finished his tea and spent the rest of the day exploring the hotel, until he had a complete map of the place in his head. Where the business center was located. Where employees congregated during breaks. The laundry room. The gym, pool, and sauna. The positions of stairwells and elevators. Where security cameras were positioned. He knew where it was safe to hide and what spots to avoid.

He was ready.

Now if only he could be rid of the shakes, headache, and anxiety, everything would be perfect.

TWENTY-SIX

Shortly before the dinner hour, Agent 47 made his way to the employees-only area on the ground floor of the hotel. As he lurked in a corner, he watched bellhops, waiters, and maids swipe keycards to get inside. He figured that beyond the door he would find a break room, personnel offices, and, most important, computers with hotel information. He considered the possibility of accessing the facility from the exterior, through an employees' entrance next to the loading dock. This was a riskier proposition in broad daylight. Eventually, though, a bellhop emerged from the office. He was dressed in the hotel uniform—brown-and-yellow tunic, dark-brown trousers, a cap, and a name tag—and he was roughly the hitman's height and weight.

47 followed him to the busy lobby, where the man immediately went to work by greeting incoming guests and loading their luggage on a cart. Once again, the assassin picked up a newspaper and sat in a chair near reception so that he could keep an eye on the fellow. After a while, a couple came in, looking harried and in a rush. 47 watched them check in and overheard the bellhop tell them that he'd be right up with their things; however, the guests replied that they were late for a dinner engagement and had just stopped to register and drop off their luggage. The bellhop politely said, "That's

fine; your things will be in the room when you return."
The couple tipped him in advance and left. 47 loitered a
little longer as the employee picked up a keycard and
then finally rolled the luggage cart toward the elevators.
One set of doors opened, revealing an empty car. The
man pushed the cart inside and pressed the button of
the floor he wanted. As the doors started to close, 47
thrust his arm between them.

"Hold it, please!"

The bellhop punched the OPEN DOORS button. 47
slipped inside.

"Thank you."

"You're welcome, sir. What floor?"

47 nodded at the bank of buttons, where only one
number was lit. "Looks like you're getting off where I
am."

They rode silently. The hitman was careful to turn his
body away from the bellhop to diminish the man's ability to identify him later. When the car stopped, the employee said, "After you, sir." 47 stepped out and held
the doors open with his arm. "Thank you," the bellhop
said as he rolled the cart out.

The assassin allowed the man to clear the elevator
bay and start pushing the cart down the hall before setting out behind him. 47 followed the bellhop until the
man reached the destination room. The hitman glanced
around to verify that no one was looking, then moved
swiftly behind the bellhop, wrapped his arm across the
man's neck, and applied pressure. The choke hold efficiently rendered the bellhop unconscious without a
sound.

The employee sagged in 47's arms like a rag doll. The
hitman unceremoniously dropped him on the cart,
searched him for the keycard, unlocked the room, and
rolled the cart inside. By now the bellhop started to stir.
47 dumped him on the bed and set to work removing

the man's uniform. When the bellhop regained ample consciousness, the assassin simply applied the choke hold again.

In five minutes, 47 was dressed in the bellhop's clothing. The hitman then removed sheets from the bed and used them to tie up and gag the employee. 47 left him on the bed, took his own discarded clothes in hand, and exited. He made a quick stop on his own floor to drop off the clothing in his room, then headed back to the first floor.

The hitman used the bellhop's keycard to gain entrance to the employees-only area. The place was crowded with hotel staff, so 47 kept his head down and moved with purpose, without looking anyone in the eyes. Hopefully others would just think he was a new employee.

He found and stepped into an empty office and shut the door. It didn't have a lock, so he'd have to take his chances. 47 sat behind the desk and booted the computer. After a moment, the Hilton splash screen appeared and he was inside the hotel records.

47 worked quickly. The first thing he did was look up Wilkins's account. He noted the reverend's suite number and then studied the entire portfolio. Wilkins had reserved a conference room in the business center for the entire next day. Food for fourteen was being brought in. Wilkins planned to check out the following morning. Special comments indicated that Wilkins was a VIP and was afforded certain amenities others guests didn't receive. For example, a Nicosia private security firm was providing additional protection, although Bruce Ashton was listed as the celebrity's director of security.

The hitman then looked up Helen McAdams's account. He saw that her room was on the same floor as Wilkins's. No special notes other than she was listed as part of Wilkins's party. 47 then pulled up Bruce Ashton's account. As expected, his room was on the same floor. The assassin smiled when he saw that the Colonel had reserved a massage in the spa for nine o'clock that evening. He'd been assigned a masseuse named Katharina. 47 quickly punched her cellphone number into his mobile.

He checked the time—he'd been at the computer for ten minutes. 47 didn't want to risk staying much longer, but he thought he'd quickly scan the names of all the guests registered that night. There were several hundred, of course, so he concentrated on any that sounded Russian. He found a few and memorized the names and room numbers. They were also listed as VIPs and had rooms near one another. The assassin then shut down the computer and left the room.

He made it out of the employees' area without incident, took the elevator to his floor, and went to his own suite. There he took his cellphone and activated the encrypted Agency app to search the database for the Russian names. One of them, Boris Komarovsky, was suspected to be the treasurer for the St. Petersburg Mafia. Another one, Vladimir Podovkin, apparently controlled funds for a criminal organization in Moscow.

47 was astounded. The assignment was becoming more of a stink by the day. What was Wilkins up to? Why was he meeting with Russian criminals in Cyprus? Who were the other attendees? Jade had said the hotel had a few high-powered VIPs in attendance, including OPEC brokers and banking executives. Might they be involved with Wilkins too? What was going on?

The killer thought about the bellhop he had left hogtied and gagged. Eventually the couple would come back to the hotel, go to their room, and discover him. Police would be brought in. The chances of being discovered would increase tenfold, especially with all the high-profile guests. Nevertheless, the hitman banked on the fact that it was a very large hotel. 47 was confident that, as long as he was diligent and made his moves with extreme caution, he would accomplish what he'd set out to do without being caught.

At eight-thirty, 47, still dressed as a bellhop, went to the hotel spa and gym. Three private rooms were set aside for massages. Two were in use, so he went in to the empty one to check it out. There was a table, of course, covered in a sheet. A counter held different types of oils and lotions. Guests could hang clothing in a small closet. 47 studied the room for a moment and then stepped back into the gym. It wasn't particularly large, but it contained a separate sauna, exercise equipment, Nautilus machines, and even a small track around the perimeter for walking and running. Since Cyprus was primarily an outdoor destination, the swimming pool and a larger track were located outside. Nevertheless, a number of guests were utilizing the facilities. 47 knew from experience that most people didn't notice the majority of what went on around them, especially when they were involved in activities such as exercise or were concentrating on external stimuli such as iPods or the flat-screen televisions on the walls. The general population also tended to ignore menial laborers, such as waiters, janitors, maids—and bellhops.

Next to the spa was a towel room. Clean, folded white towels embroidered with the Hilton logo were stacked on shelves, and a large bin for used ones sat on the floor. 47 set to "work" separating towels, folding them, unfolding them, and basically doing nothing except trying to look busy. As expected, no one in the gym paid any attention to him.

The masseuse entered the gym at 8:50. Katharina

was an attractive brunette, probably in her forties, attired in scrubs similar to what a nurse might wear. She went into the empty massage room, turned on the light, and then came over to 47 in the towel dispensary.

"Hello," she said as she grabbed a handful.

47 grunted in response.

She left and went back to her station.

Five minutes later, Colonel Ashton appeared in the gym. He was dressed in a terry-cloth robe and slippers. He looked around, saw the massage rooms, and marched to the open door. 47 saw the masseuse shake his hand and gesture for him to lie down on the table. She then closed the door.

The hitman waited five minutes and then dialed Katharina's number on his mobile.

"Yes?"

"Is this Katharina?"

"Yes?"

"This is the concierge. You're wanted in room 433. You're late for an appointment." He deliberately gave her the room number of one of the Russians.

"What? I have an appointment. I'm with him now."

"There must be some mistake. This is a VIP's reservation. The massage is booked in his suite. He specifically asked for you. Please go to him now. I'll send another masseuse up to the gym immediately to take care of your client."

She sighed. "Very well. Room 433, you say?"

"Yes. Please hurry. He's already called twice."

"All right."

47 hung up and watched. After a moment, Katharina emerged from the massage room and closed the door behind her. Once she was out of the gym, the hitman made his move. He grabbed a handful of towels, strode across the floor with purpose, and opened the door. He shut it behind him after stepping inside.

Ashton was lying naked on the table, facedown. He started to rise and turn his head so that he could approve the beauty taking Katharina's place, but before he could register what was happening, 47 rammed the bundle of cloth into the man's face. The hitman then leaped onto the table and straddled Ashton's back, simultaneously pulling the towels on either side of the Colonel's head. The man's scream was sufficiently muffled.

But the assassin hadn't counted on Ashton's highly tuned reflexes and tremendous strength. He was a man in excellent physical shape, whereas 47 was suffering from oxycodone withdrawal and had spent the last year going a bit soft. Ashton managed to buck the hitman off him, knocking 47 to the floor. The naked man pulled the towels from around his face, threw them against the wall, and then climbed off the table.

47's cap had fallen off. He lay on his back, slightly dazed. Once again, the symptoms of sickness enveloped him, causing a momentary inertness.

"You!"

Ashton's surprise at seeing a man he thought to be dead worked to 47's advantage. The Colonel faltered too, for the man didn't realize how vulnerable he was as he stood over the assassin. The pause provided 47 the precious seconds he needed to recover from the stun and see things clearly. The plan of attack was obvious.

The hitman viciously kicked his leg up and slammed his shoe into Ashton's groin. The Colonel yelled, this time a little too loudly for 47's comfort. The killer jumped to his feet as his prey fell to his knees. Ashton's face turned red from the agony, and his hands reflexively covered his privates, leaving him completely unprotected. 47 made a fist and delivered a right hook to the Colonel's jaw, knocking the man against the massage table.

The hitman retrieved the towels and continued what he'd started earlier. He wrapped a couple of them across Ashton's head, then jerked the two ends of the towel with all his might, whiplashing his victim with such force that the neck snapped and severed the spinal cord. The Colonel went limp.

47 took a breath and opened the small closet. It was empty. Ashton was heavy, but the hitman managed to carry and drop the body inside the cabinet. He had to stuff the man's arms and legs within in order to properly shut the door. Then 47 smoothed his uniform, adjusted his cap, and left the massage room. Again, none of the guests using the exercise equipment paid any attention to him. They had not heard Ashton's anguished cry of pain.

Satisfied, the hitman strode across the floor and exited the gym—only to bump into Helen.

Face-to-face.

TWENTY-SEVEN

I rarely let the unexpected throw me, but that sure did.

There she was, standing two feet in front of me, staring me right in the face. There was a moment, one of those awkward instances, when I wasn't sure how to react. Probably a remnant of the drug withdrawal. I wasn't thinking on my feet as quickly as I should have been.

At any rate, I muttered, "Excuse me," and moved past her. As if it were one of those clumsy incidents when you turn a corner and accidentally bump into someone.

Then, behind me, I heard her call, "Stan?"

I kept going. Didn't even acknowledge it. Just continued my stride toward the elevators. I was wearing the bellhop uniform and cap. Perhaps she would think I merely resembled the Stan Johnson she knew, after which she'd realize I couldn't possibly be him. A bellboy at a hotel in Cyprus? Impossible. Her imagination got the best of her.

When I reached the corner and turned toward the elevator bay, I glanced back. She was gone. Apparently I was right. She must've chalked it up to a mistake on her part and moved on. I wondered if she was looking for Ashton? She wasn't dressed for exercise.

I took the elevator to my floor and went to my room. There was nothing more I could do until tomorrow. With Helen running around the building, I knew I had to be extra cautious. I didn't want to run into her again. She might actually try to talk to me, the bellhop, and then I'd really be in trouble.

It would be so much more convenient if I were given the green light to kill Wilkins now. I could accomplish it here and be done with it. I didn't understand what the holdup was. I didn't understand anything about this crazy assignment. The reverend did have me curious as to what he was doing in Cyprus, meeting with criminal types. And moneymen. I didn't know much about American politics, but I thought it would be considered pretty shady for a presidential candidate, especially someone from the isolationist America First Party, to accept campaign dollars from such sources, if that's what he was indeed doing.

How long would it be before Ashton was missed? Would someone find him in the closet tonight? Tomorrow? What would Wilkins do?

I also wondered how safe it was for me to go back to Greenhill. They were missing two security men, and their maintenance supervisor had broken his neck falling down some stairs. If Ashton had kept my identity to himself, then I was probably all right. The big question was whether or not Wilkins knew. I had to assume that he did and play my cards accordingly. On the other hand, I had to take the chance of going back in as Stan Johnson. It was still my best bet to get close enough to the reverend to take him out.

There was also unfinished business with Helen. I had to risk returning to Greenhill for her. She was worth the gamble, and although it went against my grain, I thought I needed to protect her.

When I bumped into her, I felt as if someone had hit

me in the chest with a hammer. I'd never experienced that before. I was smart enough to know it was not a physical reaction but an emotional one.

Emotions. I had some after all. Who would have thought?

In the shower, I held my hand out flat in front of me. The shakes had diminished considerably. In fact, it was about as still as I'd seen it in months. Maybe I was kicking the painkillers faster than I thought. Then I realized the headache had disappeared as well. I hadn't noticed that before. That was a good thing.

I got into bed and fell into a much-needed sleep.

The dreams were still vivid, though.

I was back in my eight-year-old body. Little 47. From my name alone, I should have known from an even earlier age that something wasn't right with me. Who named a child "47"? When I was much older, I learned I was called that because the last two digits on my bar code were four and seven. My bar code.

So I inhabited my eight-year-old self again. I remembered the moment in question as if it were yesterday. I sat in the asylum garden near the big fountain. I'd finished with my training for the day, and I felt perturbed. I didn't understand yet why the good doctor was making me do all that stuff. I didn't like him. I didn't like the staff. I didn't like anybody.

Then I saw it in the grass. A little snake. Slithering along, minding its own business.

But I hated it. Why should that measly creature be free, when I wasn't? I was stuck in the asylum and wasn't allowed to leave. The snake could come and go as it pleased.

With lightning-fast speed that surprised me, I jumped at the reptile and caught it in my bare hands. It was gray and about ten inches long. The creature slinked *around and through my fingers. I'd never touched a snake before that. It was smoother than I expected, and yet it felt scaly and rough too. A very strange combination. I studied the thing and looked it directly in the eyes. A forked tongue rapidly slipped in and out of its mouth. It was almost as if it was asking, "Who are you? Why are you holding me? Are you my friend?"*

No. I was not your friend. Especially after you bit me.

The anger rose in me. Frustration. Confusion. Coldness.

Without thinking about it, I squeezed and crushed the snake in my hands. Its guts and bloodlike icky fluids dripped out over my skin.

I wasn't repelled.

I threw the snake's remains as far as I could. Then I sat down on the edge of the fountain and studied my palms. What had I just done? I'd killed a living thing. It bit me and I defended myself, but was that a good reason?

Right then and there—I knew. It all became clear to me. I understood why I felt like an outcast. A lab specimen. A nonhuman.

I was a born killer. I was engineered to do what I'd done.

At first I was very depressed. Sad. But a minute later the anger returned. Real fury. And I stayed incensed for weeks. Dr. Ort-Meyer kept asking me what was wrong. I told him I hated him. Several times. He laughed and patted my back, as if I was behaving exactly as he wanted. "Very good, very good!" he'd say.

Then, in the dream I was having, I tried to escape the asylum much sooner than I really did. But everywhere I turned, there were iron bars blocking my way. I ran down a hall to flee from the violence I'd inflicted in my fantasies. Dead end. I turned around and tried a different route. More obstacles.

I couldn't get away from what I was: a killer.

And then—there he was. Waiting for me at the end of a corridor.

The Faceless One. Death. He beckoned me to come closer. I refused. I sensed that he was communicating with me. He was offering me a way out of my predicament.

"What? How?" I screamed at him in my eight-year-old voice.

Death held out his hand. He had one of my Silverballers. Loaded. Ready to go. Its beauty attracted me. The sleek gunmetal finish, the pearl handle, the pure art of its design. I moved closer to Death. Reached out. Took the weapon. It was heavy in my small hands. But it felt . . . wonderful.

I peered up at Death, again trying to penetrate the blankness that covered his face. Who was he really? I was positive that he was someone I knew. Somebody familiar.

You know what to do. He didn't speak aloud, but I heard him in my head.

The way out.

Yes, I knew what to do, all right. I lifted the Silverballer and pointed the barrel at my right temple. All I had to do was squeeze the trigger and it'd all be over. I would be just another one of Ort-Meyer's failed experiments. Let 48 or 49 or 50 be his pride and joy. Not me.

Just pull the trigger. End it all.

Now.

Again, I woke up in a sweat.

So the withdrawal symptoms hadn't completely gone away.

I held out my hand. No trembles. I mentally examined my body. No headache. No fatigue.

Only the dreams. That's all that was left.

I had to beat them. I couldn't stand them anymore. And there was only one way to do so.

I had to find out who Death was. That was the key to full recovery.

I got out of bed and went to the bathroom. Stared at myself in the mirror. My eyes—well, they appeared as they always did. My skin—not as pale. That was progress.

"I'm going to beat you," I said aloud, even though I knew no one could hear me.

No one except Death.

TWENTY-EIGHT

It was the day of Wilkins's meeting.

Agent 47 fashioned himself a new costume. It wasn't safe to be a bellhop anymore, so he managed to obtain a used waiter uniform—white shirt, black pants, apron—and a white server hat to cover his bald head.

Another problem was that the Nicosia police were all over the premises. The bellhop 47 had tied up and left in a guest room had been discovered the night before. The victim made a statement that he was assaulted by a hotel guest who proceeded to steal his uniform. The police were looking for a tall man dressed as a "gaucho." The bellhop's description was wildly inaccurate, even suggesting that the perpetrator had "long, curly black hair" beneath the bandanna.

So far, Colonel Ashton's corpse had not been discovered. When Katharina, the masseuse, arrived at room 433 for the alleged reserved VIP appointment, Boris Komarovsky informed her that there was a mistake. But when he saw how attractive she was, he allowed her to come inside and perform the massage anyway. He tipped her handsomely for a happy ending, thus ensuring Katharina's silence about the incident. She never went back to the spa that night.

* * *

As for Helen McAdams, Wilkins had told her she could take the day off and lounge by the pool if she wanted, but the dedicated Church of Will member and employee had no intention of doing that. She wanted to be close to her mentor and be on hand should he end up needing her after all. Despite her natural shyness, Helen managed to assume some authority over the various bodyguards and security detail that had been assigned to the reverend. She found that she had a newfound ability to delegate instructions and give orders with confidence and firmness, which was uncharacteristic for her. In fact, even Wilkins had commented that Helen had "changed" over the last few weeks. He noticed that she had blossomed from her customary introverted self.

The truth of the matter was that she was happier than she had ever been in her life, and it was all due to Stan Johnson. While it was still early in their relationship, Helen was convinced she had found a soul mate in the quiet, intense farmer from Iowa. He was definitely an odd duck, but, then again, so was she. They fit together nicely. Helen was comfortable around him. Ever since they had revealed to each other their dependence on drugs, she felt even closer to him. She wanted badly to help him kick his habit. This desire gave her a new purpose, something that fed her own battle against past demons.

She was a bit concerned that Stan had no interest in sex. Helen firmly believed that this would change, especially after he went into recovery from the painkillers. They shared so much else, why couldn't they become intimate? Helen thought she understood him. Stan had experienced many hard knocks and apparently had suffered from a broken heart once or twice during his history. The Church of Will taught her that these things could be mended. Charlie always said to "find the Will inside oneself" and all things would come to light. The

Church's many tenets provided believers with the tools to search and locate that Will. Up until recently, Helen diligently practiced the teachings, for months and months, and hadn't succeeded. She had made no progress until Stan came into her life. For some reason, his arrival at Greenhill opened the well. It was if she had found the pipeline to a rich and abundant source of new emotions and ideas. She discovered her Will.

Helen couldn't wait to leave Cyprus and get back to Greenhill. She missed Stan terribly. She was tempted to phone him, but she resisted the urge. She wasn't even sure what the time difference was between Virginia and the island. Last night she'd actually thought she saw him in the hotel. The bellhop she'd encountered outside the gym looked *exactly* like him. The man could have been Stan's twin brother. It was uncanny. Of course, it wasn't him at all. How could it be? Helen chalked it up to a trick of her imagination. She had been thinking about Stan all day, so naturally her mind deceived her. Afterward she found it funny.

Was she in love? Possibly. She didn't want to use that word yet. Stan obviously wasn't ready for it. She wouldn't dare say it to him—it would probably scare him away. Helen would wait until he was comfortable enough to be intimate with her. Sex often broke down barriers, although she admitted it sometimes also built them.

She decided to take it one day at a time. Stan was a kind soul. She knew it. He had some secrets, to be sure, and there were things in his past that were dark and mysterious—even dangerous. But she would draw him out eventually. She believed in her heart that Stan Johnson was a good person. And that he was capable of love.

47, wearing his staff disguise, accessed the immense kitchen on the ground floor through the double doors in the Salon, where breakfast was the main attraction. He simply walked through the restaurant as if he knew what he was doing, entered the kitchen, and started loading a cart with plates, napkins, silverware, and other items that would come with a catered order.

"What are you doing?" a man in a chef's hat asked.

"They need this over in the business center," the hitman replied. "Some kind of VIP thing going on."

The chef obviously didn't recognize the tall waiter, but employees came and went in a big hotel; it was impossible to keep track of everyone.

"Very well," he said as 47 wheeled the cart out of the kitchen.

Now suitably camouflaged with not only clothing and makeup but props, the assassin could move freely about the building and no one would look twice at him. He was just another lowly kitchen worker moving a cart of dishes from one place to another. There was so much going on in Nicosia's largest and most luxurious hotel that such a sight would not be out of place. As an extra precaution, though, he slipped three steak knives and three forks into his pocket. One never knew when a weapon might be necessary.

47 noticed the police presence in the lobby and in some of the corridors. Had they finally found Ashton's corpse? If so, would that affect Wilkins's plans for the day? There was only one way to find out, and that was to check out the business center to see what was happening.

It was located on the ground floor and consisted of several meeting rooms, a boardroom/conference room, and a choice of dining spaces used for corporate gatherings. Wilkins had booked the Ahera meeting room and the boardroom. When 47 wheeled his cart into the hallway outside the Ahera, he saw that the reverend and his guests had just completed a meal there. The hitman pretended to rearrange the dishes on the cart while eyeing the men as they left the Ahera and walked down the corridor to the boardroom. Several men wearing uniforms stood at the entrances. Patches on their shoulders indicated they were employed by CYPRUS A-1 SECURITY COMPANY. 47 also recognized a couple of Greenhill bodyguards supervising the operation.

At last, Wilkins himself emerged from the Ahera. He was deep in conversation with a Saudi man dressed in a *bisht*, the traditional cloak of prestige, and the *ghutra an iqal* headdress. 47 thought he might be a prince or another member of royalty. The assassin wasn't close enough to catch any of their conversation. He continued to work with the dishes and silverware until all of the VIPs were inside the boardroom. The door was shut, and the Greenhill bodyguards stood sentry.

Interesting.

He rolled the cart into the Ahera and froze.

Helen.

He hadn't expected to see her. She was supposed to have the day off.

She was dressed in a smart business suit and stood with a clipboard in hand as she talked to a Greenhill staff member 47 recognized as George somebody, another one of Wilkins's personal assistants. Hotel employees were busy clearing away the used breakfast settings; 47 assumed that Helen and the other assistant had been present at breakfast but had been left behind once the meeting in the boardroom began. The assassin wheeled the cart closer to the pair, and then he squatted on one side, his back to them, to "arrange" the dishes again as he focused on the conversation.

". . . don't understand why we're here, George," Helen said. "Did you hear what he told me? 'Go swim in the pool.' He doesn't want me around today. Why?"

George shrugged. "I'm as clueless as you are. At least

he kept you busy yesterday. I haven't done a darned thing since we arrived."

"But why does Charlie want to meet with those guys from OPEC and those foreign banks? I thought we were supposed to be going on campaign stops."

"Honey, this *is* a campaign stop. Don't you get it? All those guys have deep pockets. They're here to give Charlie a lot of money."

She shook her head. "I guess I don't understand politics. Why are *they* giving him money?"

"Let's hope he gets what he wants," George replied. "Charlie's in a terrible mood."

"I'll say. I don't think he's ever snapped at me like he did this morning. Where could the Colonel *be*? How could he just disappear like that?"

Agent 47 smiled inwardly. Unbeknownst to everyone, the good colonel was still stuffed in the closet upstairs in the spa.

"Come on, I'll join you at the pool," George said. "Lord knows I have nothing else to do."

The pair left the meeting room. Agent 47 started to wheel his cart out of the Ahera when one of the hotel employees stepped up to him. She was a heavy woman in her forties with fierce brown eyes and a permanent frown.

"What are you doing? Are you going to help us or not?" the woman said.

The hitman shook his head. "I have the wrong room. I'm supposed to take these somewhere else."

"Where? You know all catering goes through me." She looked him up and down. "Where's your name tag? Do I know you?"

"My name is John Duncan."

"Are you new, Mr. Duncan?"

"Yes, ma'am. Yesterday was my first day."

The woman put hands on her hips. "No, it wasn't. We

didn't start any staff yesterday, and I should know. You'd better come with me."

Now what?

Agent 47 had to accept the fact that he'd been caught. She was going to march him out into the corridor, where the security detail stood at attention. The woman headed for the door and looked back at him. "Well? Are you coming, Mr. Duncan? If that is your real name?"

He had no choice. The assassin grabbed a china plate and held it behind his back as he followed her. She led him out into the corridor and then called to the two beefy men outside the boardroom. Three of the Cypriot hired guns stood nearby.

"Gentlemen, I think you need to speak to this man," she announced. But as she turned to indicate "John Duncan," the waiter smashed the plate on top of the woman's head. He knew it wouldn't kill her, but it did the job of knocking her out. Her body crumbled into a pile of arms and legs.

"Holy shit!" one of the guards managed to cough as he drew a handgun from inside his jacket. He was the fastest of the five men. By the time the other four registered what they had just witnessed, 47 had removed the three steak knives from his pocket. Like a circus performer throwing blades at an associate strapped to a spinning wheel, the hitman snapped the utensils at the first, second, and third man.

Thwack! Thwack! Thwack!

Each knife neatly penetrated the soft bull's-eye between each man's Adam's apple and the top of his sternum. The guard who had successfully drawn a gun dropped it and fell against the wall. The other two spun around in a macabre and slightly humorous dance before they, too, collapsed.

Three down, two to go.

Best to change tactics. It kept opponents guessing.

Agent 47 pulled the three forks from his pocket, positioned two in his right hand and one in his left, prongs out, and charged the two men. Being inexperienced work-for-hire employees of the Cyprus A-1 Security Company, neither had thought quickly enough to draw a gun or even put up defensive fists.

The hitman simultaneously buried two forks in the soft tissue on the underside of the first man's lower jaw and the other fork in the second man's Adam's apple. Knowing that the latter fellow would most likely scream in pain, 47 immediately bent his arm and elbowed the man hard in the stomach, knocking the breath out of him. The guard leaned forward, providing 47 with the opportunity to clasp his fists together and clobber the guy on the back of the head. He was dead before he hit the floor.

The man with the forks in his jaw struggled to pull them out, but 47 had submerged the utensils so deeply that the task was impossible. He fell to his knees and looked at 47 in shock and horror. The hitman held the man's head steady with his left hand and grabbed the forks' handles with his right.

Another shove did the trick.

Only then did the world's greatest assassin take a look behind him to confirm that no one had seen the act. It had been messy but silent. He would have liked to see Charlie Wilkins's face when the meeting was over and his cabal of criminal financiers stepped out of the boardroom to find a slaughterhouse in the corridor.

Agent 47 moved quickly down the hall, pulling off the white apron that was now soiled with blood. He wiped his hands, tossed the garment in a garbage can next to the elevators, and calmly stepped into a car going up. Three guests were inside. They paid him no mind.

In his room, he dressed in his black suit and red tie and gathered his belongings. The hitman reflected on what was really going on in Cyprus. Charlie Wilkins was soliciting campaign money from foreign contributors, obviously men of dubious morality. 47 was certain that these were men who had an interest in the future of the United States government. They all had a stake in what happened economically and politically. They wanted to see the revolution succeed.

Agent 47 didn't care. America's destiny didn't concern him.

As he took the elevator to the lobby, checked out, and rode a taxi to Larnaca Airport, he realized he hadn't experienced any painkiller side effects since he awoke that morning.

Perhaps he was superhuman after all.

TWENTY-NINE

Charlie Wilkins's entourage flew home the next day, despite the investigation going on in Nicosia regarding the murder of five security men and assaulting a female hotel employee outside the reverend's meeting. Police had interrogated Wilkins and the other participants for hours. No one had seen anything. Nobody heard a sound. There were no surveillance cameras in that hallway, so law-enforcement officials were mystified. But given Wilkins's high-profile status, they were convinced he was somehow involved, if only in an indirect way.

Several of Wilkins's VIP associates left the hotel as soon as the bloodbath was discovered. Many of them had questionable legal standings, so the last thing they wanted was to be caught up in a multiple-murder investigation. Boris Komarovsky, however, was detained by authorities regarding Bruce Ashton's disappearance; Katharina the masseuse had broken her vow of silence after the Americans had left and admitted to authorities that she was called away from Ashton's appointment by a mysterious concierge. When Komarovsky's criminal background came to light, he was arrested on charges of international racketeering. Again, this didn't reflect well on Wilkins.

Before leaving Cyprus, the reverend held a press conference at the Larnaca Airport, denying any responsibility for the killings. He was quick to blame his "political enemies" in Washington, saying that they feared his rise in popularity. "They're running scared and are resorting to drastic measures," he declared. "First they kill Dana Linder, and now they try to besmirch my good name by involving me in these heinous crimes." The tactic worked. The reverend was so well loved in America that his supporters had no doubt that he was innocent of any wrongdoing. As for Boris Komarovsky, Wilkins denied knowledge of the man's ties with the Russian Mafia. It was Komarovsky's bank that Wilkins was dealing with, not the man personally.

It was only after the Americans had arrived back in Virginia that the Colonel's body was finally uncovered in the spa closet, where curiously no one had looked. Interpol went ballistic. The media was ecstatic and the incidents made international news. Cypriot politicians decried the fact that Wilkins and his people had been allowed to leave the republic before questions had been answered. Still, the entire affair was a mess. Wilkins's political opponents milked the incident for everything it was worth. The reverend was accused of improper fund-raising and associating with criminals.

At first Helen was disillusioned. She hadn't understood why they went to Cyprus in the first place, and the Colonel's disappearance and the subsequent murders had disturbed her deeply. She thanked God that she had followed Charlie's orders and gone to the hotel's pool that morning. She hadn't seen the abattoir outside the boardroom, but the description in the newspapers horrified her.

Wilkins made a speech to his staff aboard the Learjet. He assured them that they were moving forward and the events in Cyprus would not halt his march to the White House. He said he had confidence in the Cypriot police and Interpol. In fact, he had hired his own private investigator in Cyprus, a man named Karopoulos. He would find Ashton, get to the bottom of the murders, and exonerate Wilkins of any involvement.

Helen had no choice but to believe it. Charlie Wilkins was still her mentor and reverend. He *was* the Church of Will, and it was the Church that had helped her in her time of need. By the time they landed at Greenhill, Helen had regained her complete faith in the man.

What was more disturbing was that Stan Johnson was nowhere to be found and hadn't been seen in days.

When Helen arrived at work on the morning after the return home, the reverend appeared haggard and stressed. Apparently he hadn't slept. The loss of his friend the Colonel—not to mention the murders in the hallway—had upset him greatly. The entire staff had been put on damage control since the homecoming the day before. Helen herself had only three hours of sleep. The jet lag adversely affected her, she was worried about Charlie, and she was concerned about Stan.

Where was he? Why hadn't he left word for her?

She had called his cellphone the night before and got his voice mail.

"This is Stan. Leave a message."

Helen told him she was back and wanted to see him. She asked that he please call her as soon as he could. She almost ended with, "I love you," but caught herself in time. No need to press her luck.

She had little energy to go through the pile of paperwork Charlie had left on her desk, but she perked up when her phone rang mid-morning. Helen's heart leapt with joy when she recognized the caller ID. She answered it with a breathless "Stan?"

"Hi, Helen. Are you all right?"

"Stan, where are you?"

"I had to go back to Iowa to take care of some legal matters regarding the farm. I figured I'd do it while you were gone. It took a day longer than I expected. I wanted to be back before you but was delayed. I'm sorry."

She breathed a sigh of relief. "Oh, okay, I . . . I just . . . It's good to hear your voice. When will you be back?"

"I should be there this afternoon. No worries."

"That's good. I can't wait to see you. I guess you heard about what happened in Cyprus?"

"It's all over the news. I repeat, are you all right?"

"I'm fine, but really tired. It's been very stressful. Poor Charlie is a train wreck."

"I can imagine."

"I'll tell you all about it tonight. Dinner at my place?"

"Sounds like a plan."

After Stan hung up, Helen thought he had sounded a little different. Perhaps it was only her imagination, but he seemed distant. Maybe she was being paranoid and reading nonsense into the conversation.

George stuck his head into her office and said, "Something's happening."

"What?"

"We have visitors. Some school buses with a bunch of men just came through the gate and are parking in the barn."

"Huh? Who are they?"

"I don't know."

She got up and followed him outside the mansion. Sure enough, Mitch Carson was directing traffic, pointing the way for the drivers of three yellow buses. The barn was some distance away, but it was within the restricted area, near the guardhouse. When the men climbed out of the buses, Helen noted they were of various ages, between early twenties and late forties, and were dressed in T-shirts and blue jeans or camouflage army pants. Helen thought they looked like soldiers out of uniform. In fact, they moved and acted like military men.

She watched as Carson greeted another man decked out entirely in army fatigues. He wore sunglasses and a broad cowboy hat that prevented her from seeing his face. But he walked with a limp and appeared to have mechanical pincers in place of a right hand. A prosthesis.

Carson led the man into a side entrance to the mansion. They were probably on their way to see Charlie.

Greenhill continued to grow more mysterious by the day.

Agent 47, wearing the Stan Johnson trademark overalls and flannel shirt, knocked at precisely seven o'clock. He heard her running footsteps, then the door swung open. Helen immediately threw herself at him and wrapped her arms around his tight, muscular frame.

"Stan, I'm so glad to see you!"

The hitman didn't expect the enthusiastic welcome and wasn't sure how to react. He lightly placed his arms around her. She looked up at him and then planted a kiss on his mouth. Again, he was taken aback but managed to retain character.

"I'm glad to see you too."

She released him and pulled him into the apartment by the hands. "Come in. Dinner's almost ready. I made a chicken casserole; I hope you like it. I can't believe Charlie let us go so early. I thought we'd have to continue working through the night. But I guess even *he* decided he needed to get some sleep!"

The assassin had encountered no problems reentering Greenhill. After landing at Baltimore/Washington Airport earlier that morning—there was a layover in London—the assassin picked up one of the Silverballers and the C4 from his briefcase but kept the rest of his stuff in the locker. Then he rented a car. He parked it in the compound's community lot and walked to Main Street as if he'd never been gone. His apartment was still a wreck, so he spent an hour straightening it up. He was relatively confident that Ashton and his two goons were the only security men who knew his identity. Whether or not Charlie Wilkins was also aware, time would tell. He was willing to risk the exposure. He had invested too much in the assignment to walk away now.

Helen served the meal and spent the next half hour recounting her experience in Cyprus. Even though she complained of being exhausted, she was lively and animated. Helen had not been outside the United States in years, so in many ways it had been a grand adventure. The killings obviously frightened her, and the subsequent news about the Colonel was shocking, but she seemed none the worse for wear.

47 had forgotten how much he liked listening to her voice.

"You know, I thought I *saw* you in the hotel," she said, laughing and shaking her head. "There was a bellhop I swear could've been your twin. I must've really missed you, Stan. I was seeing your face everywhere, I think."

47 chuckled with her and replied, "Well, it couldn't have been me. I was having knock-down drag-outs with men I didn't care for. It was murder."

"Where, in Iowa?"

He took a sip of wine and then nodded. "Davenport. Lawyers. IRS officers. You know, bad guys."

"Stan." She picked up her glass of wine and clinked his. "I missed your company."

After an awkward pause, 47 announced, "I have news."

"Do tell."

"I quit the pills. I'm going cold turkey."

"Really? Oh, Stan! That's wonderful!" Then she realized he looked as well as ever. "How . . . how do you feel?"

"Not bad. The first couple of days were pretty awful." He shrugged. "Now I'm fine."

"But how can that be? My God, Stan, it took me *weeks* to get through withdrawal. You can't kick the pills in three days. It's impossible." She shook her head. "I'm afraid you still have more to go through. It's not that easy."

"I guess my metabolism is different. I don't know."

"Stan, I had to go to a rehab clinic for two months. I thought I was well, and as soon as I was out, I started using again. That's when I tried to—you know." He didn't say anything, so she continued. "I went to a different clinic and they made me go cold turkey. It was a nightmare, Stan. If there's a hell, then that was it. I've been to hell and back. I *still* have trouble. There are moments when I crave it. I'll never be completely cured. I don't see how you can possibly be all right."

He didn't answer.

"You're not lying to me about quitting, are you? Just telling me what I want to hear?"

"No, I'm not lying about that."

At least that was true.

She fell asleep on the couch as they watched a movie on television. The wine and fatigue did her in. Prior to that, though, Helen had once again dropped hints that she would've liked to be intimate, but 47 couldn't bring himself to do it. He cared about her too much to hurt her like that. Because that's what would happen—she'd eventually be terribly hurt; in fact, it was inevitable. So he held her at arm's length for her own good. It was still a new and unfamiliar sensation for him to *care* about anyone.

He thought about the painkillers and how easy it had been to quit them after all. It was the genetic engineering that had done the work. What most addicts endured for weeks and months took only two or three days. No more shakes, headaches, or bad dreams. Actually, that wasn't quite the truth. 47 still had vivid dreams in which Death appeared. The hitman was no closer to discovering who the Faceless One was, but he would find out soon. He knew it.

Oddly, he wasn't tired. Jet lag never bothered him, and the assassin could always go for long periods without sleep. Nevertheless, it had been an intense few days. He should get some rest while he could. But having Helen by his side was an alien experience. Feeling her warmth, watching her breathe, smelling her perfume— *that* was about as normal as it got.

And Agent 47 came to the conclusion that he couldn't let go and enjoy it. Never in a million years.

It was a little after ten when he noticed the indicator light on his cellphone.

A message from the Agency.

Helen was still asleep. Now her head was in his lap and she had curled into a fetal position. She looked so peaceful. No troubles. Almost childlike. Without disturbing her, he picked up the mobile, signed in to his voice mail, and listened to the coded communication.

When it was over, he punched in the numbers to indicate that the message was received and acknowledged.

There were two parts. The first one directed 47 to a secure FTP site, where he could view some photos. Jade had found three pictures of Charlie Wilkins shot during or prior to 1976. The first two were from small-town newspapers in Arkansas and Maryland, dating from 1973 and 1974, respectively. The oldest picture was a shot of an early Church of Will tent, where Wilkins would have exercised his mission in a fiery, theatrical way, one that attracted local citizens who were susceptible to a fire-and-brimstone-style presentation. A young Wilkins stood with an equally youthful Mitch Carson and two others—a man and a woman. They were not identified.

The picture from 1974 displayed a newer, bigger Church of Will tent. A larger staff posed in front. Wilkins in the middle. Carson to his right. The woman and man from the first photo stood on his left. This time they were identified as Wendy and Eric Shipley. She was next to Wilkins.

The third snap, from a '76 Towson, Maryland, newspaper, revealed Wilkins emerging from the courthouse after Eric Shipley's inquest. Wendy Shipley was at his side. He had his arm around her as they avoided reporters.

Agent 47 studied the Shipley woman's body language in all three photos and came to a conclusion.

The second part of Jade's message was more significant.

The client had given the green light to assassinate Charlie Wilkins.

And it had to be done that night.

THIRTY

While Helen slept, I formulated a plan. I hoped she was so tired that she'd sleep soundly for the next couple of hours. That way, I could do what I had to do and get back to her apartment before she woke up. I could simply leave the compound, but my absence the next day would attract attention. The target was so high profile that I needed to maintain the cover a few more days, if possible. What better alibi than being asleep with one's "girlfriend"?

I carefully lifted her head off my lap and rose from the sofa. Then I draped her legs over one arm, supported her back with the other, picked her up, and carried her to the bedroom and her bed. She stirred a little and looked at me. I went ahead and did it—I kissed her—and said, "You'll be more comfortable here." I covered her with a blanket and lay beside her.

My presence seemed to be some kind of solace to her, for she easily drifted back to sleep. I waited a full ten minutes, until she was breathing slowly and deeply, before I quietly got up and left the room.

I found her purse in the living room, rummaged through it, and took her keycard.

As I went from her apartment to my own, I thought about what I was doing. There was no question that I was using her. My original scheme had succeeded. I *had become close to someone within the Church of Will and gained access to her privacy. I had secured her trust and deceived her.*

How did I feel about that? Honestly, now that I was off the painkillers, I didn't care.

I was back to my old self.

I supposed I might be a cad, a charlatan, a liar . . . but I was also an assassin. That's what defined me.

And yet a small part of me—an ounce of my heart, some grain of my soul—belonged to Helen. She had reached inside me and touched a hidden nerve I never knew existed. I was grateful for that.

It proved to me that I was more than a machine, more than a genetic monster.

And, right then and there, I vowed that I would not allow any harm to come to Helen McAdams.

In my apartment, I armed myself with the one Silver-baller I'd taken from that locker at the airport. I'd also procured the C4, blasting caps, and stopwatch I got from Birdie. I always knew these items would come in handy. I was glad I'd left the briefcase in the locker. I had a feeling I wouldn't be returning to the apartment.

By the time I left my place, it was eleven o'clock.

Charlie Wilkins sat at the desk in his office every night at midnight so he could "pray." I don't know what he got out of such a deed. It wasn't my place to judge someone's beliefs, whether he or she was a good person or not. What mattered to me was that his habit was a perfect opportunity to accomplish my mission.

Outside it was pitch black and the temperature was quite cool. The moon had disappeared behind heavy clouds. The compound's streetlights illuminated the various public paths, but between buildings it was very dark. That would be my route.

Using stealth techniques I had learned when I was a

boy at Ort-Meyer's asylum, I moved from structure to structure like a black cat. Silent and swift. Most of the residents were indoors. I heard some voices and laughter in the distance, in the Main Street area, probably in the recreation hall, where members could play pool, Ping-Pong, and other games until midnight. There wasn't a bar in Greenhill.

The path up the hill to the electrified fence and gate was exposed and well lit. That was unfortunate, but there was nothing else to do except walk with purpose, as if I knew what I was doing. After all, I was a maintenance man. I was sure I could come up with an excuse if a guard happened to stop me.

As a matter of fact, a sentry patrolled the area outside the fence. I spotted him as he passed the gate and slowly moved in the direction of the toolshed. He appeared bored and cold. He probably thought it was unlikely there could ever be any trouble at Greenhill. But I didn't want him to see me, so I moved through the shadows to the shed and crouched on one side. The man walked toward me and I waited. He paid no attention to his surroundings. He was more interested in the lake and the black sky than anything else. When he was within six feet, I made my move.

Pouncing like a leopard, I moved in behind him, wrapped the Fiberwire around his neck, and pulled the ends.

Fast, silent, and easy. He was out, but he'd live.

I grabbed him under the arms and dragged him to the shed. I quickly unlocked it and pulled the man inside. After stuffing him behind the lathe, I left and secured the door behind me.

My watch said it was 11:15. Not much time left.

I strode with impunity up the path to the gate. Not wasting any time, I swiped Helen's keycard and went through. But as I headed toward the mansion, noises from the barn attracted my attention. The lights were on in the building and the doors were ajar. Someone drove a yellow school bus from the back and stopped in front of the doors. A man got out to open the doors wider. The driver then drove the bus inside.

I wasn't sure what that was about, but it made me curious enough to investigate. Besides, I didn't want to proceed with my plan if there was a chance that men were up and about around the mansion.

So I kept to the shadows and darted from cover to cover until I reached the side of the building. I heard men talking inside. With my back to the exterior wall, I inched to the corner and stood at the edge of the opening. I dared to lean sideways and peer into the place.

There were three school buses. I counted six men moving around them. On one side of the space were several portable clothes racks made of steel pipes. Dozens of uniforms on hangers. U.S. National Guard uniforms.

Interesting.

Were these guys National Guardsmen? Somehow, I didn't think so.

I thought it best to stay on task, so I quietly moved away from the barn and dashed back to the mansion. Now I was on the east side. Not much to look at except a door that must have been an employee entrance or something, just like what was on the west side of the place facing the gardens. A few windows. I scanned the building for security cameras but didn't see any.

Slipping around to the back, I heard the water lapping on the shore. The lake was very near, and it wouldn't be difficult to slip and fall in. There wasn't anything on the ground to protect someone from doing so. I guess they figured no one would—or should—go to the back of the mansion, where Wilkins's office was located.

There it was. The wall-sized plate-glass window.

Bulletproof. The office was empty. I could see inside because it was dimly lit with a single lamp. There was no exterior illumination; that would interfere with Wilkins's scenic view. I wondered where he was at that moment. In his bedroom? When would he come to the office to prepare for his meditation? Whatever, I figured I needed to work quickly.

I set about affixing the C4 bricks along the wall below the big window and across the very bottom edge of the glass. One at the east end, one in the middle, and a third at the west end. The C4 came with an adhesive that stuck to anything when the thin film cover was removed. I inserted the blasting caps into the puttylike substance and ran the wire along the ground, connecting each brick and culminating at the third explosive. I then fastened the wire to the stopwatch, which I programmed to go off at exactly 12:02 A.M.

Done. Now to get back to Helen and—

My cellphone buzzed. I had it on silent ring, but I felt it vibrate. I pulled it out of my pocket and checked the caller ID.

Helen. She must have woken up and wondered where I'd gone. That was inopportune. I didn't answer it.

Looking back at my handiwork, I checked that everything was in place. I was confident the bricks were low enough on the window that Wilkins wouldn't see them. Then I moved to the southeast corner of the mansion, prepared to slip off into the darkness and make my way back to Helen's apartment. I was sure I could come up with some excuse to tell her. I couldn't sleep. I went for a walk. I had to go back to my apartment for something. Anything. It wasn't a big problem.

But as I rounded the corner, one of the mansion guards appeared near the front of the building. Out doing his rounds.

Between me and my path to safety.

THIRTY-ONE

It wasn't clear in which direction the guard was heading, so Agent 47 reversed his route and headed for the back of the mansion. He took the chance to cross west along the large window to the other side of the building. He thought perhaps going through the gardens would be a safer route to the gate. Glancing inside the office, he saw that Wilkins still had not arrived for his midnight prayer. Surely the reverend wouldn't skip his appointment that night?

Someone had been watering the gardens, or maybe it had rained while the assassin was in Cyprus. The ground was wet and muddy. He couldn't help stepping in it. Not good. Nevertheless, he reached the shrubbery and hid. The guard had been at the mansion's northeast corner. Would he patrol along the east side toward the back of the house? Or would he cross in front to the west side? 47 thought it best to stay put until he knew for certain. He checked his watch—11:38. Placing the explosives had taken longer than he'd expected.

He winced when he saw the guard appear at the northwest corner of the house. The man began moving down the sidewalk on the west side between the mansion and the gardens, toward the employee entrance there. How far would he go? Would he notice the footprints the assassin had left in the mud? Would the man check the back of the house? Would he see the C4?

Agent 47 held his breath and stayed still and silent.

The guard approached the employee entrance.

Go inside! The hitman silently willed.

The man continued walking toward the back. He was almost to the end.

Maybe the guard was daydreaming and not concentrating on his job, like the first man 47 had encountered that night.

The sentry came to the end of the walk, right at the edge of the muddy spot at the back. He stopped. He grabbed a flashlight from his belt, flicked it on, and shone it on the ground.

He'd seen the footprints.

Now curious, the guard moved on, crossing the mud to the south side of the house. He pointed the torch along the shore. Then he cast the light at the large picture window.

That was it. He would see the explosives.

Agent 47 removed the Fiberwire from his pocket and rushed out from behind the shrubs. Moving quickly and stealthily, he reached the guard, wrapped the wire around the man's neck, and pulled hard. The sentry dropped the flashlight and tried to scream, but the garrote mutated the sound into a gurgling sputter. The man struggled and did his best to elbow and kick backward at the assassin, but 47's grip was too strong.

The guard collapsed in the hitman's arms in less than a minute.

No time to lose. 47 dragged the guard back to the garden and dumped the body behind the shrubbery. His watch now read 11:46.

He moved north through a row of shrubs toward the front of the mansion, reaching the edge of the garden.

He'd quickly dash to the gate and hustle back to Helen's apartment before—

He froze where he was.

Helen was at the gate, talking to a guard. She was dressed, had her purse in hand, and gestured as if she had lost something. The guard swiped his keycard and the gate opened. She went through and headed toward the mansion.

No!

47 didn't want her anywhere near her office. The C4 would go off in a little over ten minutes!

As usual, she didn't go through the front entrance. She headed around the west side of the building and down the path to the employee door. The hitman watched with horror as she knocked on it since she didn't have her own keycard. Helen waited a moment and then knocked again much louder. The door finally opened, and none other than Wilkins greeted her. 47 heard her explain that she'd somehow lost her key, that she couldn't sleep, and she decided to do some work. The reverend stepped aside for her to enter, and then the door closed.

But it didn't snap shut. Wilkins obviously hadn't pushed the door hard enough, so it stood slightly ajar. Not locked.

47 had to get her out. That decision surprised him, for in the past he would have walked away and paid little attention to collateral damage resulting from a hit. This time, however, the destruction included Helen. He *did* care about her. As much as he'd used her and lied to her, he had sincerely connected with her in ways that the world's greatest assassin had never experienced.

He bolted out of his hiding place and darted to the door. 47 quietly and slowly pushed it open and peered inside.

A short foyer ended at a T-corridor, stretching north

and south. He moved forward, hugged the wall, and glanced into the passageway. To the north was a short empty corridor that took a right turn. To the south, he saw Wilkins and Helen turn left and disappear into another hallway. 47 followed them.

When he reached the turn, they had disappeared. Office doors along the hallway were closed. Which one was Helen's? In the middle of the corridor, another long passageway cut south. Exactly where Wilkins's office would be.

The hitman headed there, peripherally noticing the religious artwork and sculptures that lined the walls. The door at the end was open. 47 drew the Silverballer, flattened against the side, and moved commando-style to the threshold. A quick look inside—and he saw that the reverend wasn't there. The room was full of plants and more religious artwork. The luxurious space was dimly lit, just as it had been earlier. The picture window looked out at darkness. The assassin figured that Wilkins probably turned out the interior lights when he prayed so that he could get a good view of the water.

He looked at his watch—11:50.

"I'm going downstairs and don't wish to be disturbed," announced a familiar smooth voice. It came from the east–west hallway where the office doors were located.

Wilkins.

If the reverend was "going downstairs," did that mean he wasn't going to pray that night? Would the explosives be for naught?

Forget about the C4.

The assassin chose to kill the man as soon as he saw him. A double tap. A bullet to the chest and one to the head. He had to go to plan B. Improvise. It was what he was good at.

With weapon in hand, 47 moved back up the ornate

corridor and reached the T-intersection. He saw Wilkins round the corner to the east. The hitman followed him, reached the end, and turned north. No sign of the man, but there was a stairwell a few feet ahead and to the left. The sound of Wilkins's footsteps descending to a basement level echoed against the walls. The killer took the stairs and crept to the lower landing, waited a second, and then continued to the bottom. The only direction to go was an east–west concrete hallway parallel to the one above. 47 followed it until he reached yet another southward tunnel leading to a door identical to the one to Wilkins's office. Words on the outside read: PRIVATE—AUTHORIZED PERSONNEL ONLY. It was ajar, and flickering candlelight streamed through the opening.

47 skulked forward. There was music coming from the room beyond. Classical music. Schubert. *Ave Maria*. A piece that had many connections to the hitman and one that was extremely personal to him.

A coincidence?

Too late to back out now.

The assassin lightly pushed on the door, swinging it completely open.

The entire room, which mirrored Wilkins's office on the floor directly above it, was lit by dozens of candles. Except for a fairly empty space in the middle of the floor, there appeared to be hundreds of pieces of artwork stored there. Stacks of painted canvases leaned against the walls. Statues littered the place— reproductions of the Virgin Mary, Jesus, Buddha . . . The reverend knelt at a bizarre altar on the north end of the room, his back to 47. The hitman had never seen anything like it. A fresco adorned the entire north wall—it was a larger, near-perfect copy of a detail from Michelangelo's Sistine Chapel painting in which God reaches out to touch the index finger of Adam. Between the celebrity reverend and the fresco were erected several other iconic religious images—a cross, the Star of David, a Buddha, a green tapestry with the Arabic symbol for Allah, and others 47 didn't recognize. Was Wilkins praying *here* instead of in his office?

47 stepped inside.

Two men on either side of the door stepped out of darkness and aimed automatic weapons at him.

A third man, dressed in military camouflage, appeared from behind a concrete column on the west side of the room. He held a handgun in his left hand; his right one was a prosthesis.

"Drop your weapon," he commanded.

47 had no choice. He did.

"Kick it over to me and raise your hands."

The hitman complied.

Then Wilkins stood and turned to face the assassin. He stepped forward and looked the captive up and down.

"The legendary Agent 47," he said. "I thought you'd jump at the bait."

THIRTY-TWO

Agent 47 narrowed his eyes at the reverend.

This was a setup?

He looked back at the man with the prosthesis.

Cromwell.

His was the abnormally waxy face that appeared on telecasts made by the New Model Army when they claimed responsibility for an attack. The man's features were obviously altered by plastic surgery. It seemed clear that Cromwell had seen serious combat at some point, since he had lost an arm and walked with a limp. The hitman instinctively knew that the man should not be underestimated or taken for granted: He commanded a fierce militant force that had wreaked havoc across the United States and succeeded in establishing a mystique that had captured the imagination of the American people. Cromwell was not only a clever military strategist but also a highly intelligent leader.

And a terrorist.

47 quickly scanned his immediate surroundings for a way out of the predicament, but the room was too large. Apart from physically attacking his captors, which would result in being shot, there was nothing he could do. Instead, he bent his upraised arms enough so that he could see his watch.

It was 11:53. Nine minutes to go.

Wilkins turned to Cromwell and said, "At last we have the man who assassinated your sister, Cromwell."

The militant's nostrils flared and his eyes burned holes into 47.

Now the killer understood. The picture had been there in front of him but he didn't have the final piece of the puzzle. Cromwell was Darren Shipley. The brother of Dana Linder. The marine who was missing in action and presumed dead had in fact gone into hiding and changed his identity.

"Did you kill my sister?" he asked 47.

The hitman didn't answer.

"Of course he did," Wilkins said. "He works for the CIA and President Burdett. As I told you, he's part of a government conspiracy to wipe out the New Model Army, the Church of Will, and me. He is here at Green-hill to *assassinate* me, Cromwell. He infiltrated the Church by deceiving one of my employees. I am also convinced he was somehow responsible for the death of my friend, the Colonel." At this, he turned his attention to 47. "Ashton probably deserved it, though, for disobeying my orders when he and his guards grabbed you the other day. I expressly told him I wanted you kept alive until I returned from Cyprus, but being a man of *initiative,* he got a little carried away."

So that explains the business with almost being buried alive in cement, 47 thought.

"Inspector Karopoulos in Cyprus has confirmed that a tall bellhop matching his build was seen in the hotel gym the night the Colonel disappeared. Cromwell, this man is a professional hitman." The reverend looked at 47. "Do you deny it?"

The killer remained silent.

"We shall call the police after you are shot dead by my security team. We'll tell them that you attempted to end my life and my men acted accordingly. The world media will learn how the current administration hired you to kill Dana Linder and then sent you here to murder *me*. Such pitiful and atrocious reelection strategy! Burdett won't have a chance after this. Agent 47, Mr. Johnson, or whatever your real name is, you're looking at the next President of the United States. But before you die, we will—"

A distant female voice interrupted him. "Charlie?"

Helen. Most likely calling from the stairwell outside the door.

The reverend stiffened. "What the—" He lowered his voice to an angry whisper. "What's she doing down here? We can't let her see him." He moved past 47, Cromwell, and the two armed men, and shouted through the door, "Helen? I'll be right there! Wait for me upstairs!" Wilkins turned to Cromwell. "He's all yours. Hurt him as much as you like, just don't leave any marks. I wanted to watch, but I have to see what that stupid woman wants, and it's almost time for me to pray, goddamn it. Prolong his pain until I return. Then shoot him. Be sure to make it look like you were protecting me."

"No problem, sir," Cromwell said with a grin.

Wilkins slipped out the door and slammed it shut.

47 could have called out and warned her. *Run, Helen! Get out of the building now! The reverend is insane!*

But the job came first. If he had to sacrifice her—and himself—in the imminent detonation, he would. It was no longer possible to keep her from harm. He had failed her, but he would have completed the mission. And that's what counted.

The hitman stole a glance at his watch—11:56.

He turned his head back and forth to the two armed guards. They were standing just beyond his reach. If he jumped at one and attempted a disarming maneuver, the other one would surely shoot him. But if he could somehow get hold of Cromwell's handgun—or his own Silverballer—he might have a chance to take out both men with the split-second timing he had perfected all those years ago during his training at the asylum. He needed to distract them. Talking his way out of the situation wasn't his preferred tactic, but it was worth a shot.

"Everything he said is a lie," 47 told Cromwell.

The man laughed. "You *would* say that."

"So what happened to you, Shipley?"

Cromwell stiffened.

"You *are* Darren Shipley, aren't you?"

"That person doesn't exist anymore. He died in Iraq. Alone. Betrayed by his country's government. My name is Cromwell now."

"But you apparently still have feelings for your sister. In your heart there is still some connection to your former life."

"What do you know about it?" The terrorist gestured with the gun. "Step forward. *Slowly.*" 47 did so. "Now kneel."

The assassin was happy to do so. His Silverballer lay on the floor six feet away. Now he was that much closer to it.

"Lie facedown. Arms stretched out."

The hitman lay prone.

"I assure you, if you attempt to move, my men will drill you full of holes, although you might prefer that to what is about to happen now."

Cromwell then moved away and rolled a flat cart on wheels from behind the column. There was a box on the platform that resembled a large car battery. Wires connected it to a batonlike object. At first 47 thought it was a flashlight, but then he saw the two metal prongs on its bronze-covered end.

The militant picked up the wand and flicked a switch

on the box. The machine hummed. That confirmed 47's alarm that it was a battery containing a rheostat to raise or lower voltage.

"This is a picana, Agent 47," Cromwell said. "It is an illegal device that originated in Latin American countries, specifically for human torture. It uses the same principles as a hotshot—you know, a cattle prod—except that a picana delivers shocks of very high voltage and low current. The voltage is ample enough to cause significant pain, but the low current means that it is less likely to kill you or leave marks on the skin. I'll give you a little taste now. When Charlie returns, we'll really have some fun. We'll strip you, tie you down, and use the picana to abuse all the sensitive areas of your body, and, believe me, there are more than you can possibly imagine when it comes to electric shocks. And the authorities will never know when they perform your autopsy."

With that, Cromwell thrust the prod forward and held it against the back of 47's outstretched hand. The pain was sharp and intense, causing the hitman to involuntarily jerk his arm away.

The terrorist laughed. "Now do you see? Is the situation perfectly clear to you? Imagine what it will be like when you are restrained and can't avoid the agony."

The man poked 47 on his shoulder blade, causing the hitman to roll to his side. Another jab went to a kidney. A further nudge attacked the ribs. Despite the pain, the assassin did his best to rotate his body closer to the handgun.

"Do you feel that? That's what it was like there," Cromwell said. "Iraq, I mean. It was torture. Yes, I was a marine. I believed in America, so I enlisted. I believed in the cause. Charlie taught me that. I found the Will inside me, and that's what it told me to do. I *wanted* to serve my country." Cromwell laughed wryly. "Boy, was

I wrong. It wasn't long before I found myself questioning authority as my squad grew more and more unhappy."

47 couldn't help watching Cromwell's face. The man's
eyes clouded over and he seemed to disappear into a
painful memory, forgetting who he was addressing.
Suddenly the man thrust the picana into the hitman's
lower back, delivering a few seconds of misery. Then he
resumed his reverie.

"My sister was in politics, and I figured my enlistment
would help her. Good PR. That's what Charlie told me,
and I'd do anything for Dana and for Charlie. Reverend
Wilkins taught us that when we were young. We had
lost our parents, and Charlie, well, he became like a
father to us."

There was indeed a darkness that ate at Cromwell's
soul. The man paced back and forth, gesturing with the
picana as if it were a general's sword. The hitman eyed
the handgun, now five feet away. His watch read 11:59.

Three minutes!

47 feigned distress and groaned, rolling a foot closer
to the weapon. Cromwell didn't notice as he continued
his rant. "I'm gonna enjoy killing you. My superior officer was a lot like you. Smug and arrogant and in it
only for the glory. We were ordered to destroy a building that I knew was simply a preschool center. Nothing
but women and young kids inside. But the *lieutenant*
was convinced they were hiding weapons and al-Qaeda
operatives. He ordered me to burn it to the ground."

Cromwell approached 47 and crouched beside him.
He whispered, "So I did what I was told. We were
armed with Mk 153 SMAW rocket launchers. We had
thermobaric novel explosives, SMAW-NEs. We were
loaded and ready to fire at the building. The lieutenant
was trigger-happy, and he gave the order over the radio
to go ahead and fire. But then I saw a woman with a

child in her arms standing by a window. I told the men to wait. I decided to defy orders and investigate. I wanted to be *sure*, you know? So I ran to the building, followed all the rules of entry into a possible hostile space, and it turned out I was right. No one there but frightened women and children."

Cromwell paused, stood, and took a deep breath. 47's watch read 12:00. Was Wilkins in his office for his ritual prayer? What kind of damage would the C4 do to this basement room, which was directly underneath the blast point?

"But the lieutenant couldn't wait. He gave the order to fire. My men knew I was in there, but they followed orders. They fired four rounds of powerful incendiary explosives. The building went up in flames. I lost an arm, my leg was badly injured, and my face was mutilated. But I managed to crawl out the back and run. The women and children weren't so lucky. I had no desire to go back to my so-called fellow marines. The media said I'd died a hero. But no one in the marines admitted it was 'friendly fire.' Hell, it was deliberate!"

The time was 12:01. It was now or never.

"I hid in Iraq and allowed the world to believe I was dead. The only ones who knew were Dana and Charlie. At that point, I hated our government. I hated our policies and our arrogance. So I decided to do something about it. I had money stashed away, but it was Charlie who helped me. He gave me the means to start a new life. I had plastic surgery, made my way back to the States, and became who I am today. Through social-media websites, I tapped into the current dissatisfaction that existed all over the country and invited men to join me. They came by the dozens. Ex-military men, mercenaries, and civilians who simply wanted to make a difference. The New Model Army was born. And, thanks to Charlie's support, we grew and began our assault. We started the New Revolution!"

47 managed to speak. His voice cracked as he forced his mouth to form words. "Darren . . . Did you know . . . Wilkins . . . had your father killed . . . so he could be with your mother?"

Cromwell blinked and slowly turned his head toward his prisoner.

"What the fuck did you say?" Again, a jab of the picana.

47 shouted in agony, then gathered the strength to groan when his tormentor pulled the instrument away. "You know that, right? . . . Wilkins bumped off your father and covered it up—"

Again, the picana. Over and over.

"You lie!"

The fact of the matter was that 47 took a gamble by suggesting the notion. The photos Jade had sent were telling. In the 1973 picture, Wendy Shipley held Wilkins's hand while looking up at him lovingly. The 1974 photo indicated even greater intimacy. The hitman might not have had much experience in relationships, but he knew how to read body language. He would have bet a fortune that Wilkins and Mrs. Shipley had an affair. It was in her expression. Eric Shipley was the clueless, cuckolded husband.

"No! No! I'll kill you!" Cromwell spent the next ten seconds jabbing the picana into different parts of 47's body, plunging knives of anguish through the hitman's senses.

Apparently the hitman had touched a nerve. Perhaps it *was* the truth.

And then the clock struck 12:02.

THIRTY-THREE

When Helen awoke suddenly at 11:25, she was surprised to find herself in bed, completely dressed. Then she remembered that Stan had carried her there. She had drunk a little too much wine and was exhausted to begin with; the combination knocked her right out.

"Stan?"

When he didn't answer, she forced herself to sit up. Was he in the living room? She heard the television, so he must have fallen asleep on the couch. Still a little groggy, Helen managed to stand and leave the bedroom. Sure enough, the TV was on, but Stan wasn't in sight.

"Stan?"

He wasn't in the kitchen either.

At first she thought she should be perturbed at him for leaving, although she was the one who'd fallen asleep on him. But, then again, he'd also shown no interest in kissing or making out or even going to bed with her. He *was* an odd duck, and now that he had left her alone, she wasn't sure what to think about him.

After going to the bathroom and splashing water on her face, she found her cellphone on the coffee table and dialed his number.

"This is Stan. Leave a message."

"Stan, where are you? I woke up and you were gone."

She looked at her watch. "It's eleven thirty-five. Call me back. I'm awake. Sorry I passed out on you. I wish you hadn't left, though. Anyway . . . uh, yeah, call me back."

She sat on the sofa and switched off the TV with the remote.

What was she going to do about him? It was clear to her that she cared a great deal for him, and at first he seemed to share that sentiment toward her. And yet he was a "cold fish" when it came to intimacy. It was as if he didn't know how to be a lover. And after her return from Cyprus he had acted differently. His former warmth toward her had vanished. His attitude this evening was detached and distant. Was there someone else in his life? No, Helen didn't think that was possible. How many hints did she have to drop? Didn't all men want to have sex? She had already ruled out that he might not like women, but, again, that didn't feel right either. She had heard of some people being asexual. Perhaps that was the case with Stan. Whatever it was, there was something in his past that prevented him from letting go and being totally *with* her.

Who *was* Stan Johnson?

Helen considered undressing and going back to bed, but the fog of sleep had lifted. Now she was wide awake. What she really wanted was—

Oh, no.

The idea of shooting heroin suddenly occurred to her. Though she felt the urge from time to time, it had been largely absent for a few years. Now, though, the urge to get high was stronger than ever. Was it the anxiety over Stan that caused it? The last few days had been very stressful. When she was under pressure, whether it was from work or personal matters, she craved the drugs she'd fought so hard to forget.

Think of the Will! The Will inside the soul!

As much as she attempted to block it, the craving was

more powerful than anything she'd experienced since quitting. If she'd possessed some, she would have definitely used it. If she'd had a source to phone, she would have certainly called.

Find the Will! Fight the evil!

She had to get busy. Occupy her mind. Distract herself with something. Anything.

There was all that paperwork still to do up at the mansion. Charlie was probably there, getting ready for his nightly prayer in his office. He was leaving on a campaign trip in the morning. Why not go up the hill and do some work?

Helen returned to the bathroom and freshened her makeup. Then she poured tap water into a cup and drank it. There were tranquilizers in the medicine cabinet, but she didn't like to take them. The side effects were very unpleasant.

What the heck. Stan didn't love her, she'd be a spinster the rest of her life, and she was a drug addict. . . .

She got the bottle of Xanax and took one.

Back in the living room, she checked her mobile. Stan hadn't returned her message. She stuck the phone in her purse, put on a jacket, and left the apartment.

Fall was in full swing. Brown, red, yellow, and golden leaves littered the ground. A chilly breeze spread through Greenhill as Helen walked up the hill to the fence. It wasn't one of her favorite times of the year. Things died in the autumn. It was also the harbinger of the holiday season, which she dreaded. She hated the commercialism and phony "good cheer" that everyone put on. All her life she had been an outcast, a misfit, someone who'd never received a kiss under the mistletoe or had family with which to share presents. No man had ever given her a gift, wrapped and tied with a red bow. She was never invited to Christmas parties. When Helen was in college, strung out on drugs, her roommate flatly told her that she was "no fun," and that's why she was left out of so many social activities.

There *had* been one man. A boy, really. He had introduced her to heroin. *They* had been intimate. *They* were in love. For a while.

Then he overdosed and she fell into the darkest depression. After she dropped out of school, the drugs turned her into a misanthrope nobody wanted to know. Or love.

Why was she dwelling on this? Was she that upset about Stan?

She reached the gate and dug in her purse for the keycard. It wasn't there. Frowning, she opened the bag wider and thoroughly searched it. She could have sworn she'd put it there. It's where she always kept it. Had it fallen out? Was it in her apartment?

Annoyed, she didn't want to walk all the way back to her building, but there was nothing else she could do. Then she noticed one of the night guards patrolling in front of the fence to the west.

"Excuse me!" she called and waved. The guard acknowledged her and hurried to see what she wanted. "I'm sorry, I can't find my keycard. I must have lost it, or it's in my apartment, and I don't want to go back and look. It's cold out. Can you let me in? I want to do some work for Charlie."

"Sure, Miss McAdams," the guard said. She might not have many friends at Greenhill, but nearly everyone knew her. He used his card to unlock the gate, and Helen pushed through. She thanked him and walked up the path. As usual, she took the right fork and hurried up the west side of the mansion. When she got to the employees' entrance, she could have kicked herself.

She didn't have her keycard! Duh!

So Helen knocked. Surely Charlie or someone else was inside and would hear her. She knocked again, louder. And again. Finally, she heard Charlie's voice.

"Just a second!" Then, when he was closer to the door, "Who's there?"

"It's Helen, Charlie. I don't have my key!"

The door opened and the reverend held it for her. "What are you doing here at this time of night?"

"I couldn't sleep, so I decided to catch up on some work. Sorry to disturb you."

"It's not a problem." He let the door go behind them as he ushered her inside. Usually Helen made sure the door was shut tightly and locked, but Wilkins had an arm around her shoulders and escorted her out of the foyer and into the corridor.

"It's almost prayer time," she said.

"Yes, it is. Helen, you really don't have to be here. Why don't you go on back home and try to sleep? You know the Will allows you to drift off when you concentrate properly."

"Charlie, that never works for me. Sorry."

He nodded as if he understood. "No need to apologize. It's like meditation. Some people get it, some don't. You'll learn."

They reached her office. She said, "Call me if you need me."

"I'm going downstairs and don't wish to be disturbed," he said. "But I'll be back up in time to pray."

He left her and moved on. She opened her office door, went inside, shut it behind her, flicked on the lights, and booted up her computer.

Wilkins was leaving on the campaign trail. There was a lot to do. She had to work on itineraries, set up meetings, and make copies of speeches he had written. She needed to coordinate all the traveling logistics with the campaign committee. Helen wasn't sure how much she could do that late at night with most businesses closed, but she would try.

The clock on her wall read 11:51.

Where was Stan?

Once again, she pulled out her mobile and dialed his number.

"This is Stan. Leave a message."

She chose not to do so. Instead, she hung up and focused on her computer monitor. Opening a folder, she stared at the text on the screen and sighed. She didn't feel like working at all. What was wrong with her? Too anxious to sleep and too apathetic to work.

It was all Stan's fault.

The office phone rang. The blinking light indicated it was Charlie's "hot" line, as opposed to the regular office line. He gave the number out only to important people to whom he'd want to talk no matter what. She picked up the receiver.

"Charlie Wilkins's office," she announced.

"Who is this?"

"Helen McAdams, personal assistant to Reverend Wilkins."

The man spoke in a thick accent. "This is Inspector Karopoulos calling from Cyprus. I expected him to answer; I'm sorry. I need to speak to the reverend immediately. It is important."

Charlie didn't want to be disturbed, but Helen thought this was serious enough to interrupt him. She asked the inspector to hold while she fetched him. Helen got up, left the office, and ran to the stairwell.

"Charlie?" she called.

No answer.

She went down to the first landing and faced the basement floor below. There was no doubt the reverend was in the room that was off-limits to everyone but a few people. The storage space for all the alleged treasures.

Louder. "Charlie?"

After a moment, his voice came from behind the closed door. "Helen? I'll be right there! Wait for me upstairs!"

She did as he instructed, ascended to the ground floor, and lingered. Eventually he appeared. There was a strange, wild look in his eyes, and he didn't appear happy.

"What is it?" he snapped.

"Inspector Karopoulos in Cyprus wants you on your hot line. He says it's important."

Wilkins made a face and nodded. "Thank you, Helen. I'll take it in your office, since that's closer, if you don't mind."

"Not at all."

She followed him as he hurried down the corridor to her open door. "Charlie? You haven't seen Stan, have you?"

Wilkins whirled around. "Who?"

"Stan Johnson. You know, my friend? The new maintenance man?"

"Oh, right. Stan. No, I haven't. I'm a little busy, Helen."

He went into the office and shut the door, leaving her in the hallway. She could hear his voice inside but couldn't understand what he was saying. Helen glanced at her watch. It was 11:59. Time for Charlie to pray in his office. Would he miss it? She supposed that it wasn't a hard-and-fast necessity for him. After all, he could always pray at five minutes after the hour, or ten minutes after. What did it matter?

The conversation in her office went on as she patiently waited. She felt awkward standing there. Perhaps she should go to the kitchen and get a cup of coffee or something. Maybe a snack. A candy bar out of the vending machine.

The time was 12:01.

She started to walk away when the door opened and Charlie stepped out. His face was red, as if he was struggling to keep an angry outburst in check.

"Is everything all right, sir?" Helen asked.

"Oh, yes, Helen," he answered through clenched teeth. "Everything is just fine."

And then the clock struck 12:02.

THIRTY-FOUR

*The entire building shook as if a tremendous earth-
quake had struck. The ceiling collapsed in huge chunks
of concrete. The blast so surprised Cromwell that he
dropped the picana and screamed like a baby. In his
mind he was back in Iraq. Back inside that preschool
center as it blew up around him.*

*Despite my weakened state from the torture, I used
that opportunity to leap for my Silverballer, which
would have disappeared, buried under tons of falling
rubble, had I not snatched it and continued to roll
toward the pillar. I was banking on the hope that the
column was acting as a support and that perhaps it
wouldn't tumble, and I was right. Nevertheless, huge
blocks of cinder hit me and showered around Cromwell. I hoped he'd be killed, but he kept on yelling and
moving toward the door. I aimed the Silverballer at
him, but a mass of ceiling dropped between us just as I
squeezed the trigger. Looking back at the entrance, I
saw that the two guards had been crushed to death by
large lumps of concrete. The only way out was by
climbing over the rubble to the door, which, surprisingly, still stood in its frame.*

*Suddenly flames erupted around me. The explosion
had ignited flammable material somewhere in Wilkins's
office or down here, and the whole room became an*

inferno. Once again, I heard Cromwell cry in terror. Fire must've been his Achilles' heel, after his experience in Iraq. I couldn't see him; the room was filled with smoke and dust. It was difficult to breathe. I knew I had to get out of there or I would perish in seconds. I shoved away from the pillar and blindly made my way toward the door. A large amount of wreckage blocked my way, so I scrambled up on top of it. From there I made out a dark human shape scrambling over the mountain of debris in front of the entrance. Cromwell. I pointed the handgun and fired. I was sure I missed as he disappeared on the other side. He was free. I stumbled and tripped off the junk I was on and landed in a patch of flames. My suit caught fire. Too pumped up on adrenaline to notice the pain, I simply rolled out of the blaze into a mound of dust and ceiling particles, which extinguished my burning clothes. I immediately got up and started climbing the ruins in front of the door. Once I made it down the other side, I found myself in the hallway outside the demolished room. I quickly took stock of my body. My clothes were singed and would need replacing, but I hadn't suffered any serious burns. The Silverballer was still in hand. I had survived and was, as they say in America, ready to rumble.

The space to the stairs was cloudy and thick with all that smoke and dust. It was still difficult to breathe. I thought the air would be better on the ground floor. The stairway was undamaged. No place to go but up.

As soon as I reached the top, one of Greenhill's guards rushed past. I swiftly pointed my gun at him, but he kept on running to the south. He was probably intent on finding Wilkins and missed seeing me altogether. I figured he was headed in the right direction, so I followed him. I darted to the corner and looked west. About eight feet away, the same guard was aiming a

Browning 9mm at me! He must have heard me after all.

I dropped to the floor as he fired. The bullet sliced the dusty air above me. In less than a second, I aimed the Silverballer at him with both hands by supporting my elbows on the floor. My two rounds struck the chest and head. Double tap.

On my feet again, I navigated toward the T-intersection to see if Wilkins was in what was left of his office. The air was the worst that close to the blast point. The long corridor was full of even thicker smoke and dust. All that expensive artwork that lined the hallway—ruined. As far as I could tell, there wasn't much left of the south wall of the mansion, and Wilkins's office was completely destroyed. There was absolutely no way a human being could have survived there.

I turned back, reached the T-intersection, and ran into—

Helen and Wilkins. Together.

They appeared frightened. In shock. They seemed disoriented and were coughing a lot but were otherwise unharmed.

I should have raised the Silverballer and fired right then and there. But Helen was standing next to him and was staring at me as if she were looking at a monster. I have to admit that seeing her threw me. I hesitated.

Wilkins pointed at me and shouted, "There he is, Helen! The one I told you about! He's responsible for this! Agent 47! He's a hired assassin from the government!"

I held out my left hand. "Come with me, Helen, I'll get you out of here."

Tears were in her eyes.

"Is it true?" she asked.

"Come on, Helen, there isn't time. You have to get out of here."

She shook her head. "The inspector in Cyprus just confirmed who you are. The bellhop you left tied up in a room identified you from photos. Stan, is it true?"

I saw two guards, way in back of her at the end of the hallway, running toward us. Guns drawn. With my left hand, I instinctually moved in and grabbed her by the wrist—one she had once taken a razor blade to—and pulled her toward me. I raised the Silverballer while forcing her down at my side. Two shots. The guards fell.

I guess that answered her question.

She cried out as if I'd stabbed her in the heart.

Actually, I guess I had done that.

Never mind. Wilkins had already taken off down the hall to the east. Helen wriggled out of my grip and ran west. Both directions led to exits on those sides of the house. Confident that Helen would make it to safety on her own, I chose to run after Wilkins.

The atmosphere was so different outside it was like strapping on an oxygen mask and breathing sweet, fresh air from a tank. Still, I didn't rush out the door without stopping first to see what was waiting for me out there. Sure enough, two more guards were headed my way. I went down on one knee, held the grip with both hands, and fired twice. The guards fell.

I ran out onto the grass.

Wilkins had already made it down to the gate. Helen had crossed from the east side of the mansion to the front and would reach the gate in a few seconds. But I was forced to abort the mission. There was no way I could follow them into the compound. It seemed that the entire population of Greenhill was on the other side of the fence. And a couple of dozen armed men were *charging out of the barn. But I knew who they really were.*

The New Model Army. And Cromwell was there, commanding them to kill me.

So I ran toward the lake. I'd survived in cold water before.

I could do it again.

THIRTY-FIVE

When he jumped into the frigid water, Agent 47 quickly tucked the Silverballer into the waist of his trousers and swam. He swam, knowing his life depended on it. The men on the shore were looking for him, but it was too dark on the water for them to see the escaping figure. He figured they didn't have a spotlight on hand to shine on the surface, or they would have.

It took nearly a half hour to reach a small island in the eastern half of the lake. It was uninhabited. Nothing but trees and rocks. By then the police and fire-department personnel were swarming over Greenhill. 47 could see the lights and hear the sirens, so he still felt too close to the compound for comfort. It wouldn't be long before they sent out boats to look for him. The roads around the shore would be monitored. He was a wanted man. He had tried to kill a presidential candidate.

Badly needing a rest but refusing one, the hitman walked to the eastern side of the island. The opposite shore appeared to be approximately three hundred feet away. He could swim that, no problem, so he did. The assassin hated getting back in the cold water, but what was he going to do when he emerged?

It wasn't as difficult as the first lap. He made it to the bank in five minutes and climbed up. Nothing but dense woods all around. 47 knew that County Road 658 was a couple of miles to the east, through the forest. If he just headed in a straight line, eventually he would hit it. He would worry about what to do next when he got there.

The woods were dark and thick with rough terrain. Several times he thought he heard animals. There were bears and other predators in the forest, and he didn't particularly want to meet any of them. The Silverballer was wet and most likely useless until he had the time to take it apart, dry it out, and clean it. He had faced dangers in his career worse than bears, but it wasn't something he wanted on his résumé.

47 had a good sense of direction. Others would have easily become lost. Whenever trees blocked his path, he went around them but was careful to return to the line he'd been following. After a while he felt an extreme chill. His clothes hadn't dried yet. What he wouldn't give for a cup of hot coffee at that moment.

He trudged on. It wasn't easy but necessary to avoid hypothermia.

It was nearly morning when he finally reached the road. His watch told him it was 5:22. He felt as if three days had gone by since he sat across the dinner table from Helen. Hard to believe that was only the previous evening.

County Road 658, also called Brent Point Road, was a lonely north–south two-laner that wound through the forest, up and down slopes, and connected nothing to nowhere. 47 chose to walk north. At least the going was painless. He was hungry and thirsty but he was in one piece.

The sun rose and the temperature increased slightly. His clothes finally dried, but they were stiff and felt like sheets of ice on his skin. He had been walking for more than an hour when he reached a fork in the road.

County Road 658 continued north. Quarry Road jutted off southwest, toward Greenhill. Best not go that way. 47 stayed on 658.

There were a few houses along the highway there. Nice, expensive homes. The hitman considered picking one, knocking on the door, and forcing the occupants to feed him and give him an automobile. But that was something a desperate man would do. A hardened criminal. 47 wasn't a criminal.

Yeah, right.

Brent Point Road dead-ended at east–west Decatur Road, and it was there that a Virginia State Police car slowly rounded the T-intersection. A silver Dodge Charger. The driver noticed 47 across the street on 658 and slowed even more.

This didn't worry the hitman. He saw it as an *opportunity.*

The vehicle stopped. The red and blue lights flashed and twirled. The patrolman got out of his car, drew his weapon, and leaned over the hood.

"Stop right there! Hands up where I can see them!"

Agent 47 did as he was told.

"Now cross the street. Slowly. Keep your hands in the air!"

The hitman walked across the road and stood on the other side of the car.

"Hands on top. Now!"

Agent 47 looked around the intersection. No pedestrians. No other cars. No witnesses. He put his hands on the patrol car as instructed.

The state trooper moved around the front of the vehicle, his gun still pointed at the killer. "Where's your ID, sir? What pocket do you keep it in?"

"Right front," 47 answered. He could tell the guy was nervous. Good.

"I'm going to frisk you. Then I'm going to reach into

your pocket and get your ID. Don't move. Backup is on the way."

The hitman knew that was a lie. He had watched the officer from the road. The man never picked up his radio. He hadn't had time to call for backup.

The trooper stepped behind 47 and then found himself in a predicament. In order to frisk the suspect, he'd need both hands. If he holstered his weapon, he'd be vulnerable.

"Don't move," he ordered again.

47 found it incomprehensible that the patrolman actually believed his suspect would obey the command. He could have easily disarmed the cop, but the assassin decided to make it simple. The officer did indeed holster the handgun and reach under the hitman's armpits to begin the search. 47 swiftly removed his hands from the car, snatched the man's wrists, and simultaneously delivered a back kick to the officer's right kneecap.

The policeman screamed in agony.

The hitman turned and slugged the trooper hard in the jaw, shutting up his temporarily disabled victim. He then quickly went around the car to the driver's side and opened the latch to the trunk. 47 sprinted back to the unconscious man, picked him up, laid him inside, and shut the lid.

It was a long drive ahead. 47 didn't want any interruptions.

He got in the driver's seat, turned off the flashing lights, and took off north on Decatur. The cop's radio sputtered with bulletins from headquarters. Every few minutes, the operator said, "Be on the lookout for a white male, between six and seven feet tall, bald head, good physical shape. Armed and dangerous. Wanted in connection with terrorist attack at Greenhill Church of Will compound." Along the way, several cars passed him going the opposite way. 47 looked over and saw the officer's hat on the passenger seat. He grabbed it and put it on. It was a fortuitous act, for a minute later another state police car passed him on the road. The driver waved as he went by. 47 returned the greeting.

He took a left on County Road 611, eventually hit Jefferson Davis Highway 1, and then merged onto the interstate toward Washington.

Agent 47 lay in bed in a hotel room at the River Inn on 25th Street NW in Washington, D.C. The room-service meal of a medium-rare steak, potatoes, and steamed vegetables wasn't as good as he'd hoped, but it was satisfying.

It had been a grueling twenty-four hours. He had driven to the Baltimore/Washington Airport to pick up his briefcase from the locker and fresh clothes from an Agency drop point. He ditched the Virginia State Police cruiser in the long-term parking lot and then rented another car. By the time he'd checked into the hotel, it was the evening of the day following his dinner date with Helen.

47 wondered what she was doing. He was certain that she hated him.

He was happy that she was alive, but it didn't matter. The job came first.

He switched on the television to watch the news.

His handiwork was on every channel. The attack on the Greenhill mansion had made international news. Charlie Wilkins had escaped injury. Nine deaths were reported, apparently all security men. The FBI was called in to investigate. Wilkins held a press conference that afternoon and accused President Burdett's government of sending an assassin to Greenhill to kill the one presidential candidate who would "lead the country to greater glory." He blamed the failed attempt on the

CIA. A fairly accurate police sketch of 47 circulated around the globe. Protests by masses of ordinary citizens occurred across the country. Cries for civil war were louder than President Burdett's appeals for calm and denials of involvement.

It was a volatile situation.

There had been no mention in the news reports about the dozens of armed men that had emerged from the barn. 47 suspected that they had left the premises before the police and FBI arrived. Cromwell was most likely in hiding or traveling with his men. And yet the New Model Army struck in retaliation just hours before the hitman checked in to the hotel. The group had attacked CIA headquarters in Langley, Virginia, in a bold maneuver that left eleven federal agents dead. The NMA lost three men, then retreated into the forest and vanished before government reinforcements could arrive.

Agent 47 was now wise to Wilkins. It was all very clear now.

The reverend was obviously in cahoots with Cromwell, the man who was once Darren Shipley. Wilkins had known both Darren and Dana when the Shipleys were young and had forged an unbreakable bond with them. Considering that the children had grown up in the communelike atmosphere of the early Church of Will, they would have been extremely susceptible to his influence. If it was true that their mother had been involved with the man, then that relationship would have been potent. 47 wouldn't have been surprised if Wilkins was the twins' real father. Whatever the case, Wilkins had definitely used the twins for his own means.

By her own admission, Dana had been pushed by the reverend to run for public office, to advance the America First Party and put forward a public face besides his own to indoctrinate the people.

The New Model Army was also Wilkins's tool. Although he claimed not to have any connection to it, it
was he who was really commander-in-chief. Darren
Shipley—Cromwell—simply followed orders and was
fueled by a mad desire to get back at the America he
thought betrayed him.

Wilkins wanted to change the United States to fit his
own ideals. Being a beloved celebrity, television personality, fast-food restaurateur, and leader of the Church of
Will wasn't enough. He had to be president and saturate
Congress with the America First Party, and the election
was only six days away. If he succeeded, then a true
revolution could take place in the United States. Laws
the party didn't like would be changed or overturned,
and new legislation would be enacted. It was an all-too-
familiar scenario, one that had taken place over and
over around the world throughout history. Although
the American population didn't realize it, they were
about to elect a Fascist to office. All it would take was
one more incendiary incident to assure Wilkins's vic-
tory.

Agent 47 was pretty sure he knew when that event
would take place. In two days, Wilkins was holding a
massive rally on the National Mall in Washington,
D.C.; he wanted volunteers from the Church to ride
there on school buses and protest the current administration. Helen would be attending.

The bigger question was: What would that incident be?

The hitman checked his messages and saw that the
Agency had tried several times to reach him. He figured
he should return the call and get it over with. It wasn't
going to be pretty.

It took an unusually long time to be patched through
to Jade, for codes had been changed and security fire-
walls had been strengthened. Only operatives at 47's

level knew how to bypass them—it was just more complicated.

"It's nice to hear that you're alive," she said. "Where are you?"

"D.C."

"Benjamin wants to speak to you. Hold on."

After a few seconds, Travis got on the line. "What the hell happened, 47? What the hell did you *do*?"

"I blew up part of the target's mansion. Unfortunately, the target wasn't in the right place at the time."

"You do realize the mission is a disaster? The client has walked away. He hasn't paid the next installment and I doubt we'll hear from him. We'll probably be forced to give back most of the fee to prevent him from exposing the ICA. And it's *your* fucking fault! Hell, we could have found out who he is if you hadn't blown it."

Agent 47 bristled but kept his temper under control. "What do you mean?"

"Our encryption experts finally traced his last call to the Agency. It came from Greenhill. The client was at Greenhill all along."

That's when it made perfect sense to the hitman. The pieces of the puzzle fell into place.

"Travis. I know who the client is."

"You do? Who?"

"The good reverend himself, Charlie Wilkins."

"What the hell are you talking about?"

"He's the only person at Greenhill who had the clout and means to reach the Agency. He ordered the hit on Dana Linder to advance his own position and put him in place to be president. Then he ordered the hit on himself."

"On himself? Are you crazy?"

"Listen. His plan was to catch me in the act before the hit was carried out. That was why we had to wait for the green light. He wanted to kill *me* before I killed *him*, and then he could blame the current administration and the CIA for the assassination attempt too, right on the heels of killing Linder. It would give him even more sympathy and support from the American public and increase his chances of becoming president. Calling the hit on himself would also clear him of suspicion for the assassination of Linder, in case it was ever traced back to us. That phony colonel, Bruce Ashton, tried to kill me first against Wilkins's orders. When that didn't work, Wilkins gave you the go-ahead for me to hit him, and Cromwell and his New Model Army were supposed to stop me. They failed. Now he's running scared and is planning some kind of catastrophe four days before the election. At a campaign rally in D.C."

Travis was silent on the other end.

"Well, Travis?"

"This is completely mad, 47."

"Charlie Wilkins *is* mad. And I intend to carry out the hit. I'm going to finish the job I started."

THIRTY-SIX

A day passed.

I rested. I trained. I returned to the land of the living. Or maybe it's the land of the dead, considering what I do for a "living."

I cleaned and oiled the Silverballer that took a bath in Aquia Lake. I took both weapons to a shooting range in D.C. and made sure they were up to snuff.

All remnants of the drug addiction were gone. No more bad dreams. I hadn't seen Death or felt his icy-cold breath on my neck. I still hadn't figured out who he was. It was like when something was on the tip of your tongue. I felt like I knew his identity, somewhere in the recesses of my mind—and that disturbed me. Nevertheless, I hadn't felt this good since before the incident in Nepal, just over a year ago.

Travis told me they were closing in on Diana. The Agency might have found her. It appeared that would be my next assignment. But I had to finish this one first. Travis told me to go ahead and complete the hit on Wilkins, because the guy knew too much about the Agency. I didn't care. It was a matter of principle. For me, it was personal. Charlie Wilkins tried to trick me and then kill me. Normally I was not someone who went after a target simply for revenge or because I held some kind of grudge. That wasn't me. But this time, it was different. I couldn't explain why, and I didn't think there was a psychiatrist in the world who could. Maybe it had something to do with Helen. During the course of the mission, I came close to being a "normal" person. At least, closer than I ever had before. Whatever that meant. For the first time in my life I entered the personal sphere of another human being—a woman, no less—and became part of her existence. And she did the same thing to me. I wanted to keep my promise that I'd do my best to make sure no harm came to her.

And as long as she was around Charlie Wilkins, she was in danger.

I also believed the so-called reverend was a threat not only to the United States but to the rest of the world. If he gained control of America, there would be a domino effect across the globe. Alliances would change. The international economy would splinter and collapse. Wars would be fought.

That was *unacceptable.*

It had happened too many times throughout history. Mankind never learned from its mistakes, but I did.

Wilkins had to be stopped.

The National Mall was an impressive site, even for a jaded and nonpolitical person such as myself. All those magnificent sculptures and statues and plaques and buildings built to honor the dead. I often wondered why nothing was ever erected to honor the living. Wasn't it more important and more meaningful to be alive?

This, coming from a man whose hands would always have blood on them.

Thousands of people turned out for Wilkins's afternoon campaign rally. The mall was packed. Police were all over the place. The National Guard lined the streets.

The authorities attempted to keep the supporters separated from the protesters, but they weren't doing a very good job. Even before I arrived on the scene, there had been several arrests; people had gotten into arguments and started brawling. I felt the tension as the taxi I was in approached the site. The driver couldn't get near, so I had to get out and walk from the Smithsonian area. All traffic had been halted for blocks around the mall. The masses spilled out onto the avenues and spread in all directions. I'd never seen anything like it. This place was a powder keg ready for the spark.

I didn't bother with a disguise. I wore my black suit. White shirt. Red tie. Armed with both Silverballers. Briefcase in hand.

Agent 47, the hitman, was back.

I walked right past the police line. No one paid any attention to me. The officers were all focused on the crowd, looking for troublemakers. I guess I must have been just another businessman to them.

The action was set to take place on a portable stage that had been built southwest of the Washington Memorial Driveway, a circular road surrounding the monument. A large east–west sidewalk was directly in front of the stage, which faced north so that Wilkins's throng of admirers could have enough room—barely—to see and hear him speak. A huge banner spread across the top of the proscenium shouted: WILKINS–BAINES! *The reverend had chosen an America First Party senator named Marshall Baines to be his running mate. The stage appeared to be pretty flimsy. Made of wood, canvas, and some curtains. A limousine was parked behind it. I was sure the reverend was inside, waiting for his big moment.*

The naysayers were relegated to the side of the mall east of the monument. Police sawhorses created a north–south line dissecting the mall. There was no question that the supporters outnumbered the protesters by the thousands. It was almost comical that there were also food and drink vendors stationed around the mall. Heaven forbid that the maniacs became thirsty or hungry.

Lots of people held signs and banners. They read: America First Party! Wilkins for President! Down with Burdett! The CIA are Terrorists! Impeach Burdett! Revolution NOW! The Rebellion is HERE! Wilkins/Baines! And, my favorite, Wilkins Is a Survivor! We'd see about that. A lot of his campaign propaganda capitalized on the fact that he had endured more than one assassination attempt and therefore was somehow divine.

I spotted the three yellow school buses on the north side of the mall. My instincts told me that, whatever Wilkins had planned, it would involve those Church members who'd traveled from Greenhill to Washington. I wondered if I would see Helen. I wondered how I would react. I wondered if she would see me and how she would respond.

So I pushed and shoved and wormed my way through the crowd. Since it was chilly—it was November 1, after all—everyone wore coats. At one point, I passed a guy wearing a black robe and hood. He turned to me, and I would have sworn he was Death, standing right there in front of me. The Faceless One. My old nemesis. It startled me and I felt a rush of adrenaline. But I blinked and it turned out it was just some guy who had painted his face white and was "acting" the part of the stereotypical persona of Death. He held a fake scythe, to which a sign was attached. It read: America Is Dead! Long Live America! Whatever that meant.

I made it to the area where the buses were parked,

*right there on the grass. Standing among a horde of
people, I scanned the scene. I recognized several members from Greenhill, all holding protest signs and sing-
ing Church songs. Helen was with them. She was
unavoidable. She wore a bright blouse. I felt a twinge
of pain in my chest when I saw her.*

*She looked beautiful. But she also appeared nervous
and frightened.*

I made sure she didn't see me.

*Just north of the school buses, on Constitution Ave-
nue, there were several National Guard trucks parked
at the curb. Four of them. I couldn't tell if anyone was
inside.*

*The angry shouts of an anti-Wilkins group were dis-
turbing. They were clustered nearby, although a few
policemen kept them behind a line of barricades. They
taunted the Church members, almost as if they were
looking for a fight. Not surprisingly, TV crews from all
the major stations had cameras pointed at them and
everywhere else.*

*So far, though, I hadn't seen anything that might be a
harbinger of Wilkins's plan. Not knowing what he was
going to do was a disadvantage, of course, but I could
usually spot telltale signs of mischief. Everything seemed
to be exactly what he'd advertised. He'd brought along
a small group of his most ardent followers to be a visual aide to his propaganda, and there was nothing else
sinister about it. I didn't think I was wrong about the
guy, but I almost felt disappointed.*

*Music began, blasted throughout the mall by large
speakers mounted near the stage. It was then I thought
it odd that Wilkins had placed his Church people so far
away, at the very back of the crowd. From there the
stage was probably a thousand feet or more to the
south. Why the separation?*

It was some high school band on the stage, playing American patriotic songs, similar to the ones played at Dana Linder's rally. Déjà vu.

After a ten-minute overture, the vice presidential candidate, Baines, took the stage and addressed the audience. He was met with an enthusiastic ovation.

"I'm not going to spend too much time up here," he said. He was a squirrelly type, what you'd expect a bookworm nerd to look like. Clark Kent without the Superman persona to back him up. A ninety-eight-pound weakling. A real nobody. "I know you all are anxious to get to the main event. When I was young and went to rock concerts, I always hated when there was an opening act before the band I paid money to see. So, without further ado, let me introduce to you the next President of the United States, the one and only Reverend Charlie Wilkins!"

The entire mall erupted in a tumultuous roar. It was deafening. I could have sworn the ground shook. The attendees from the other side were completely crushed by the enthusiasm. The excitement was impossible to ignore. I didn't care one whit about the election, and yet the thrill was contagious. I craned my neck to get a better view of the stage.

My target stepped into view. He was a tiny dot of a figure from where I was standing, but he still exuded a massive aura. His charisma could be felt even at the north end of the mall. It was uncanny. It was no wonder some people thought he was the Second Coming.

It took nearly another ten minutes for the crowd to be quiet. Wilkins kept pleading for people to settle down, but his voice was drowned out by the cacophony. Eventually, though, he was able to talk. His smooth, musical voice floated over the mall and spread an unexpected tranquillity over the place. It was as if the very act of his speaking did something magical to the audience. I didn't buy it for one second, but I understood why he was well loved by the sheep that lived in America.

"Greetings, my fellow Americans!"

Cheers.

"Welcome to the beginning of the New Age!"

Roars.

"The Rebellion is now!"

Frenzy.

Then—it happened. Almost as if it were on cue, and I suppose it was.

As soon as Wilkins had started to talk, dozens of men dressed in National Guard uniforms piled out of the back of the trucks parked behind the school buses. They immediately organized into ranks and stood at attention.

There was something familiar about them.

My heart started to pound. I recognized some of the faces. Men from Greenhill. The ones that stormed out of the barn. They were wearing the uniforms I'd seen on the racks. These were not really National Guardsmen.

They were the New Model Army.

And then their leader appeared. Limping. He shouted a command I couldn't understand, but it was obvious to me who he was.

Cromwell.

Before I could move, before I could do a single, solitary thing, the NMA attacked the civilians. They drew weapons and started firing at the unarmed, innocent, but misguided followers of Charlie Wilkins. When the people realized what was happening, many of them screamed and ran. The "Guard" started picking them off, one by one. Some of the militant soldiers drew clubs and, Gestapo-style, beat the supporters who had tripped or cowered before being shot.

It was horrific.

Within moments the throng caught on to what was happening. Even the real police and National Guard were slow to react.

Then it was mass chaos. Gunshots everywhere. Panic. A stampede.

In sixty seconds, the National Mall had become a death trap for thousands of human beings, and I was caught in the middle.

One could barely hear Wilkins, calling from the stage for everyone to keep calm. It was certainly too late for that. The place had erupted in mass hysteria.

It was all so clear now. The headlines would read: NATIONAL GUARD FIRES ON CHURCH OF WILL MEMBERS AT RALLY! *The man was sacrificing his own people in the name of gaining sympathy and support for the election.*

Unbelievable.

I drew both Silverballers, one in each hand, and started picking off New Model Army soldiers. But there were so many civilians running about that it was difficult to get clear shots at the correct targets.

Then I saw her on the ground. Helen. She had fallen and was attempting to crawl to safety. She was about to be trampled. Killed. Right in front of my eyes.

I holstered one weapon and ran to her, shoving and punching anyone who was an obstacle. Before I reached her, I was forced to blow away an NMA guy who blocked my path. The man fell on top of her, so I roughly grabbed him by the shirt collar and pulled him off. I then crouched beside her and took her hand.

"Helen."

She looked at me with confused, terrified eyes. She didn't know who I was, probably because she hadn't expected to see me there. I was a face that didn't belong.

"It's me, Helen. I need to get you to safety. Can you stand?"

Then her expression changed. Naked fury boiled to the surface.

"YOU!" she cried.

The ferocity shocked me.

"This is all your doing!" she spat.

THIRTY-SEVEN

Helen jerked her hand out of 47's grasp and leaped to her feet. "Get away from me!"

The hitman clasped her by the waist to keep her from running. "Stay with me! It's not safe to—"

He pointed the Silverballer over her shoulder and fired at three New Model Army men headed in their direction. Two militants dropped, but one was still alive; although wounded, he crouched and took aim at 47 with an assault rifle that would have mowed down Helen and the assassin. 47 shoved Helen away, spun, and blasted a hole through the man's head. By then the immediate space around 47 was crowded with people running and dodging bullets. He turned to take Helen's hand again, but she had fled into the multitude.

"Helen!"

She slipped through a clump of Church members who were rushing toward him with terrified, panicked expressions on their faces. NMA soldiers behind them fired, and several victims fell to the grass. Enraged, 47 drew his second Silverballer and fought two-handed. He was forced to dart about to avoid being hit, but he managed to wound or kill six men in the space of three seconds. Then he looked back but couldn't see Helen anywhere.

Sirens blasted throughout the mall. The D.C. police

had bolted into action, but it was unclear to them what the hell was going on. If the National Guard was shooting at civilians, then their targets must have done something terribly wrong. *They* began to chase down the Church members too, without realizing the phony Guardsmen were the enemy. Meanwhile, the *real* National Guard was busy all over the mall, attempting to control the mad dash of humanity trying to escape the mêlée. Confusion and pandemonium reigned, producing a fog of misinterpretation of every single action. The result was that many more rally attendees besides the Greenhill volunteers were being attacked, wounded, or killed.

The tear gas came next. Grenades sailed through the sky in arcs, landing amid clusters of civilians.

The disaster was completely out of control.

Agent 47 frantically searched for Helen while simultaneously defending himself and aggressively attacking the enemy. It was ultimately terribly difficult to pinpoint which Guardsmen were NMA men. Washington city police now mixed with them, firing blindly at uncertain targets. One D.C. policeman spotted 47 wielding two weapons, took aim, and fired, clipping the outside of 47's right thigh. The assassin fell and rolled to his stomach, placed his elbows on the ground, and instinctively blasted the patrolman with both barrels. He hadn't wanted to waste bullets, but the situation had become so perverse that it was impossible to keep anything straight. The blanket of cloudy gas made visibility even worse.

While on the ground, the assassin took a few seconds to examine his leg. The wound was superficial but would most likely need a few stitches. 47 got to his feet, winced at the pain, and rejoined the mayhem. Then, out of the corner of his eye, a moving blue blur flashed through the smoke.

Helen's blouse. Twenty-five feet away.

"Helen!"

She turned to him. He held out his hand, but she hesitated.

"It's all right, Helen!"

Terrified, she knew of nothing else to do. Helen ran to him.

But gunshots echoed through the murky air and bullets littered the ground between the couple. Helen's body jerked and she faltered. Her eyes grew wide in shock.

"No!"

She fell forward and collapsed on the grass.

Agent 47 fired both Silverballers at the two New Model Army men who were responsible for the barrage. Bulletproof vests protected their torsos but not their faces—47 hit the targets dead-on.

Helen rolled and lay on her back. 47 crouched beside her, laid his guns on the ground, and took her hands. Her blouse was covered in crimson wetness, and her eyes were glazed over, focused on the sky. Her breathing was labored. The hitman saw that she had been shot through the lungs, and he knew she wouldn't survive.

"Helen," he whispered.

She choked as blood gushed from her mouth. 47 rolled her to the side, but the maneuver was useless. She had maybe a minute of agony left before she was gone. The hitman chose to spare her that torment. He picked up one Silverballer and held the barrel to her chest, exactly in position over her heart.

"Helen, I'm sorry."

For once, Agent 47 squeezed the trigger as an act of compassion.

He wasn't sure how long he stayed at her side. It might have been a few seconds, or it could have been ten minutes. The turmoil raged around him, but he shut it out for those precious moments. Then he reached out with a bloody hand and closed her eyelids.

The hitman retrieved the other weapon and stood.

Now he was *really* angry.

It didn't matter if they were authentic National Guardsmen or the New Model Army in disguise. 47 started blasting at anyone wearing the uniform. He carried extra magazines in his jacket pocket, and within the next five minutes the hitman went through six of them. Ejecting a used magazine and inserting a new one took all of 1.6 seconds, a feat he'd learned when he was only twelve years old.

47 knew the best strategy was to keep moving; thus, in the heat of battle, he found himself moving backward, heading north toward the school buses. It was there that he encountered Cromwell. The man saw him and aimed an M16, the standard issue for the U.S. Marines, directly at 47. The assassin leaped sideways as the militant spray-fired, hitting several innocent people who were cowering near the buses. He completely missed the hitman. 47 rolled onto his back and pointed his weapons backward over his head for a rapid-fire assault at Cromwell, but the man had already jumped into the open door of one of the buses and shut it. The vehicle pulled out of its space just as 47 got to his feet. Cromwell drove the bus like a maniac, turned south, and mowed over anyone in his way.

There was only one thing to do. Agent 47 bolted into one of the other buses. Gratified to find the keys in the ignition, he used the manual handle to close the door, revved the engine, and took off after the first bus.

Both vehicles had been riddled with bullets, but the tires were sound. Cromwell had a good lead, but 47 quickly switched gears and slammed the gas pedal to the floor. Both drivers were forced to swerve and dodge masses of pedestrians, but Cromwell took less care—

his bus invariably hit horrific-sounding bumps as it zoomed across the mall.

At last 47 caught up to Cromwell. He held steady on his prey's left side as both buses sped neck and neck. The militant turned to grimace at his pursuer through his window, intent on making it to the stage first. 47 grabbed the manual handle and opened his door. Then, with his left hand on the steering wheel and a Silverballer in his right, the assassin carefully aimed the gun and squeezed the trigger. The bullet went through the open door and shattered the driver's window of the other bus. Cromwell's head exploded as the slug penetrated the man's skull and exited the other side.

The militant's bus swerved wildly out of control and veered to the mall's western edge. Police unloaded a firestorm of ammunition at it, not realizing the driver was already dead. The bus made a final careen, tipped over thirty degrees, and plowed into a food vendor's stand. The vehicle crashed onto its side and slid another twenty feet before it came to a screeching, sickening halt.

Agent 47 ignored all that and focused on getting Wilkins. He headed full speed toward the stage. Crowds parted like the Red Sea in front of him as he blasted the bus's horn.

Charlie Wilkins stood frozen on the stage, watching with revulsion what he had wrought.

Oh Lord, I didn't mean for it to be like this!

The plan had been for Cromwell and his men to shoot a few of the Church members, disappear into the crowd to mingle with the real National Guard, and eventually get away to safety. But Cromwell got carried away. The man who was once an American hero—he had attempted to save lives in Iraq—had become a monster willing to massacre his own countrymen. He had ordered the New Model Army to slaughter everyone in sight. Just as Darren Shipley had lost any semblance of humanity, Wilkins, too, had fallen into depravity.

And it had become . . . *this.*

"Charlie! Get down!"

Wilkins thought he heard a voice calling him, but he wasn't sure. He kept staring at the carnage that spread across the mall in front of him. And then there were the two school buses. One crashed; who was driving it? The other one—it was speeding straight at him, on a collision course with the stage.

"Reverend!"

Wilkins looked down. Mitch Carson was on the ground, his hands out.

"Jump, damn it! Jump! We can take the limo!"

For the first time in his life, the Church leader couldn't speak. He was immobile. Wilkins reached into his soul to find the Will, but it wasn't there. Everything he had learned, all he had taught, was nothing but a void.

The Will had failed him.

Finally, Carson grabbed Wilkins's ankles and jerked. The reverend fell on his back, which jolted him to his senses. Carson continued to pull the man's legs until he had the reverend on the stage apron.

"Come *on*, Charlie!"

Wilkins, dazed and in shock, nodded and whispered, "Show me where to go."

Carson helped him to the ground and led him by the arm around the side of the stage. They ran to the limousine, the doors of which were already open. Wilkins ducked into the back while Carson got in the driver's seat. The doors slammed shut, and they were off. Carson turned the car around and drove south toward the edge of the mall and Independence Avenue.

* * *

Agent 47 lost sight of the reverend, but he also knew the man's limousine was behind the stage. There was no time to steer around the flimsy structure. The bus was sturdy enough. He hoped.

Fifty feet until impact.

The hitman glanced in the right side mirror. Police vehicles were hot on his tail, lights flashing.

Thirty feet.

He glanced in the left side mirror.

The Faceless One stared back. Death.

47 averted his eyes and stared straight ahead.

Ten feet.

Two feet.

The bus tore into the stage, ripping right through it as if it were made of paper. The sides collapsed and the WILKINS–BAINES! banner floated down and crumpled limply on top of the wreckage. The police cars were forced to swerve to the right and left to avoid hitting the ruins.

And the chase continued, with the limousine in front and 47's bus trailing closely behind.

THIRTY-EIGHT

The limo shot south, jumped the sidewalk, and tore onto Independence Avenue, on the westbound-only side. Luckily, traffic had been halted there due to the rally, but police cars and other emergency vehicles lined the road. Instead of turning the limo and following the avenue west, though, Carson navigated between a fire truck and an ambulance, dissected the street, and continued south, jumping onto the grass again.

"What the hell are you doing?" shouted Wilkins from the backseat.

"I know a way out!" the driver yelled.

The limo cut between trees and then slammed hard onto westbound Maine Avenue SW.

"You're going to kill us!" the reverend screamed.

"Shut the fuck up, Charlie!"

The car was back on the grass, still pointed south. A wide-open patch of grass and trees lay between them and eastbound Independence Avenue, which had *not* been closed to traffic.

Behind them, Agent 47 tightly gripped the bus's steering wheel as the heavy vehicle bounced and bumped across westbound Independence Avenue, over the grass, and dissected Maine Avenue. Despite the siren-shrieking police cars behind him, he was intent on staying with his prey.

For a moment he imagined ending his days on earth in a hail of bullets from law-enforcement personnel. Even if he did catch up to Wilkins and manage to kill the man, how would he get away from the police? Hundreds were after him. If this was to be the day he died, then so be it. He would shuffle off this mortal coil with the knowledge that he had done his duty, completed the assignment, and rid the world of a nasty and dangerous criminal. What more could he ask for?

The love of a woman?

No. That was impossible. He'd almost had that and he intentionally rejected it. The flirtation with a normal relationship had been a learning experience and one that he would treasure for the rest of his life, but it wasn't for him. Not for a man who constantly remained one step ahead of Death, the Faceless One whose identity 47 still had to expose.

The bus approached eastbound Independence Avenue, closing the distance between it and the limo, which was now fifty yards ahead. The hitman noted the heavy traffic on the road and realized they'd never get across without a major collision. He figured the driver planned to merge into traffic and drive east with the flow. It would be a difficult maneuver, but the limo could do it.

The bus would not be so accommodating. It was too big and cumbersome. 47 would be forced to slow considerably in order to do so, and by then the police would be on top of him and the limo would be long gone.

Whatever.

The assassin kept his foot on the pedal and stayed the course.

* * *

"Are you *mad*? You're going to kill us!" Wilkins shouted again.

"Seriously, shut the fuck up, Charlie!" Carson screamed.

The Greenhill employee knew it would be a do-or-die maneuver. The oncoming traffic on Independence Avenue was heavy and fast, with no breaks in the lines of cars and trucks. Carson's only hope was that the other drivers would see the limousine ripping through the grass, followed by a huge yellow school bus and dozens of police cars with sirens blaring. Surely they would stop!

The car approached the road at a speed of seventy miles per hour.

"Hold on, Charlie!" Carson commanded. The reverend braced himself.

And then they were there.

The limousine hopped the curb and dropped onto the avenue as Carson spun the wheel to change directions—

—and a U-Haul truck slammed ferociously into the vehicle.

Then an SUV plowed into the truck.

Three passenger cars collided with one another while attempting to avoid the catastrophe.

The pileup dominoed down the line as horns blasted, tires screeched, and an ugly, crunching, crashing cacophony topped the police sirens in decibels.

The limousine flipped and rolled once, twice, three times—before it slid, upside down, a hundred feet along the road and came to a stop.

Charlie Wilkins, secure in a seat belt, had hit his head on the window. At first he thought he was dead, for the world was topsy-turvy. It took him a moment to realize that the limo was upside down. He took stock of his body. There was a lot of blood, but he could move his arms and legs.

He was alive.

"Mitch?" he called.

The same could not be said for Carson. The driver slumped in his seat at an obscene angle. The man's face was completely crimson.

Then Wilkins remembered what was happening. He heard the sirens, looked toward the National Mall, and saw the yellow bus about to jump the curb and come crashing down on the road.

The Agency's hitman was almost upon him.

Wilkins struggled to unbuckle his seat belt, kicked the door open, and crawled out of the wreckage. As he stood, the earth spun and he almost collapsed. But the sight of the bus, now plowing through other wrecked vehicles and heading toward the limo, motivated him to move.

He ran south toward the Tidal Basin.

Agent 47 witnessed the horrific pileup but didn't slow down. The bus entered the foray at full speed, barely dodging the ruined vehicles and adding insult to injury.

Stay on target.

The hitman turned the steering wheel sharply toward the east, almost overturning the bus. Two wheels lifted off the ground but then slammed heavily back on the asphalt. The overturned limousine lay a hundred yards ahead on the highway. 47 saw a man emerge from the wreckage and stagger.

Wilkins. Still alive.

But not for long.

The man saw the bus bearing down on him, and he ran south off the road and onto the grass. He was headed for a group of trees that stood between the avenue and the water. 47 couldn't allow him to get that far, for the trees would act as obstacles and prevent the bus from following the reverend. The assassin had to head him off; luckily, the bus was faster than a running man.

47 pulled the bus in a curve, around and in front of Wilkins, so that the man's route was blocked. The hitman continued the pursuit, this time chasing the reverend straight for the basin.

Wilkins was out of breath and in pain.

But the Supreme One would stop this attack! Charlie Wilkins was not destined to end his time on earth like this!

Find the Will! You can do it!

But the Will had deserted him.

Stop the bus! Where is the Will? Do it!

When nothing happened, the reverend cursed at the sky and then snapped back to reality. He had to get out of there. A paddleboat-rental facility was located farther southeast along the shore. The parking lot for the attraction was now between Wilkins and the basin. Many cars had taken up slots and therefore created yet another barrier for the bus. That was promising, so the reverend ran through the lot. But then he found himself dead-ended at the bank. What next? He could run along the shore to the boathouse. That was it. He would be safe there. He'd find a policeman or somebody who would protect him from the madman on his heels.

The Supreme One would intervene.

Wouldn't he?

It was as if Agent 47 had put on blinders. Nothing in his peripheral vision was significant. The crosshairs were on Charlie Wilkins as the man stood on the basin shore like a deer caught in the headlights.

Finish the job.

The assassin didn't let up on the gas. The bus was a locomotive, barreling across the grass and into the parking lot. The yellow juggernaut crashed through several parked vehicles, catapulting them in opposite directions as if they were insects. Now nothing stood in the way of the hitman and his target.

Wilkins dropped to his knees and folded his hands in front of him.

He was praying.

How's that working out for you? 47 thought.

For the assassin, the last two seconds stretched into a time slip. The fast-paced, nonstop action suddenly switched to slow motion. All sounds ceased and were replaced by a vacuum. Agent 47 was aware only of his own heartbeat as it pounded in his chest and echoed in his brain.

He locked eyes with Wilkins. For those brief moments, the two adversaries understood each other. 47 saw that the confidence the reverend usually displayed was gone. In its place were fear, despair, and the realization that he had lost. Wilkins had lost his faith and it was replaced by the hand of Death.

The man opened his mouth to scream, but it was too late.

This was it.

The bus broke through the railing, sailed into the air six feet off the ground, and then dropped in an arc. The behemoth's front end smashed into Wilkins with tremendous force and carried his body fifty feet over the water; then the vehicle pierced the surface and disappeared into the dark green-brown murkiness.

* * *

Emergency crews worked feverishly for an hour to find Reverend Wilkins. Scuba divers finally recovered the battered body and brought it ashore, where it was then taken to the city morgue for an official autopsy.

Area hospitals were overwhelmed by the influx of wounded rally attendees. It was too early to tabulate the number of deaths.

Some of the New Model Army men who were arrested had already begun to talk. The truth of what happened was going to come out.

The school bus was pulled out of the water and thoroughly examined by the FBI. There was no trace of the driver. Divers continued to search the basin bottom and found a lot of garbage, broken bottles, a couple of old tires, and other odd items, but they uncovered no other corpses. One curious retrieved item, which investigators didn't attribute to the events of November 1, was an empty briefcase bearing a strange fleur-de-lis insignia on its exterior.

A few witnesses reported that it had all happened so quickly that they never saw the man driving the bus. Even more onlookers claimed that *no one* was at the wheel—that the figure in the driver's seat was some kind of "faceless shadow." At any rate, the person who killed Charlie Wilkins had vanished.

It was just one more mystery added to a list of many regarding that fateful day in Washington, D.C.

THIRTY-NINE

The *Jean Danjou II* gently rocked at anchor off the coast of Sardinia. She had spent the last week island-hopping, perpetuating the pretense that the yacht was owned by a wealthy tycoon who had nothing better to do than sail around the Mediterranean for no reason at all.

Deep within the ship's bowels, however, it was business as usual in the Agency's command center. At least six different operations were active around the globe. Handlers monitored their assassins' progress every step of the way. Managers initiated contracts with clients and supervised the handlers. The money poured in to the ICA's coffers. Personnel were paid, expenses were met, and life—and death—went on.

Benjamin Travis sat in his cabin/office studying the latest reports from America.

What a mess . . .

He hadn't slept, had a cranium-busting headache, and was fighting a cold. On top of that, upper management was pressuring him for an update on his pet project and demanding answers for what was perceived as a monumental screwup in Washington, D.C.

The Agency's top assassin was missing. No one knew if Agent 47 was alive or dead. Travis knew the operative well enough to believe that the hitman had gone into hiding. Again. Since law-enforcement authorities in the States had failed to recover a body in D.C.'s Tidal Basin, it could only mean that 47 had indeed escaped and was holed up somewhere, biding his time.

The fact of the matter was that the ICA's greatest killer had succeeded against all odds. No one could have pulled off the spectacular hit on Charlie Wilkins. Sure, there was a tremendous amount of collateral damage. That was unfortunate but, given the circumstances, unavoidable. That kind of thing came with the territory. Nevertheless, the hitman had proven that he was still at the top of his game.

Now if they could only find him, bring him in, debrief, and move on to the next stage.

Travis was more concerned about the Diana Burnwood situation. Until the traitorous bitch was located, his pet project was in jeopardy. Upper management was breathing down his neck. Where was the money going? Where were the results? Why was he being so secretive?

He didn't want to tell them the truth. Travis couldn't reveal what Burnwood had done. So far only a few select individuals knew about it, and that was a few too many. Sooner or later, management would find out, and Travis's head would roll. Until then, he would work continuously on damage control, spin tales, stall reports, and wait with frustration as Jade did her magic. The lead to Burnwood's whereabouts in the midwestern United States seemed promising at first, but the trail had gone cold. Travis had given his assistant a severe reprimand, which the stoic woman brushed off as just another of her boss's outbursts. Jade was one tough customer. He knew that someday she would have his job if he didn't watch out.

The manager stood, rubbed his weary red eyes, and moved to the stand where he kept a coffeemaker. He poured a cup and swigged it down, black. He'd consumed so much caffeine in the past several days that he had the shakes.

Travis considered bailing. Pack a bag, get off at the next island, and try to disappear. If Burnwood wasn't found soon, then the shit would indeed hit the fan. No one was simply fired from the Agency. They didn't hand out a pink slip and severance package. Failure had far more serious consequences. He wouldn't be able to just revamp a résumé and go knocking on doors for new employment. It didn't work that way in the ICA.

To be an employee for the Agency, you put your life on the line. It's why you were paid the big bucks.

There was a knock on the cabin door.

"Yeah?"

It opened to reveal his assistant, looking marvelous as usual in her sexy business suit, glasses, and high heels. Travis often fantasized about nailing Jade in a moment of unbridled passion, but he knew it would never happen.

Dream on, Travis, he thought to himself.

"What is it?" he asked.

There was a hint of a smile on her face.

"What?"

"You'd better be ready to kiss my ass," Jade said.

He almost snapped at her, but Travis took a breath and calmly replied, "I really don't have time for this. What do you want?"

"You'll have time for *this*. We found her."

Travis blinked. "What?"

"Burnwood. We got her. She's in Illinois, just like I thought. We know exactly where she is. And she's got the package with her."

He wanted to kiss the woman, but Travis refrained. "That's excellent news."

"I thought it would make your day."

"It does. Now you know what your next priority is."

"Find Agent 47."

"Precisely."

She nodded, left the cabin, and closed the door.

Benjamin Travis sighed with relief, went to his bunk, and lay down.

He was finally able to sleep.

FORTY

The sun was always hot and bright in the "sophisticated metropolitan capital of Guadalajara," as the travel brochures liked to describe it.

Sitting in the shade of the outdoor bar at the Hotel Universo, I sipped cold ice water and relished the fresh, warm air. I was content to do nothing, and I'd practiced that pleasurable activity for a month.

I felt fine. The gunshot wound on my right thigh was healing nicely. The oxycodone was completely out of my system, and I had no desire to ever pop a pill again. It felt wonderful to sleep late every morning and indulge myself with decadently expensive meals. Except for the daily exercises that I'd performed habitually since I was a child, I absolutely refused to do anything constructive.

The Agency was trying to reach me; I knew that. I'd contact them in due time. Luckily, they were unaware of this hideaway in Guadalajara. It was a necessary destination after the events in Washington. I needed a new briefcase, and my arms dealer in the city was the only man I trusted to accurately re-create it—just as the guy had done nearly a year ago. Some might say it was nothing short of miraculous that I managed to escape the States with both Silverballers and my Fiberwire. The briefcase was more problematic, so I had to ditch it in the Tidal Basin.

I owed my survival to three things: my physical prowess, which I'd always maintained, except during that period a few months ago when I was a drug addict; what Ort-Meyer used to call "tenacity"; and, well, luck.

Just before the school bus had crashed into the water, I filled my lungs with as much air as they could hold. As soon as the vehicle was submerged, I swam out the door, with the Silverballers tucked into the waist of my trousers. I dropped the briefcase on the basin floor and swam toward that paddleboat place. I knew it was there. I'd mapped out all possible escape routes beforehand.

I didn't come up for air for nearly five minutes. By then I was at the pier where the little boats were docked. It was easy to steal one, for the attention of every person in the facility was focused on the goings-on farther northwest, where all the action was. No one noticed me paddling away and eventually setting shore near the Titanic Memorial at the southern end of the long lake. I rested and dried off there among the trees and then walked along P Street until I found a taxi. The cab took me to the motel on the outskirts of the city where I'd left changes of clothing, passports, and money. From there, it was easy to leave the country under one of my many false identities.

I didn't look back.

The temperature was very warm, so I decided to step inside and splash some cold water on my face. As I did so, I stared at myself in the mirror and continued to think about what happened.

The aftermath of Wilkins's debacle was significant. Captured New Model Army members had revealed what they knew under interrogation. The body of Cromwell was successfully identified as that of Darren Shipley by using dental records. The truth of the reverend's involvement with the NMA was revealed after the FBI stormed Greenhill and thoroughly searched what was left of the mansion office.

The election went on as scheduled. On November 4, Mark Burdett was reelected president. He vowed to work toward healing the nation's scars and meeting the demands of the people. All but three America First Party congressmen were voted out of office. The United States was back to a two-party country, and before long it would be business as usual.

Not that it mattered to me.

One hundred ninety-three people died during the "National Mall Riot," as it was dubbed by the media. Seven hundred fifty-eight were wounded or maimed. After all was said and done, the blame was placed solely on Charlie Wilkins.

He deserved it.

Greenhill was shut down and the remaining residents moved out. Other Church of Will branches slowly fizzled. Every Charlie's restaurant in the country was avoided like the plague. The chain was on its way to bankruptcy and would close within weeks. No American celebrity had suffered such a fall from grace as had Reverend Charlie Wilkins.

I'd laugh if I found it funny.

To tell the truth, I paid little attention to the news from the States. My thoughts did, however, occasionally settle on Helen McAdams.

Yes, I missed her.

For a while there, I thought I had the potential to be normal. It was an interesting exercise. Granted, it was necessary for the assignment, but I had never been that close to another human being before, both mentally and emotionally.

She gave me something I'd never experienced in my life—the realization that I did have emotions.

I guess I failed her in a lot of ways. I betrayed her

trust and I couldn't keep her out of harm's way. I don't know if there will be a judgment someday, but I suppose that'll be on my record. So be it.

I'm who I am. I'm what I am. Nothing can change that.

I know, because I finally figured out who the Faceless One is. The shadow man of my dreams. Death. His features finally formed out of the blur one night as I slept. I recognized him instantly. He was probably my only friend.

He was me, you see.

I was Death.

I was damned for all time to be him. I always was and always will be.

Forever.

EPILOGUE

She had rented the large mansion in Illinois for a song. With the real estate market being what it was, it was impossible to sell a home but quite easy to rent or buy. Her refuge was even more perfect because it was built on the edge of a cliff overlooking Lake Michigan.

Diana Burnwood performed all the necessary due diligence, covered her tracks, and set up her new identity with great care. For all intents and purposes, county records showed that the structure was still vacant. It was secluded enough that it was off the radar. No one knew where she was. It was just her—and the package she had taken from the Agency.

As she sat in a rocking chair on the wooden porch, wrapped in a fur blanket, and watched the snow fall, Diana knew it was only a matter of time.

Her days were numbered.

The Agency *would* find her.

And if Agent 47 was alive, they would send *him*.

It was inevitable. The question was . . . when?

The best she could do in the meantime was simply live. Take care of the package and wait out the days and nights until that fateful moment of—

Absolution